breaking up
is hard to do

breaking up is hard to do

a miracle girls novel

Anne Dayton and May Vanderbilt

NEW YORK BOSTON NASHVILLE

FaithWords
Hachette Book Group
237 Park Avenue
New York, NY 10017

Visit our Web site at www.faithwords.com.

Printed in the United States of America

First Edition: April 2009
10 9 8 7 6 5 4 3 2 1

FaithWords is a division of Hachette Book Group, Inc.
The FaithWords name and logo are trademarks of Hachette Book Group, Inc.

Library of Congress Cataloging-in-Publication Data
Dayton, Anne.
    Breaking up is hard to do / Anne Dayton & May Vanderbilt. — 1st ed.
        p. cm.
    ISBN 978-0-446-40756-4
    1. Teenage girls—Fiction.   2. High school students—Fiction.
I. Vanderbilt, May.   II. Title.

PS3604.A989B74 2009
813'.6—dc22

                                                                        2008030404

Anne

For Wayne.

May

For Sandy, a better sister than I ever deserved.

acknowledgments

Anne: Thanks to the friends who love to talk about writing and don't mind that I don't (especially Jeff, Donna, Annie, Carey, Nicci, and May). And to the friends who put up with the writing (especially Annie and the Beths). You guys keep me going. And thanks to Wayne, who makes it all worthwhile.

May: I feel like such a lucky girl because I have not one, but two incredible families. Thanks to my Colusa family for always coming through in a pinch and supporting us no matter what. And thanks to my original family for holding me tight and welcoming the newest member.

And thanks to Nathan. I know I get forever with you, but it doesn't feel long enough. Thank you for all the unseen, thankless hours of holding us together while I peck away at my computer late into the night.

And huge thanks to the whole FaithWords team, especially Anne Horch, for their dedication and hard work on this book.

breaking up
is hard to do

t looks like a cheerleader's soul exploded all over the gym."
I scrunch up my nose and catch a glimpse of my nose ring.
It still surprises me to see it there.

Ana laughs at my joke, but Zoe rolls her eyes and starts
clapping loudly, probably to cover for our silence. The bleachers shake as everyone around us gets pumped up on school
spirit. Everywhere you look, there's garnet and gold bunting,
streamers, and posters—one of which is misspelled. At least
I don't think the cheer-nerds meant to say "Starfish Have
School Sprit." It's bad enough that our mascot is the Starfish, but if people find out we have "sprit" too, we'll be the
laughingstock of the county.

It's first period of the first day back in school. I rarely feel all
that peppy on a very good day, and I'm certainly not chipper
on a day like this. At least we were allowed to sit with anyone
we wanted. The only requirement was that we had to sit by
class. So here are the Miracle Girls, after an incredible summer together, parked under the big "Sophomores" sign. Woo.

The cheerleaders tumble onto the basketball court as the
band cues up to play our fight song. Riley trails behind the
tumblers, galloping sideways and "sparkling" her fingers at
the crowd. The doctors don't want her tumbling this year. I
give her a nod. She waves back.

"Go, Riley!" Zoe shouts. As a sophomore, Zoe doesn't get to play her piccolo at the pep rallies. That's a "privilege" reserved for the seniors.

"You guys," Zoe groans at us, "cheer for Riley at least."

Ana obliges, but she's careful to look cool doing it. She claps her hands gently, as if she's at a golf game, and lets out the occasional scream. I give Zoe a look. I know we all changed some over the summer, but I'm still Christine Lee. I couldn't care less about school spirit. That's never going to change.

The cheerleaders separate out by grade level and begin to lead each section in a chant. Riley stands in front of us and kicks off the cheer for our grade. We all know it from last year, and Ana and Zoe scream along with the rest of our class. The object is to be the loudest class and earn the title of having the most *sprit*. Which is really an honor, let me assure you. A real treat.

"*S-o-p-h-o!*" Riley yells.

"*M-o-r-e-s!*" the crowd screams with her.

"Sophomores. Sophomores. Sophomores are the best!"

The juniors and seniors are doing the same thing, yelling as loudly as they can, while the freshmen just look confused. Sheer pandemonium reigns. That part isn't so bad.

"Scream!" Zoe yells at me over the fuss. "We have to be the loudest!" Zoe is wearing a long lavender skirt and some kind of loose tie-dyed top. Her red hair falls in a long curtain down her back.

"Sophomores!" Ana screams at the top of her lungs, getting into it now that the noise level in the gym is reaching decibels that can be heard two counties over. Ana spent a good part of the summer shopping in San Francisco with her mom, and she looks like a J.Crew ad. Since when did she care about clothes? With her new wardrobe, her sun-kissed hair, her deep tan, and the fact that she's shot up two inches, she looks nothing like the lonely little freshman I met a year ago.

Ms. Lovchuck comes out on the gym floor, and the cheer dies. I've never been so happy to see our principal. She stands at the podium and adjusts the mic for a moment. We all sit down. Well, everyone else sits down. I wasn't exactly standing.

"Students, welcome to another exciting year at Marina Vista High School!" Ms. Lovchuck pauses, as if expecting a roar of applause. She sighs at the silence, then trudges onward. She begins to drone on, making boring announcements about new school initiatives and rules.

I try to zone out, but out of the corner of my eye I see movement and turn to watch a scrawny guy with mousy brown hair climb over people, coming toward us. Oh no. Marcus Farcus. I lean forward to peek at Zoe, and her face is bright red.

"Hey, Marcus." I wave at him and flash a big debutante smile.

"Christine, always a pleasure," he says in a hushed tone.

Zoe shoots poison darts out of her eyes.

"Zoe, I'm so glad I found you," he says, pushing past and forcing himself into a nonexistent space next to Zoe. "This school is crazy."

Marcus moved into the house next door to Zoe this summer. Well, technically, he moved into a section of the woods next to Zoe and then bulldozed it and built a giant McMansion in the old growth forest. Of course, it was Marcus's parents who actually did all those things, but that hasn't kept Zoe from holding it against Marcus. Unfortunately, Marcus latched onto Zoe, who's too nice to tell him to go away, and has been following her around like a puppy dog. "Maybe you should sit with your class," Zoe says quietly, shrugging his arm off her shoulder. I stifle a laugh. She's so annoyed with him that she could scream, but she's still trying to be kind.

"Nah," he says, gesturing toward the freshman section dismissively. "I'll get to know them eventually. I'd rather be with you."

"Thanks," Zoe says, her voice flatter than a pancake.

Poor kid. He never had a chance. His parents gave him a rough start in life. If your last name is Farcus and you have a son, the only name in the world you can't give him is Marcus. That's very clear. And if you do, you're violating the laws of the social universe, condemning him to outsider status forever. Parents willing to do that to their child are obviously not right in the head.

"Hey, Marcus," Ana says, raising her hand in a wave that makes Zoe cringe. Ana finds Marcus as annoying as the rest of us do, but she has this weird sympathy for him since he's new in town. Far too charitable, if you ask me.

"And without further ado, I give you your quarterback, Zach Abramo!" Ms. Lovchuck screams. She steps away from the podium and gestures at a huge painted piece of paper with a fighting Starfish on it. The gym fills with noise, Zach bursts through the paper, and the crowd goes wild, as if it is an actual feat to tear a piece of paper. My stomach suddenly feels pumped full of lead.

"What's up, Marina Vista?" Zach screams. All the clueless sophomore twits around us clap and whistle for him. At least this creep is a senior. Unless he fails, this is the last year we'll have to deal with him. I watch Riley. All the other cheerleaders jump and cheer for him, but she remains completely still. After what he did to her, I have to fight the urge to stand up and shout, "Coward! Traitor!"

"This year we're going all the way to State with our mighty fighting Starfish football team!" Zach pumps his fist in the air. The thunderous applause nearly bursts my eardrums. We really should have reported Zach to the police, or at least told everyone exactly what he did, but Riley asked us not to. She's trying to forgive him.

"Woo! Go, Marina Vista!" Zach yells, ending his little speech. Everyone but the Miracle Girls cheers for him, and he drinks it in. As he struts to the side of the gym, Ashley Anderson, Riley's ex-best friend, gives him a hug. They've been dating all summer, which makes me twice as ill, so I try to focus my eyes on the floor. The band starts to play our fight song again, and the cheerleaders lead us in a chant that spells out *Starfish*.

A group of girls next to me lean toward each other and form a huddle. I lean back a little to see if I can hear what they're saying.

"It was Zach's," a scratchy girl's voice says.

Ooh, dirt on the quarterback. This could be good.

"She doesn't look like she just had a baby," a girl says. I recognize the voice as Hailey, a decent sketch artist from my art class last year.

"When a girl disappears for five months, it can only mean one thing." The first knowing voice sounds smug, and it suddenly hits me what—I mean *who*—they're talking about. "That's why she got her hair chopped off."

I clench my fist. First of all, everyone knows Riley dropped out of school last year because she fell off a cliff, not because she was pregnant with Zach's baby. Second, what does that have to do with her hair? And who do these girls think they are, anyway, talking about this stuff in front of anyone, but especially in front of us? Don't they realize they're sitting behind, like, Riley's best friends?

"He said he wouldn't marry her, and she went crazy and started chopping at her hair, like Britney."

"What do you think she did with the baby?" Hailey asks, giggling. As the band plays the final notes to our fight song, it hits me. No, these girls probably don't know that Riley is our friend. We spent all summer together, just the Miracle Girls, and it was an amazing time, goofing around at Zoe's house with the horses, going down to the beach to watch Riley surf, hanging around with Ana and Dave—unending days of fun, far far away from the pressures of school. The Miracle Girls have become everything to me.

But these girls don't know that. Riley became our friend at the end of last year, just before her accident. No one at school knows the first thing about our incredible summer together, or the secrets in our past that make our bond special.

"Probably gave it up for adoption. A lot of people do that and then pretend it never happened."

I can't listen to this anymore. Anger floods my veins, and

the whole world drops away. I don't know where I am or what is going on around me. I only know that I must defend Riley. I stand up and lunge at Hailey, grabbing her shirt and pulling her out of her seat.

"That...is...not true." I hiss at her, my nostrils flaring. Hailey and her stupid friend stare at me, eyes wide.

"What?" She tries to lean away from my face, but I have her shirt balled up in my fists.

"Nothing you said is true." I feel something tugging at my right arm, and then my left. Ana and Zoe are pulling me back. I grab Hailey's shirt tighter, but they begin to overpower me, forcing me to let go.

And then it's like I come to. Somehow, the entire jamboree has screeched to a halt and everyone is staring at me. I swallow and slide down into the bleachers, but it's too late. Ms. Lovchuck points at me viciously with her thin, crooked finger, then points at the gym door.

I know what she means, and I begin to pick my way over people, tripping on bags and shoes and jackets. I fight the impulse to say, "Pardon me, freak show walking." Everyone is staring at me as I plunk down the stairs. When I get to the door, I glance back one last time at the Miracle Girls and see Zoe's worried face. I know what that look means. Like me, she's worried that being back at school means everything is about to change.

Just great, Christine. It took you less than one hour to completely ruin this year too.

2

walk into the house at 4:45. Detention was no big deal, and it's the worst Ms. Lovchuck will ever give me because I'm "at risk." Her words. The only person who has figured out that I actually like detention is Ms. Moore. It represents one less hour with The Bimbo.

"Hiiiiiii, Christine," Candace, The Bimbo, sings from the kitchen. She's my dad's fiancée. I really don't know if I can take her after the day I've had.

"Hey," I say quietly and walk as fast as possible to my room. If I can just make it to my bedroom, she'll forget I'm here. Honestly, I don't know why my dad thinks Candace needs to watch me after school, but I'm turning sixteen soon, so I don't have much longer to suffer through this awkward arrangement.

"Hey!" Emma jumps around a corner. She's thirteen and a total spaz.

"Move it, Em." I push past her. As of May, Emma will be my stepsister, and while I think she's a nice enough kid, I have my art and the Miracle Girls and, well, there's not a lot of space in my life.

Emma takes a deep breath. "So today was my first day as a seventh grader and you know what? It's way less lame than being a sixth grader."

"Oh?" I start shutting my bedroom door a little. I don't want to hurt her feelings, but she's going to attract her mom's attention, and right now, I need to be alone.

"Because when you're a sixth grader everyone's like, 'Oooh, look at the little babies,' but now we're kind of in charge, you know? My friend Sylvie is going to run for class president and..."

"Uh huh." I get the door almost closed, but she sticks her foot in it.

"And I said to Sylvie, 'Well, why don't I run for Vice President? My sister Christine'"—I wince every time she says this, but Emma never notices—"'is the most amazing artist in the world and she does this amazing calligraphy and she can help us make campaign posters.'"

"Yep, that sounds *amazing*." I nudge her foot out of the way and finally get the door shut.

"Okay," Emma says through the door. "You promised!"

"Fine." I flop onto my bed. I'd make a deal with the devil to be alone right now.

Emma lingers outside my door, but eventually I hear her steps grow distant down the hallway. I exhale and plug my iPod into the speaker dock to flood my room with the music of a local surf rock band.

For the whole first song, I don't think about anything. My brain flatlines. On the next song, I go through the pep rally incident again in my head. I don't really know why I did it. One moment I was fine; the next moment I was up to my ears in Hailey's shirt. I trace the pattern of my duvet cover with my finger. Maybe the school is right. I am a total freak, and someday I'm going to go postal and pull a letter opener on someone.

Emma knocks on my door.

"Later!" I scream over the music, but the door opens anyway and a smiling Candace comes right in, turning off my music as she passes the sound dock.

"Hey, Christine." Candace sits on my bed stiffly. "How was the first day back?" Candace used to come over to watch me while my dad was at work or out of town, but lately she's been around all the time, trying to butt in and be my new mommy.

I slide away from her. Sitting this close on a twin bed is kind of weird, but Candace loves physical contact. She's already hugged me more times in the year that I've known her than my dad has hugged me in my entire life.

"It was..." I look at Candace's perky face. My dad met her at the Fourth of July parade two months after my mother died, when they were both riding on the City of Half Moon Bay float. She's a former Miss California, and she's always dressed perfectly, ever at the ready to answer questions about how she'd solve world hunger with a hug. I really don't know what she and my dad could possibly have in common because she's nothing like my mom.

"School was really great, you know. Um, all my friends and stuff were there. My classes look cool."

Candace tilts her head to the side. "Oh, that's so good to hear. It must be nice not to be a freshman anymore. Now you're going to be a big woman on campus. The famous Christine Lee."

I struggle not to laugh, because after all, she's right. I am famous. I'm the freak show who almost throttled someone at the pep rally today. "Um, yep."

Candace stares at me for a moment, and a silence fills the room. Our silences are not the companionable kind. Someone of weaker willpower would crumble and talk to Candace, but not me. It's my room, and I don't have to talk. She doesn't even live here, and if I have anything to say about it, she never will. I've been working on a plan to end this whole stupid marriage idea.

"Welllll," Candace says after a long moment. I have the distinct feeling she's trying to pull her nerves together, so I brace myself. "I did want to talk to you about something."

"Okkkaayyy," I sing back to her in the exact same tone.

Her lips squash into a thin line. "I was poking around the house today, and I got curious about the studio in the backyard."

I feel my features begin to collect in the middle of my face. That's my mom's studio.

I used to love to go out there and watch Mom paint for what seemed like hours. She had a slow, precise style, and I would lie on Grandma Ba's old floral couch and let my mind drift. *Bà* is Vietnamese for grandmother, but I couldn't say it right as a kid, so I called her Grandma Ba, which means "Grandma grandma," but whatever.

"You probably haven't been out there in ages, but it's really a mess, full of paintbrushes and half-finished canvases and a dusty old couch."

When Mom died, Dad's method of grieving involved putting everything that Mom ever breathed near in boxes and shoving them into the attic. He even took down all the photographs of her. So far, he's ignored her studio, but I still go there to be near her things sometimes. It makes me feel close to her.

"So I thought we could go out there, you and me, and go through everything. We'll salvage what's useable, clean it up really nice."

"That studio was my mother's." I ball my fists up. Candace has no right to be out there. That's my place. "Stay out of there."

"But—"

"*No*. Don't touch anything in that studio. Stay away from her."

"Christine, I'm sorry." She opens and closes her mouth. How could she bring my mom into this mess they call a relationship? "I thought it would be a nice thing to do. We could put one of her paintings in your room."

I push myself off the bed. She has no right. She has no right to discuss my mother with me—she shouldn't even be thinking about my mother who was an amazing, unique, one-of-a-kind person who cannot be replaced. I shake my head and scan the room for my sketchbook. I need to get out of here.

"Christine, let's talk about this. I didn't mean to hurt you. We don't have to clean up the studio." Candace's face is pale. Somewhere deep inside I think I know she only did this because she thought I'd appreciate it, but I push that down, down, so deep that I'll never have to think about it. She's the one trying to take my mom's place.

I remember that my sketchbook is in my backpack, and I reach in and snatch the smooth leather book. I slam the door to my bedroom, shutting Candace inside, and start walking toward the back door.

"Christine, wait," she says, throwing the bedroom door open again. "You can't just keep running off."

I turn back for a moment and see her standing at the end of the dark hallway, the one that used to be lined with pictures of our family. Of course I can.

I yank the sliding glass door open and look across the backyard to the studio. The cool evening air hits my face, and it feels good. I close the door behind me, then step out into the yard and look up at the sky. This can't continue. This madness stops now. I don't care what it takes. I am going to figure out a way to stop this wedding.

3

One of the cool things about having all the adults at your high school think you're crazy is that you get to skip PE once a week. Someone high up decided that meeting with the school counselor to talk about my feelings is more important than getting smacked in the head playing dodgeball. After all, talking about your feelings is very, very important. Just look at how many famines and wars have been stopped by people taking a little time out of their day to sit around and talk about their feelings. I've absolutely lost count.

I knock on my counselor's door. It's just a courtesy, really. I've been coming here every single Tuesday afternoon since I started high school, so I know she's waiting for me.

"It's open."

I walk into her office and nod hello. How can she stand it in here? It's so cluttered, with books on every single surface.

"Christine, welcome back. I assume you've missed our little sessions exactly as much as I think you have?" Ms. Moore gives me a sly smile and gestures at the chair across from her.

"Least I'm not in PE." I plop down in the swivel chair and toss my book bag on the floor. The real school counselor is Mrs. Canning, but she only lasted two sessions with me.

That's when they tapped Ms. Moore to work with the freak show. I don't think the other girls know who I meet with. They know I see a counselor, but I never really mentioned who it is, so it's our little secret.

"I'm surprised to hear you say that, after all the interest you showed in full-frontal contact at the pep rally yesterday." She crosses her arms across her chest and bores her eyes into me.

Jeez. I just got here. It's a little early for the third degree.

"I was showing Hailey how to scrunch her shirt up around the collar. It's the latest thing."

Ms. Moore refuses to laugh.

"How was your summer?" I ask. "Did you make it all the way through that, um, weird book you wanted to read?"

I pull my hair back into a ponytail as she talks. This summer I decided to give up dyeing my hair. It's so "troubled teen," and I'm really fine, no matter how much adults treat me like I'm going to break. Plus, Zoe and I went to San Francisco one day and got my nose pierced and my hair cut. My hair is shoulder-length and choppy now, and the little diamond stud I got looks so cool.

"*Ulysses*. James Joyce. And yes I did, thank you." She clears her throat. "So. A new year. A whole new chance to talk about—"

"Did you like it?" Talking about books is the easiest way to keep Ms. Moore distracted. The more boring the book, the more she loves it.

"I did. But I want to talk about what happened at the pep rally yesterday."

"Did the freshmen seem tiny to you? I know it's only been a year, but I just can't believe we were ever that small."

Ms. Moore locks eyes with me, and for a moment we stare at one another.

"Christine, what do you think made you do that at the pep rally?"

I shrug.

"I'll tell you what *I* think. I think you have so many questions bottled up inside of you, boiling and churning around, that you occasionally bubble over in ways that surprise even you." Ms. Moore waits as if she thinks I will explode on her.

I laugh instead. It's always better to play this stuff off as a joke. "I never really saw myself as a bubbly person, to tell you the truth. Now Riley—"

"Christine." Ms. Moore stands up, presses her hands flat on her desk, and leans across it. "It's been a year. It's time to start talking about the accident."

I lean back in my chair and jut out my chin. Why do people always want me to talk about it? There's nothing to say. My mom croaked, my life is miserable now, and I can wallow in it or just move on. "I gotta get going. I've got art class next, and Mr. Dumas will hate it if I'm late."

"We will talk about it this year." Ms. Moore nods. "That's my goal."

I stand up and slowly pick up my book bag, wondering if Ms. Moore will try to stop me. We both know that it's ages until the bell rings, and no art teacher since the dawn of time has ever cared about students being late to class, especially Mr. Dumas.

"You're going to have to report back to PE. I can't let you wander the halls." She narrows her eyes at me. "Seems better to take a seat and talk about the accident with me."

"Actually, I'm feeling kind of sporty all of a sudden." I walk toward the door. "Well, uh, see ya, I guess."

Ms. Moore says nothing. Time seems to creep by. She has one of those industrial standard-issue wall clocks, and now that I notice it, I can hear the second hand tick.

"Okay, bye then." I rush out the door and steal down the hall as quickly as possible, tears streaming down my face.

4

ast year Ana was always after me to come to church with her, especially because Zoe goes with her pretty regularly now, but it wasn't until the white-water rafting trip they took this summer that I actually braved it. I mean, sitting around singing "Kumbaya" and talking about Jesus is fine if you're into that kind of thing, but river rafting is really more my speed. I guess that's how they sucker you into it because the next thing I know I'm sitting in church on a normal Sunday evening, wondering how I got here.

And tonight they made me endure a long service *and* song time. I was so relieved when the last chord was strummed and the lights finally came up. Now the fun could begin. But instead Riley, Ana, Dave, and Zoe planted themselves on couches that look like they'd give you a rash, so I was forced to engineer this plan to liven things up.

I used to be pretty into the whole God thing when I was younger. My mom was very religious, and we went to church just about every week, but Dad and I don't go anymore. Everything changed after the accident. Still, I play along. The Miracle Girls have a way of sensing things, so I wonder if they suspect my dirty little secret. Knowing Ana, this might be exactly why she's always pressing me to come to church with her.

"I can't believe we're doing this," Zoe says, wobbling out onto the sloped church roof. She really shouldn't have been the first one up because she's a total scaredy-cat, but it took all of us to push her up to the roof. I learned tonight that Zoe does not actually have arms. She has wet noodles attached to her shoulders.

Riley goes up on the roof next. She throws her right leg up, as if she's doing nothing more than stepping into a pair of jeans, and then pushes herself upright. I can see her triceps glistening in the moonlight, and it's nearly impossible not to hate her.

Then it's Ana's turn. She pulls herself up on the roof with a little boost from Dave, who goes to great and very hilarious lengths not to touch her butt. Dave is Ana's pseudoboyfriend. Ana's not technically allowed to date, but those two are together so much it doesn't really make any difference at this point. She ends up stepping on his face, but he seems to admire her all the more for it. Love is a very serious sickness.

I shimmy up before Dave can touch me, then slide out of the way, and Dave is on the roof behind me in a matter of seconds.

Zoe, Ana, and Riley are already lying on their backs on the sharp incline. It took some time to convince them that stargazing from the roof would be fun and not get us into too much trouble, but now I'm not hearing any complaining. Typical. Dave and I walk over to join them.

The warm shingles feel good against my back as the night cools off. Down below us we can see members of the youth group congregating around cars and playing basketball.

"They'd better not scratch Emily." Dave points at his new (to him) Chevette, which already has a dent in the front fender from where he hit a light post last week.

I spy Tyler Drake and Tommy Chu, Dave's bandmates, sprawled out on the hood of the youth director's, Fritz's, car. I had a thing for Tyler last year, but one evening at an art gallery was all I needed to figure out we are not a match made in high school heaven. When I compared one of the artists in the show to Klee, he said, "Oh, yeah, I guess clay is cool, when you're a kid and everything."

The rhythmic sound of the basketball hitting the pavement begins to lull me into a peaceful state. It's nice up here, looking down at the ants below. What would it be like if I could orchestrate their lives? If I were God, I'd make only good things happen to people. No more war or hunger or...

"Hey, Riley." Ana sits up and brushes the dirt off her hands. "What did you get on the *Middlemarch* test in Ms. Moore's?"

Riley laughs. "I don't even want to think about it."

Ana bites her lip a little. "It doesn't really matter since I bombed the first trig test—"

I nudge Zoe. "Bombed means she got a B+." Ana and Riley are on the accelerated paths to college, jockeying for the spot at the top of our class. Meanwhile, Zoe and I are bumping along. It doesn't matter that I'm no good at algebra because someday I'm going to move to the East Village and be a painter, and Zoe's going to...I don't know, join the Peace Corps? She doesn't need math to dig wells in Papua New Guinea.

Zoe laughs, and Ana waves me off. "When you're up against a genius like Riley, a B+ matters."

"Hey, Dave, have you scaled back your hours at Pizza King now that school's started?" Riley smiles at Dave, who nods. Completely oblivious to Riley's attempt to change the subject, he continues to watch the basketball game below.

"Anyway, after I bombed that trig test I reworked our class standing and you were ahead of me by a long shot. So even if you didn't do so well on the *Middlemarch* test"—Ana studies Riley's face at the suggestion—"it wouldn't matter too much. I might catch up a little, but you'd still be ahead."

Zoe's face shows that she's going into panic mode. Neither of us has ever mentioned it, but I suspect she worries about those two as much as I do. There's this weird competitiveness between them sometimes.

"Nerd alert," I say and roll my eyes. "It's like the third week of school. How can you already have reworked the standings?"

"It's important, Christine." Ana gives me a lopsided smile, then turns to Riley. "Sorry, you were saying?"

Riley laughs a little. She has taken off her worn Cal hoodie and is using it as a pillow, staring up at the sky. "I hate talking about school." Ana continues to stare at her until Riley sighs. "Fine. I got a 98."

Ana collapses back on the roof. "Congratulations," she mutters. "I got a 99, but it's not enough to make a difference."

In the awkward silence that follows, I sense it happening. School is already beginning to come between us. I bite my lip and fight off the feeling that it's all starting to slip away.

"Isn't this the most perfect evening ever?" Zoe says. She's

trying to change the subject. Good Zoe. "You can see so many more stars from up here."

"Mos def," Dave says and takes Ana's hand, and they smile at each other, but I sort of want to gag. It's easy to say that God is awesome and cool and totally radical when he's given you everything you want, plus a hot boyfriend. Too bad God has forgotten the rest of us down here in the sewer of life also known as high school.

What if I told them that I'd left my faith in that ditch with our mangled car? I stare at the Miracle Girls and think about the perfect summer we had together, away from the distractions and pressures of school. If I told them, we'd have nothing left in common. It's better to keep quiet.

5

As Candace grips the sharp knife, I swallow hard. If an evil stepmom-to-be wanted me to go away and never come back, the last thing I would hand her is a knife. But then beauty queens aren't really known for their brainpower, and besides, she has to pretend to like me until the wedding. Though if my plan works, she won't like me after tonight. I can't wait to see Dad's expression when she drops the goody-goody act and shows her true colors.

When Candace appeared on our doorstep wielding a bag of carving supplies and four handpicked pumpkins, her hair shellacked into place, I tried to escape to my room, but Dad came home and forced me to come out and "be nice," to use his words. Well, Dad doesn't make too many guest appearances during waking hours these days, and when he does show his face he's usually making goo-goo eyes at Candace, so the fact that he was willing to spend some time with his only daughter was enough to get me to come out. I never promised anything about being nice.

Emma plunges the knife into the top of her pumpkin without even making any kind of sketch of what she's going to carve. That's either really brave or really stupid, I'm not sure which.

"I wish my dad was here. He's like a pumpkin-carving

genius." The knife slips through the flesh cleanly, as Emma hacks away at the top of the poor gourd. "Last year he helped Sylvie and me carve a puking pumpkin. Do you know what that is, Christine?"

I shrug, staring at the blank canvas of my little orange specimen. You know, in this light, it kind of looks like Candace when she goes a little crazy with her bronzer.

"It's hilarious." Emma looks up from her pumpkin. "You have the pumpkin's guts coming out of his mouth. You know, like he's ralphing or something?"

I laugh a little.

"You would have loved it, Christine. You'll have to meet my dad soon. He lives over in San Mateo. You can come along sometime when he picks me up."

Ohh! Why don't I carve this pumpkin as a caricature of Candace, and then my dad will look at the hideous orange vegetable and realize he's about to marry its human equivalent.

"He can fix anything, and he's like a genius with wood and carving and stuff. Isn't he, Mom?" Emma smiles at her mother, and for a moment I wonder if she's up to something. Candace divorced Emma's dad a few years ago, and Emma goes to stay with him every other weekend, which is not nearly enough in my opinion.

Candace clears her throat. "I think I'm just going to go with a classic design this year." She's wearing a navy pants suit, high heels, and full makeup. She's a Barbie nightmare come true. Candace sticks her tongue out a bit while she concentrates on penciling her design onto her pumpkin. She draws dorky googly eyes, a triangle nose, and a wide mouth with a couple of wonky teeth and pretends not to hear as Emma talks about the year she and her father carved an entire pumpkin village. I begin to sketch what I've decided to lovingly entitle Miss California Pumpkin.

Miss California — okay, well maybe I'd better call it Glamour Pumpkin just so Dad doesn't kill me — is not going to be that hard to accomplish. The pumpkin's skin is the perfect shade. Plus, I have a wig in my closet from the year I dressed up as Cleopatra for Halloween, so I'll flop that on its head. My sketch has plump lips, heavily made-up round eyes, high cheekbones, and even a little beauty mark. In short, it's a perfect rendition of Candace, except that her hair is a little pouffier.

It's not that hard to create a really intricate design if you take the time to sketch it out and then carve very carefully. Right now it just looks like a bunch of strange lines, but once I cut away the right places and stick a candle inside, I think it will look exactly like my evil stepmom-to-be. Maybe I should put a tea light inside. She's not that bright.

"Oh, he's turning out so perfectly!" Candace claps her hands and admires her pumpkin, which is not turning out perfectly and does in fact have a crooked mouth.

I study her as she continues to carve. What is my dad thinking? I'll admit that she's pretty, in a fake kind of way, but she's way too high maintenance for us. I need to expose her for what she is, or someday he's going to wake up and realize that he made a mistake, that they are nothing alike and never have been, and it will be too late. I'm outta here in three years, but he'll be stuck waking up to her mug for the rest of his life unless I fix this.

I scan the face of my pumpkin. Satisfied that I have the design copied accurately, I pick up the knife and begin to cut a hole around the stem.

"This year Dad's out of town so we have to carve pumpkins here. But maybe when he gets back, Christine, you can meet him." Emma's pumpkin has three eyes, no nose, and a few teeth.

"Yeah, cool," I say. She smiles at me.

I saw methodically, up and down, up and down, careful to keep my motions steady.

"Do you know what I'm reading right now, Christine?" Candace stops carving for a moment.

These two are like the conversation cavalry. Can't they tell I don't want to talk?

"John Steinbeck's *East of Eden*. It was an Oprah pick."

Wahoo, she's literate. Give that woman a gold star. I nod, trying to appear interested.

"Christine loves Steinbeck." Dad gestures at me with his knife.

What is he talking about? I've never read Steinbeck. I might have mentioned that Ms. Moore loves *East of Eden*, but I don't. How do rumors like this get started?

I finish cutting around the stem, then lift the lid off carefully. Candace doesn't shut up.

I use the edge of my knife to scrape away the pulpy mess from the lid, then reach inside. There's something so satisfying about pulling out pumpkin guts. The way the stringy sinews squish between your fingers is calming. I scrape as much as I can from the walls, then grasp a big glob in my hand. This is my chance.

"I think it's about mankind's essentially *sinful* nature, the sin buried in all of us ever since Eve took a bite of the apple," Candace says.

That's when I toss the seeds. They soar across the room and my heart swells, but I have to suppress a smile and play my best shocked expression as the gooey mass hits Candace in the face. "I'm so sorry!"

Dad sits up quickly, as if awakened from a dream, and Emma stares at me with a bit of wonder in her eyes. But instead of the disgust and horror I expect to see on Candace's face, there is an expressionless calm.

"Christine!" Dad stands up, nearly knocking over his stool.

Candace wipes the pumpkin goo off with her hand. I try not to be disappointed that her makeup doesn't all come off with it. She's about to lose her composure and drop the whole nice routine.

"I didn't mean to get it all over you," I say quickly.

"Sure you did." Wait, why isn't she shrieking?

"Go to your room," Dad says through clenched teeth. At least I finally got his attention, though if he had been paying attention at all for the past year, he might have known being sent to my room is not exactly a punishment. Emma is watching me carefully.

"It's okay." Candace has a wry smile on her face and doesn't look like she's about to burst into tears or anything. Then, before I can prepare, she's slinging pumpkin goo right back at me. I screech a little when it hits my face. Did she really just do that?

She's already got another handful from the pile in front of

her, and I take a step back, but this one she tosses lightly at my dad. He looks stunned when it lands over his left eye.

I feel a moment of triumph, certain my plot has worked. How can he like her after she threw pumpkin guts at him? Surely he's about to lose it. But then, incredulously, he breaks into a slow smile.

Dad grabs a handful for himself, and within moments the kitchen has turned into a war zone, pumpkins forgotten, goo flying across the room from all sides. Candace is laughing as she scrapes seeds out of her hair and launches them at Emma, Dad is chuckling as he reaches for another handful, and sneaky little Emma is double-fisting, reaching for one pile of guts with one hand while she's midfling with the other.

I dig into my pumpkin for a handful to throw at Emma, who has landed a batch in my hair. Candace wipes pumpkin seeds off the front of her designer suit, laughing, not shrieking, pretending for all the world that she's having a grand old time. My dad begins to guffaw and can't stop, bracing himself with his arms. I realize with a jolt that this is the first time I've heard him laugh in months. In fact, everyone is laughing, except me.

6

An icy breeze blows past my ears. I hear a whisper and turn around out of reflex, but there's nothing there.

I swear I'm being haunted. Well, not haunted in the traditional sense because I'm not being chased around by something in a bedsheet with eyeholes. It's more like the air grows icy and then this faint noise starts. It's probably in my head, but it has happened before and it has definitely crossed my mind that it might be my mother's spirit. Heck, if my husband were marrying a former Miss California so soon after my death, you'd better believe I'd be angry enough to come back from the grave and make my daughter do something about it.

The beach is peaceful this early. The only sound is the pounding of the waves on the hard sand. I pull the strings of my hoodie tighter around my face and hunch over my sketchbook. I had to bring an extra sweatshirt with me this morning, which means that fall will be here before we know it. It's usually foggy in Half Moon Bay, especially before the sun burns away the marine layer, but today there's a bite in the air that wasn't there a few weeks ago.

Riley is wearing her full-body wet suit, so I know she feels it too. She's not allowed to surf alone (she never was allowed to, but now she's actually obeying that rule), and I like drawing without having an annoying little twerp bothering me every five seconds about how awesome middle school is, so I figured if I came along, I could relax a little.

And the truth is, I love hanging out with Riley. I like Ana and Zoe too, but they have such perfect families who love them to little tiny pieces that it's hard to open up to them. It's easier to talk to Riley, especially when it's just the two of us. The McGees love their children, but their home life is anything but sane. Thanks to Michael's autism, they live their lives in the spaces between chaos and crisis.

The hair on my arms stands on end. I rub my hands together and try to get warm.

I wish I believed in God because then everything would be so much more convenient. My mom would be in heaven playing a harp—no wait, she'd never play a harp—instead of down here, freaking me out. I turn around again, but no one is there.

Soon Riley drags herself out of the water, and when I see her staggering up the beach toward me, her board balanced under one arm, I sigh and flip my sketchbook closed. The sun is starting to break through the mist, and the light bounces off her glistening black wet suit. She looks lean and powerful in the getup, and she's laughing as she approaches.

"How can you scowl when you're lying on a beach?" She tosses her board down on the sand, and it lands with a satisfying thud. I scowl again to make her laugh, and she plops down next to me. "I've got to get you out there with me someday. You'll love it once you try it." I doubt that very much but don't bother to say so. She leans back on her arms and takes a deep breath. "You ready to head back?"

"Sure."

"Liar." Her dopey cheerleader grin flashes across her face.

The wind picks up for a moment and a howling echoes in my ear, like a woman wailing. I try to shake it off. "No, seriously. I'm ready. "

The sun is burning off the fog as we trudge back to the parking area. It feels a little brighter now, a little less, well, ghostly, especially since there are more people around here, but I still can't shake the feeling. It's freaking me out. Riley is chattering on about a new kind of treatment they're doing for Michael. Who knows if I'll ever have the guts to talk to her about this again... Mentioning that your mom is a spook who's pestering you because she wants you to break up your dad's impending marriage doesn't exactly just roll off the tongue.

"Hey, Riley?"

She smiles and stops talking. The weak sunlight glints off her hair.

"Can I ask you something?"

"As long as it's not what I got on my last test, sure." She rolls her eyes.

"Um, do you ever..." How do I say this exactly? I don't want her to think I'm totally crazy.

"I mean, she's insane, right?" Riley laughs, filling in the space. "She's totally obsessed. Don't get me wrong. I love her to death, but don't you think she's taking this whole getting into Princeton thing a little too far?" She steps up onto the narrow curb that edges the parking area.

"Uh...," I falter. Ana. She's talking about Ana. Why is she talking about Ana? We never really talked about one another this summer because we were always together, all four of us.

"I know, I know. I should be nicer. It's just that she makes me so crazy sometimes." Her eyes scan the road. "Why does everything have to be a competition?"

"Yeah. Crazy." I try to smile because Riley seems like she's been waiting to get that out of her system for a while. And I bite my lip to keep from saying anything about my mom. Maybe now's not a good time to talk about the haunting. Plus, she'd probably have no idea what I was talking about anyway. That's why I'm the freak. I step up onto the curb with her.

"Anyway, sorry." When Riley turns back to me, her face is a little sad. Maybe I was supposed to agree with her about Ana. Is that what a friend would do? What about a friend to both of them? "I really do like her. You know that." I nod. "What were you saying?"

"Um..." I look around frantically and make a quick decision. Now is not the time. "I have to use the bathroom."

Riley gestures toward the squat cinder-block building at the end of the parking area. "I'll call my mom while you're inside."

I nod and duck into the stinky concrete bathroom. The floor in here is damp and gritty, and every noise I make echoes. I can barely make out my reflection in the mottled mirror.

In August it felt like we shared everything in the world, but now I don't know. It's not just the competitiveness. Everyone is always doing other stuff these days. The cheerleaders are busy with football season, Ana is always preoccupied with school or Dave, and Zoe is tied up with the marching band, practicing odd formations that never look quite right even during the halftime show.

I run my hands under the cold water, then splash some on my face and try to get my breathing under control.

I'm not like Riley. I don't have a mom I can confide in, I don't have other friends I can turn to, and I haven't talked to the kids from middle school since... before. The Miracle Girls are everything to me, and if we grow apart, I don't know what I'll do.

I stay in the bathroom until I feel calm enough to face her again. When I finally come outside, Riley is talking to some guy, which is hardly surprising to me anymore. That girl could wear a potato sack and guys would still drool over her. This one is leaning against an old white truck, his arms crossed over his chest. Riley is laughing and touching his arm. His hair is shaved short and it's dark, and I can see a tattoo peeking out from under his short-sleeved wet suit. I eye him warily.

"This is my friend Christine," Riley says, gesturing to me, then turning her megawatt smile back to him.

"Hi," I say quietly, not really up to making much effort. His wet suit is dripping onto the asphalt, the water collecting in shallow pools at his feet.

"Tom." He holds out his hand, and I take it uncertainly, while Riley giggles for no apparent reason.

"Charmed." It's not that I don't want Riley to find someone. That's not it at all. It's just that we need Riley, the three of us, and if she dates someone...

"Tom's a senior at Abraham Lincoln in San Francisco. He was telling me about Mavericks." Riley rubs her hands up and down her arms, trying to get warm. Mavericks is a legendary surfing spot a little bit north of Half Moon Bay with huge waves. Professionals die out there all the time, getting knocked against the underwater rocks and pulled under by raging riptides.

"Rumor has it the competition is going to be early this year," he says, brushing some water out of his short hair.

"We should come watch," Riley says, winking at me. Every year they hold a huge competition here. The only problem is, they have to do it when the conditions are just right, so once they make a decision the surfers only have forty-eight hours to show up here or forfeit their entry.

"Boy, that sounds *swell*..." I wait to see if anyone catches my surfing pun, but they don't, of course. "It will probably be tough, though. We're both very busy in *Half Moon Bay*." I clear my throat at Tom. Maybe since this guy lives in the city I can convince him to leave Riley alone. There must be girls in San Francisco he could date.

"I can pick you up on my way in from the city, if that's the problem," Tom says. I cross my arms over my chest and look away.

"Riley, isn't that your mom?" I point toward a blue minivan pulling into the parking area. Plastered on the sides are giant magnetic signs of Mrs. McGee's face. When she started selling real estate, she hung those things all over town.

"Yeah." She doesn't even seem embarrassed by her mother's ridiculous car. "See you around." She gives him her most charming smile, then struts over to pick up her board, still resting on the sand. As we walk toward her mom's van, I cast a quick glance over my shoulder and see that Tom is still watching Riley walk away. *Please go away,* I chant to him in my head.

7

By the time the sky is dark enough to be deemed night, we have run into half the high school kids in town, developed three new inside jokes, and laughed until our sides ache—and I can't help but pat myself on the back.

It's been ages since we were all in the same place at the same time. But October marks the Half Moon Bay Art & Pumpkin Festival, and this gave me an idea: bring the Miracle Girls together at the festival. The face painting I did last year for the Earth First table was "such a hit" (Ms. Moore is becoming delusional in her old age) that the environmental club ditched the whole pumpkin-bar thing and set up a face-painting booth this year. That made my job easy. All I had to do was make sure each girl signed up for a shift at the face-painting booth, then talk them into hanging around afterward.

And now as the autumn sun slips behind the hills and the booths begin to close up for the day, electricity ripples through the air. By day, the festival is little more than schmucks selling pumpkin goods and tacky handicrafts ("art"), but after dark the haunted house and carnival games make this an actual fair.

We walk in a group, laughing and snacking on buttered

popcorn and hot chocolate, and join the long snaking line for the haunted barn. The line drags as the people ahead of us shuffle inside in groups, but that's okay. It's the four of us together, just like I planned. We could be waiting in line to take a math test for all I care.

Actually, there are five of us. You have to count Dave, who may as well be one of Ana's appendages. Ana is on probation, but she somehow seems to have more freedom than ever before. Her parents are insane. As long as she gets parental approval before she goes out and doesn't lie about where she is, she can go pretty much anywhere.

Marcus Farcus spotted us in line for hot chocolate, much to Zoe's dismay, and hasn't left Zoe's side since. So make that six. But still, we're all here and having a good time.

We inch forward as a scream sounds from inside. I did the haunted barn last year, but each season the local theater company revamps it entirely, enlisting their scenery department to create elaborate sets and getting actors to dress up like corpses and jump out at you from hidden corners. Last year they had a guy hanging from the ceiling. It was sick.

Eventually we make it to the front of the line. Ana and Dave hand over their tickets, then grab each other's hands and step inside the dark room. Zoe goes in next, with Marcus trailing right behind her. Marcus and his parents stopped by the Earth First booth earlier, and Marcus got so excited talking about one of those Narnia movies he accidentally spit on Zoe. It was just a little bit, but it was totally hilarious.

Riley and I exchange a look, realizing we're couple #3. She gives me a wry grin as we walk toward the entrance.

"You ready for this?" she asks, her blue eyes sparkling in the footlights. I nod as Zoe shrieks and my eardrums explode. Riley and I rush into the pitch-dark hallway, disoriented by the inky blackness.

The air smells a little like hay as we all walk through the house in pairs, shrieking when zombies jump out at us, touching peeled grapes the "ghosts" insist are eyeballs, and turning away from the corpses in every corner. It is kind of spooky, but it's really fun too in this big group. It's like we're all in this together somehow.

Zoe screams a lot, and one time Marcus tries to put his arm around her, but even in the dark you can see the look of death she gives him.

When we get to the finale, a long hallway where things fly at us and a zombie chases us with a fake chainsaw, the Miracle Girls all put their arms around each other and Zoe screams at the hilariously bad sound effects, which sets the rest of us off laughing. My plan is working. The Miracle Girls are here together, and if you squint a little, it's just like old times.

"You guys want to go again?" I ask as we stumble through the exit. "Or maybe hit up some of the games?"

"Can't," Ana says, sliding the face of her shiny gold watch around. "I gotta get going." She sighs, even as Zoe's face falls. "My mom will be here to pick me up in ten minutes, and you know what happens if I'm late." She pretends to hang herself with a noose, sticking out her tongue. "Anyone need a ride?"

I shake my head, wondering if there's a way I can make Ana stay. But my heart sinks when I remember that her parents are like jailers. It's probably better to let her go. Okay, well, even if Ana leaves, the rest of us can still hang out.

"I'll walk you there," Dave says, gesturing toward the parking area beyond all the food booths. Ana smiles at him, then gives us each a hug in turn, except for Marcus, to whom she gives a little army salute. Dave turns and bows to us, charming as always, then puts his arm around Ana's waist as they begin to walk away. I fight the urge to scream after them as their silhouettes dissolve into the inky night.

"How about you, Riley? Want to go again?" Zoe smiles at her, but Riley doesn't seem to hear her. She's scanning the crowd behind us and biting her lip.

"I can't," she says, lifting herself up on her tiptoes and squinting. "I'm...meeting someone."

"I'll go again," Marcus says, but Zoe pretends she doesn't hear him.

"What? Who on earth are you meeting?" I nudge Riley playfully, trying to cover the edge in my voice. "Stay and hang with us instead. Who could be more important than us?" I hook my arm around Zoe's, and we both smile at Riley. I hope my desperation isn't as obvious as it seems to be.

"It's no one." Riley cranes her neck to see above the heads around us, and finally, her eyes light up. She waves to someone over my shoulder, then smiles at us. "It was great to see you guys." Before we can even protest, she's gone, bouncing up the dusty hillside. For a moment I think of chasing her down and asking if I can tag along, but I can't seem to make myself do anything.

"Who's that?" Zoe shrieks. I turn in time to see Riley give that surfer guy Tom a hug, and he smiles down at her.

Him? I open and close my mouth. What is she doing with him? I watch as he takes her hand and they turn away, her smile wide. I guess on some level I should be happy that she's happy. I should. But watching her walk away, it's hard to keep that in mind.

"Come on, Zoe," Marcus says, pointing to the line at the front of the haunted house again. He looks so hopeful it's almost sad. That kid has got it bad for Zoe. "You wanna go again?"

"It's some surfer guy she knows from San Francisco," I mumble. "Tom." I wonder if Riley has told the others about him yet.

"Who?" Zoe bites her lip.

"Come on. Let's get in line for the haunted barn, or we could get some pumpkin pie. You want some pumpkin pie?" Marcus tries to put a hand on Zoe's shoulder, but she deftly dodges it.

She shakes her head. "Sorry, Marcus. I've got to meet Ed by the giant pumpkin soon," she says, sighing.

"Oh, come on." I give her a pleading smile. "You don't have to go yet." This is Zoe, my true blue, and even she's deserting me.

"Your dad told my parents he'd give me a ride home, so I'll go with you." Marcus grabs for her hand, but Zoe moves it away quickly. She glares at him, then turns to me.

"I'm tired, and everybody else..." She trails off, and I catch the look of defeat in her eyes. So much for my big plan for us to spend a little time together. "Do you need a ride?"

I shrug.

"Okay." She watches me for a minute, but I don't move. "Call me," she mouths, then begins trudging up the hill. I nod. They walk away, Zoe taking slow, labored steps while Marcus skips next to her, yammering away.

And suddenly I'm completely alone. A group of middle school girls falls through the exit of the haunted barn. Their high-pitched shrieking is earsplitting.

I wander away in a cloud of confusion. When did all of the Miracle Girls get boyfriends? Okay, Zoe would never call Marcus a boyfriend, but he likes her at least. It's something.

I turn around and spot a lonely booth in a shiny beam of moonlight. It's a milk-can toss. Without knowing why, I walk over to it and saddle up to the counter, though the haggard college student manning it seems in no mood to shill it to me.

"One play, three dollars. Two plays, five dollars." He speaks so quietly I can barely hear him.

I hand him three singles, and he gives me a softball and then moves out of the way. He stares off into the distance, and I find myself wondering if he is all alone in the world too.

I pull my arm back and launch the ball as hard as I can.

All six milk cans clatter to the ground with a satisfying crash.

"What can I get for that?"

The greasy-haired booth attendant gestures toward the rows of prizes. "You can take any of the prizes on the middle shelf," he mumbles, waving his hand vaguely in the direction of generic stuffed animals behind him. "Or you can throw another ball and try for the top row." He halfheartedly moves his arm toward the top shelf, filled with giant pink monkeys and purple gorillas larger than most children. "Or you can get a fish." He points to the small tank of sickly looking goldfish at his feet and shrugs.

"Do I get to choose which fish?" I squint at the algae-covered walls of the tank and try to pick out which one will be least likely to die on me. The attendant looks at me, disdain in his eyes, and I sigh. "I'll take the fish." He scoops one out with a net, tosses it into a plastic bag, and hands it to me.

"Thank you for playing." He's already turned away before I can utter thanks back.

I hold the bag up to my face and look into his little fishy eyes.

"What should I call you?" The fish looks at me, and for a moment he seems to understand. Wait, is it a he? How can you tell the sex of a fish? I hold the bag up in the moonlight. Nope. Hmm...He really looks like a guy. He swims to the far side of the bag and ignores me. Okay, he's definitely a dude.

I walk behind the back of the haunted barn and pull out my phone, then flip it open, and the soft glow of the screen lights up the night. No new messages. I speed-dial my dad, who predictably does not answer, but I leave him a message asking to be picked up. Man, I can't wait until I get my license. It's less than a month away now, and I'm getting pretty good behind the wheel; even Dad says so.

I trudge up to the parking lot, cursing under my breath. Why didn't I get a ride home with Ana or Zoe? Who knows how long it will be before my dad checks his messages. As I walk through the brightly lit corridor lined with food stands, I try not to think about the real reason I didn't get a ride.

Because I didn't want to go home. Because we were having so much fun I wanted to hold on to the feeling. I wanted them to stay, just the four of us. Even when Ana left, I clung to Riley, and then Zoe. I exit the bright corridor and scuff my feet along the dirt path that leads to the parking area. Stupid, stupid, stupid. I know it's useless to cling to people because they always move on. Everyone leaves.

I plop down on a hay bale at the end of the parking lot, holding my fish's bag carefully. I guess it's me and him now. Voices sound all around me, people walking to their cars laughing in the cool moist night as I try my dad again. No answer.

Now that I'm not a part of it, the noises of the festival—the clanging of the milk cans against the cold concrete, the high-pitched screeching from the haunted barn, the canned music playing over the sound system—are no longer festive. They only seem sad. Real life is going on around me, but I'm here, struggling to hang on. Behind me, people are eating and making friends and falling in love, and I'm waiting in a dark parking lot with my fish.

"You all alone, little lady?"

I gasp, clutching the fish to my body to protect him, then sigh as Ms. Moore plops down beside me.

She laughs quietly. "You okay?"

"Oh yeah." I give her my typical smile and try to sound confident. "Me and Joe here are fine." I hold up his bag.

She watches me; then a slow smile breaks across her face. "What kind of name is Joe for a fish?"

I shrug. A generic one, a forgettable one. It's the name of a loner, which is fitting if he's going to join my family. "I thought about Bruce."

"Bruce Lee?"

"Yeah, but fish are no good at kung fu."

"What are you still doing here?" She peers behind my back, turning from side to side as if a Miracle Girl or two might pop out. "Is someone coming to get you?"

I pretend to be engrossed with Joe, holding his bag up to study his face. He looks a little thin.

"Did you call your dad?"

He's really kind of a silvery color, not actually very gold at all.

"He didn't answer." She says this with an eerie kind of certainty.

Where do you get fish food? I'll have to remember to find a pet store around here.

"Okay." She pulls me in a little closer. My back stiffens reflexively, but I force myself to relax. "We'll wait."

Behind us, we hear the shrieks and laughter of carnival goers, but on this little bale of hay, all I can hear is my own breath, growing soft and even. Maybe I'm not utterly alone. There is at least one person who cares about me, and that's a start.

8

As I slide into art class, I breathe a sigh of relief. I'm not entirely sure, but I think Ms. Lewis, my gym teacher, might be a witch. She wears a lot of black, has a funny bump on her crooked nose, and is bone thin, and sometimes when she looks at me I get the distinct impression she's about to cackle in delight and throw me into a pot with some eye of newt. Also, I'm getting a C in her class.

The art teacher, Mr. Dumas, on the other hand, is plump, scatterbrained, and lets us sit anywhere we want at long communal tables. He has messy, whitish hair and wears Buddy Holly glasses and cardigans with holes in them. We don't have to be on time or even attend his class. Even the freshmen figure out by Christmas that he simply marks everyone present every day no matter what. I choose a seat in the back left-hand corner, pull out my sketchbook, and start thinking about the piece I've been working on.

A couple of weeks ago I brought in a very old picture I found in the attic. At the time, I was looking for that stupid wig for my Miss California Pumpkin, and I came across an old wooden box from when I was a little girl. Inside were pictures of my mother's ancestors. I'm not sure who any of them are except for my grandparents, but one of the pictures really grabbed me. It was of a small, weathered woman wearing a *nón lá*, the traditional Vietnamese hat that looks like an upside-down top, standing in front of a little wooden house smiling like she didn't have a care in the world.

"That picture is so amazing." Andrew Cutchins slips into the seat next to me as the bell rings.

I slide my arm over the picture to cover it, then look at him out of the corner of my eye. Andrew is one of the most popular guys in the entire school, and he's also probably the best artist in the class. He's been sitting across the room the whole year, ignoring me, so I'm a bit skeptical about his sudden interest in my project. People like Andrew make me uncomfortable. They're so ra-ra-ra and I'm so... invisible.

"Um, thanks." I wait for him to move. Surely he was just sitting next to me for a moment? He tosses his backpack onto the floor and hooks his legs around the bars of the chair, then grins at me.

"All right, all right. Simmer down, you wild animals." Mr. Dumas walks lazily to the front of the class. His brand of humor is all about pretending we annoy him no end, but even we know that he lives for this job.

"Today let's keep working on our reinterpretations of old photos. I'll be at my desk if you need to harass me, either for sport or with just cause. Try not to disgrace the muses too much." He rolls his eyes and trudges back to his antique wooden desk in the corner. Currently Mr. Dumas is working on some sort of acrylic painting.

"Love that guy," Andrew says, laughing.

I stare at him. Is he talking to me? I glance around, but

there's no one behind me. Huh. Is this when normal girls giggle? Would Riley? I decide that she definitely would, but I can't. On the other hand, I can't just say nothing either. "Yeah."

Right when the word comes out of my mouth, I hate myself. The one and only Andrew Cutchins deigns to speak to me, and all I come out with is *yeah*? Christine Lee, you are definitely doomed to the lonely life of an artist.

"By the way, I've been wanting to tell you how amazing that painting you did last month was. I thought it showed a lot of Gustav Klimt."

My heart slams around in my chest. As Ana has observed out loud on several embarrassing occasions, I'm the most confident girl in the world, except where guys are concerned. Take for instance that disastrous date with Tyler this summer. I don't think I breathed a word the entire time we walked around the gallery, and galleries are really quiet. The silence was pounding in my ears.

"Really?" I turn to him. "The trees in the painting are in my friend Zoe's backyard," I say quickly. "We were over there one day, and I snapped this incredible picture of the light hitting them just the right way. I'd been itching to paint it."

"I wanted to say something earlier, but my painting was so bad." He runs his hands through his blond hair. His eyes are such a pale blue that they're almost gray. He's got a lanky frame and big hands with short, pristine nails.

"Oh please. Yours was the best in the class." I startle even myself with this comment. For some reason this guy isn't so intimidating. Not like Tyler.

"Hey now. It's not nice to tease a simple preacher's son like me."

"Give me a break." I wave off his joke. There is no way a guy like Andrew is a preacher's son. Preachers' kids always smell a little funny, quote Monty Python movies, and have exotic allergies.

"Really, I am. I swear!" He puts his big hand across his chest and my heart begins to thump a little faster as I notice how built he is.

"Whatever." He seems serious about this, but it's better not to find out. Just when I start to believe him, he'll admit he was teasing me and I'll feel like a loser. I uncover the photo and try to settle down and get a little work done.

"That's looking really good."

I drop my pencil and turn back to him. Okay, seriously. Why pick on the poor lonely freak girl? I've got enough troubles as it is. I narrow my eyes at him.

"So why the sudden interest in my work?"

"It's not sudden." My heartbeat picks up again as Andrew pulls a pencil out of his backpack and flips his sketchbook open. "You're hard to talk to. Last year you were molting, so..."

I touch my poor, dye-fried hair. "I was going through my Gwen Stefani phase."

"The pink was my favorite." He hesitates for a moment and then lowers his voice. "But I think I like it black best of all. And the nose ring is really cool too."

The compliment hangs in the air, creating a tangible awkwardness. My cheeks burn, and my head is trying to make sense of what is happening. Andrew Cutchins is talking to me, and as far as I can tell, he's not doing it to tease me. Actually, I think he might be flirting with me. Why oh why aren't any of the Miracle Girls good at art so I could get a second opinion?!

Mr. Dumas clears his throat dramatically. "Ms. Lee, Mr. Cutchins. This is art class, not *The Bachelor*. Please stop flirting before the rest of us lose our appetites altogether."

I stare wide-eyed at Mr. Dumas. He gives me a sarcastic smile, and I glance quickly around the room, expecting people to be pointing and laughing, but instead I see a few girls giving me a look I recognize all too well. I used it when I saw people talking to Tyler last year. It's jealousy.

I swallow and pick up my pencil, trying to focus on the picture I'm supposed to be reinterpreting, willing myself with all my might not to steal a glance at Andrew. After fifteen minutes, though, I can no longer fight the urge. I glance at him and catch him looking at me out of the corner of his eye. I jolt my eyes back to my paper. Is it true? Was Andrew Cutchins flirting with me?

Finally, after a long, grueling hour of *not* looking at him, the bell rings and Andrew throws his sketchbook into his bag, runs his long fingers through his hair, and walks toward the door. He is so cute, devastatingly cute. And he knows art—no, he doesn't just know art, he can create art. I shake my head at this unreal day.

Packing my things away, I make my way for the door, hitting my hip on one of the desks on my way out.

"Be careful out there, Christine." Mr. Dumas crosses his arms over his chest and smirks as I leave. "It seems you might have come down with something."

9

O kay, give it a leeeettle gas." Dad seems totally relaxed.

This sleepy little town is a great place to learn to drive because you can't possibly hit anything, but no matter how many times I tell myself this, I can't seem to calm down. They never tell you how difficult driving is. You only get to use one foot. That's like hopping or something.

I press my foot gently on the gas, and we begin to back out of the driveway, passing a little too close to the mailbox, which Dad is nice enough not to mention. In fact he only winces a little as it passes so close to my sideview mirror that I could touch it, and then we're off.

We're headed to the ice cream shop, just Dad and "his girls." That would be me and Emma. I wouldn't even bother except that I need the hours behind the wheel, and Dad is finding it hard to pencil me in these days. He's an assemblyman, and his official office is in Sacramento, which is two hours away without traffic. Usually when the legislature is in session he stays there all week and The Bimbo watches me and Emma.

Five minutes into the drive, I relax my death grip on the steering wheel a little. I still keep my hands at 10 and 2, but I lean back a little in my seat. When I'm nervous, I drive like a grandma, leaning way forward, and it's kind of embarrassing.

But nothing has happened so far, and I'm starting to feel pretty comfortable behind the wheel.

I see an intersection coming up and begin to slow the car. Dad and Emma seem to have an unspoken agreement that it's probably better for their own safety if they don't talk, and in the blessed silence, my thoughts drift to Andrew. We've been chatting in class all week, and every new detail I discover about him makes me like him a little bit more. He is, in fact, a preacher's son. He can drive already. Sometimes he takes his mother's station wagon to school, but usually he rides with his friend Ben.

I bring the car to a slow crawl at a stop sign and look both ways. There's no one in the intersection, so I push the gas pedal down slightly and continue forward.

"*Christine!*" Dad screams.

I slam on the brakes. A bad smell fills the air, and I hear honking. A car is stopped outside the window on my dad's side, and the driver is leaning on the horn.

"It's okay," Dad says in a calm, soothing voice. "You thought it was a stop sign, but it was a stoplight. Just look both ways and continue on through the intersection. Backing up would be too dangerous at this point."

I gulp and look around. Aside from the angry driver next to us, there's no one around. I ease the car forward while Dad smiles and waves to the other driver like a maniac. I feel jittery and shaken. I almost got us killed.

And before I can push the thoughts down like I usually do, make them go to that place in my mind where I keep them locked up and safe, the wreck flashes across my eyes. I see the trees rushing toward us, I remember the sense of falling, I feel myself flying through the windshield, and I see it all happening in slow motion.

I feel my dad's hand on my shoulder. "It's okay. It happens to everyone. You just need to stay focused on the road." Emma, in the backseat, is biting her lip, and her face is pale.

A tear traces my nose, then crosses the barrier of my top lip and lands in my mouth. The salt tastes good, and Dad keeps talking to me in a reassuring voice until we reach the ice cream shop.

I decide to wait in the car while Dad and Emma go in to get ice cream, and they don't argue. The car is silent, empty. I climb into the passenger seat and lower the back of the seat so I'm staring up at the fabric ceiling. I'm sealed off from the world in here, and it feels good.

I want to learn to drive so I can be a normal teenager and get away from this madness at home, but that day with my mom will always be with me. What if I kill someone with my car? What if I die?

Emma and Dad are laughing when they come back to the car, and mercifully, Dad offers to drive home.

Emma smacks her lips as she digs into her ice cream cone, and I stare out the window and try to tune her out.

We ride in silence for a while until Dad clears his throat. "So, girls. I actually have an exciting announcement that I think you're both going to be pretty stoked about." Dad doesn't take his eyes off the road as he steers toward home.

"Stoked?" I raise an eyebrow at him.

"Emma taught me that."

She cracks up in the backseat.

Dad snaps the radio off, then flicks on the blinker and

pulls the car onto our block. Down at the end of the street, there's one tree that turns bright orange with the cool autumn air every year. While fall is generally pretty unexciting around here, that one tree always gives me a strange feeling of hope. Ms. Moore would have a field day if I told her about that.

"Candace got a great offer on her house, and she's going to take it."

I yawn. Whoop-de-do.

"But the buyer had one condition. He needs to be in the house in two weeks."

"We're moving?!" Emma asks.

Dad pulls into the garage and shuts the car off. "I hope you don't mind me telling you instead of your mom. I was so excited that I couldn't wait."

Emma looks unsure.

Dad swivels around to face her. "We're going to have you move into our house. Your mom will live in the office in the backyard, and after the wedding she'll move into the house. How does that sound?"

I stare at the floor, unable to process the horrible words coming out of my dad's mouth. What did he just say? "It's not an office." I cover my face with my hands for a moment. "We have an office. It's the third bedroom in the house, and it's yours, in case you forgot. What's in the backyard is not an office."

"Well, it kind of is," Dad mumbles.

"You can't," I whisper, unable to keep the pleading out of my voice. What's he going to do with all of Mom's half-finished canvases? Her palette and brushes? Grandma Ba's couch?

"Why doesn't Candace just move into the house? It's not like she doesn't spend the night there half the time anyway."

Dad gives a fake cough. "We...uh..." His voice falters. Good. Let him be embarrassed. It's not like I haven't noticed. "It, uh, looks better. For political...things."

Awesome. So they're pretending to be all chaste so Dad can get reelected. When voters look into his personal life, they'll see that James Lee didn't live with Candace before the wedding. What a crock.

"No one ever uses the old painting studio anyway." Dad puts a hand on my shoulder, but it sounds like he's talking from far away. "We'll move anything that's in there to the attic, and I'll donate Grandma Ba's couch to The Salvation Army. Candace has a nice daybed at her place she can bring, and we'll set it up in the studio." He shifts uncomfortably in his seat.

Inside I am screaming, but I keep silent. My lips feel like they're not even attached to my body, and I'm sure they're unable to move or form sounds. This man sitting next to me, who calls himself my father, knows nothing about me. He has no idea what this place meant to Mom, and how it is so sacred to me. "No."

"You want to keep the couch? We can put it in my office if you really like it that much." Dad leans forward to try to see my face, but I look out the window. My old tricycle is still in our garage, rusting and broken, and one of the handles has foil streamers coming out of it.

"I think when you go off to college, it will be nice to have an extra bedroom out there. You'll want to bring friends home." He clears his throat.

"Am I going to stay with Mom in the painting studio?" Emma's voice shakes.

"Actually," he nudges me and I scoot away, "we were going to ask your big sis here if you guys could share a room."

"What?!" I reach for the door handle. I'll start running and never, ever look back. I could go to Uncle Peter, or maybe Mom has some relatives somewhere who will take me in. Maybe in Manhattan. I could switch to an art school.

"You mean I get to share a room with Christine? Like real sisters?" Emma's voice is full of something disgusting, like hope.

"If Christine says it's okay," Dad says, glancing at me. "If not, we'll figure something out. But since Christine wants to keep her grandmother's couch, I think it's the best option. My office won't fit a couch and a bed."

"Oh, please, Christine!" Emma says. She starts bouncing around in the backseat, making the car shake.

"What do you say?" Dads asks.

What do I say? How about no? How about I need my space? I say that I've been ambushed, hijacked. I'm a sophomore in high school. I'm practically an adult and she's a seventh grader, plus we have absolutely nothing in common. Never mind the fact that The Bimbo will be invading Mom's old painting studio and will be around even more than she already is. But Dad knows I can't say no in front of Emma. I might not be Humanitarian of the Year, but I have a heart.

"What do you say? Huh?"

I swallow hard, give my dad a cold stare, then muster, "Sure," with zero enthusiasm.

Emma's screams can be heard by dogs in outer space.

10

By the time I arrive at Half Moon Bay Coffee Company, Ana and Zoe are already seated at a table for four in the corner. This place is packed tonight, and I see a few kids from school huddled over their drinks as I thread my way through the narrow café. Zoe and I declared this Friday a "girls' night"—it's going to be just the four of us, without any extras like Dave. Ana took it pretty well. It had to be done for my plan to work. We need this time together so things can go back to normal.

"In one short week," I say, grabbing a wrought-iron chair and plopping down, "this carless humiliation will all be over."

"For you." Ana sighs. California has this weird rule that for the first year after you get your license, you can't drive anyone under twenty around without an adult in the car, which pretty much defeats the whole purpose of getting a license to escape your parents. But even though I can't drive them around, it means the start of all kinds of new freedoms for me.

"And for the rest of us eventually," Zoe says. She breaks out her floral-covered day planner. "Ooh. What are we doing on your birthday?" Zoe's not really all that organized, but people are the most important thing to her, so she keeps track of birthdays and special events like her life depends on them. "I've got next Saturday put aside for you, but what should we do?"

I shrug. I hate to plan. "I may fail the test. So we might not have anything to celebrate." This isn't the whole truth. I might fail, but I'm kind of afraid I might not even make it to the test. I haven't been able to put my fears about driving into words. I want to tell the girls about it, but it brings up too much about my mom and that day, so I keep quiet. No need to worry them about my driving anyway.

Ana scoots her chair forward. "Listen to me. You will not fail. Do you hear me, Christine Lee? Think positive."

I slip off my jacket and leave it on a chair, then head to the counter. The mousy woman at the register with a name tag that says "Marge, Manager" doesn't look me in the eye as she takes my money and makes my mocha. It's clear from the furtive glances she keeps giving us that she's not thrilled to have her shop invaded by teenagers. I take the coffee back to the table and sit down to a brainstorming session.

You'd think after sixteen years of longing for wheels, we could think of something fun to do once I could actually drive.

Ten minutes later Riley appears, soaking wet, with her brother, Michael, following behind her. My heart sinks. So much for our girls' night.

Riley rushes over to us. "I'm so sorry, guys. One of Mom's clients demanded that they drive clear over to Emeryville to look at a condo tonight. And my dad's out of town." Riley holds Michael's shoulders protectively. His blue Windbreaker hangs loose on his thin shoulders, and water drips off his sandy blond hair onto the stone floor.

"Don't worry about it at all," Zoe says and sounds like

she actually means it. She scurries across the room to get another chair.

Riley smiles at me, but then she spies someone beyond me, over my head, who makes her face light up. I turn and see a table full of people waving at her. She laughs and waves back at them.

Michael sits down without taking off his raincoat, soaking the chair Zoe brought him. Riley starts to say something, but stops herself.

"Rats have small pouches in their cheeks where they can store food." Michael looks at me for a reaction. Michael is almost fourteen, but he doesn't act like most eighth graders. He has autism and is for the most part completely unaware of social niceties.

"Efficient," I say. He nods.

"What are you guys drinking?" Riley squints at the menu.

"Mochas," we say in unison.

"I want a mocha," Michael says.

"Doesn't that have caffeine?" Riley whispers to Ana, who nods back.

"I want a mocha!" Michael almost yells.

"Okay, Michael. Coming right up." Riley winks at me and walks to the counter to place her order.

"Rats use their whiskers to feel around because they have poor vision. They can only see certain colors." Michael looks around the café nervously.

"What got you so interested in rats?" Ana asks, taking a sip of her drink and trying to play along.

"*Ratatouille*," Michael says, nodding. "It's an animated

film about a rat who likes to cook, but that's stupid. Rats can do a lot of things, but they can't talk or cook."

"Did you like *Ratatouille*? I did." Zoe is trying to steer the conversation away from every girl's least favorite vermin.

Michael shakes his head. "The writers didn't know anything about rats."

We all nod. Can't really argue with his logic, I guess. Riley is way better at this stuff than we are. I look up to see if her drinks are almost ready, only Riley's not at the counter. I scan the room for her. Ah. There's her freakishly blonde hair, by the other wall.

Wait. She's standing in front of a table packed with cheer-nerds. Their heads are bobbing every which way as they talk, and Riley, clutching a paper cup in both hands, is leaning over and laughing at something one of them is saying.

"We could go to San Francisco Saturday night," Ana says, bringing the subject back around to my upcoming birthday. "There's got to be something fun to do there, right?"

I turn back to our little table, hoping the other girls don't notice that we've been ditched, but I'm too late. Zoe hears Riley's loud, boyish laugh across the café and turns to watch her talking with her other friends.

"All the restaurants in San Francisco have rats." Michael chews on his bottom lip.

Zoe turns back around and smiles twice as big. "Or Santa Cruz? We have to do something big and exciting. I wonder if the Boardwalk is still open this time of year."

"I went to the Boardwalk once. I puked on the carousel," Michael says. "There were seventy-three horses on the carousel."

I hear Riley's laugh again. What is she doing? It's one thing to be forced to bring your brother along, but it's something else to abandon him—and us for that matter.

"Or we could stay in town," Zoe says, shrugging her shoulders. "As long as we're together, it doesn't matter to me."

"Where's Riley? She always has the best ideas." Ana glances toward the counter, squinting, then looks around the table in front of us and stops suddenly. She rolls her eyes, and I turn in time to see Riley squishing in to share a chair with Kayleen, or Kylee, or Kaylee, or whatever. Some bouncy blonde. "Oh."

"You guys, she's just saying hi. She'll be here in a minute," Zoe says quietly.

Michael begins tapping his fingers against the table in a rhythmic beat.

Zoe's probably right. Riley will probably come back and sit with us in a minute, but that doesn't make me feel much better. The truth is, she could leave. Without us, Riley would be fine because she has other friends, popular friends, but what about the rest of us? What's going to happen to us when she moves on?

I try not to be too obvious, but I steal a peek over my shoulder and see Riley leaning into Kayleen, sitting halfway on her chair.

I turn back around, paste a smile on my face, and attempt to reason with myself. It's okay that she has other friends. That doesn't mean she'll forget about us. It's not written anywhere that Miracle Girls can't have other friends. Plus, she's involved in so many things in school that she can't help but know lots of people.

I hear someone at her table scream her name, and my hopes plummet. She's pulling away. "Who are those people?" Zoe squints across the room.

"Riley has a lot of friends." Michael begins to tap out a beat on the table. It sounds familiar, but I can't quite place its rhythm.

We continue to ignore him, absorbed in the drama of the moment.

"She'll go along with whatever," Zoe says, smoothing down the page of her day planner. "Why don't we decide, and we'll fill Riley in?"

"Fine with me." Ana lets out a long breath, but her shoulders stay tense. "What could they possibly have to say for this long?"

"The Miracle Girls are Riley's friends, but she has lots and lots of friends." Michael sounds like a tape recorder playing back something he has heard on more than one occasion.

I stare down at the table, and we all wait, silently listening to Michael's rhythmic tapping. She'll come and sit with us soon, but will it already be too late for the Miracle Girls when she does?

11

So far, being sixteen is nerve-wracking. Dad and Candace took me to the DMV before school, and I passed my driver's test on the first try, which must have been some kind of mistake because I was only half awake and shaking hysterically. Then Dad let me drive his car to school as a special birthday treat, but I spent so much time adjusting mirrors and checking over my shoulder before doing anything that now I have to hurry to make it to class on time.

When the school gates come into sight, I slow down to a crawl and relax a little. It's almost over now. I did it. I ease over the speed bump, pass through the parking lot's chain-link fence, and enter a new planet of cool.

I find a parking spot and turn the car off, then lay my head on the steering wheel and let out a huge sigh as tears of relief threaten to fill my eyes. I got here safely, and aside from one near miss with a mailbox, I didn't come close to hitting anything or anyone.

Something is pounding on the passenger-side door. I yank my head up and laugh. Zoe is clawing at the door handle and Riley is pounding on the hood. A second later, a door swings open, and Ana climbs in.

"Happy birthday!" Ana throws her arms around me from

the backseat. I reach over and unlock the passenger door, and Zoe jumps in, and a second later, Riley slides into the backseat next to Ana.

"Were you guys lying in wait or something?" I unbuckle my seatbelt and turn to face them.

"Something like that." Zoe starts digging around in her bag.

"Oh, look!" Ana says and points at a red-haired figure standing by a car in the next row. It takes me a second to recognize Ashley Anderson, cheerleader extraordinaire. "Riley, quick! Wave at her. She'll go blind with jealousy."

Riley laughs but is careful not to make eye contact with Ashley. "I'm not going to get on her bad side. The number one rule of cheerleading is never, ever get dragged into a battle. Stay above it."

Ana glares out the window at Ashley. "Well, I'm waving. She used to call me God Girl."

Ana flashes a huge smile and waves, and Ashley mouths something that would get Ana grounded for life. We dissolve into laughter.

"I found it," Zoe says, pulling a paper sack out of her school bag. "Okay, Christine, you have to change your clothes."

I glance down at my outfit. Sure, it's nothing special—a green T-shirt that hugs my body in a sort of pleasing way, my vintage Levi's 501s, and my favorite pair of black Chuck Taylors—but there's nothing wrong with it. Andrew said he likes green.

"I like what I'm wearing."

"But do you like it as much as this?" Zoe asks and hands a white T-shirt up to the front.

I hold up the shirt in the morning light. It's just a basic white men's undershirt with some wonky hand lettering on it.

"We argued about what it should say for weeks," Riley says.

"Do you like it?" Zoe asks.

"Doesn't matter." Riley laughs. "She's wearing it no matter what, even if I have to pin her down and pull it over her head myself."

In black block letters, it says, "It's my birthday."

"Thanks, guys." I chuckle, thinking of them trying to make the shirt.

"Turn it around," Zoe says, nudging me.

I turn the shirt around and see that the back of it says, "Woo."

"Now *that's* a birthday shirt."

"Happy birthday, freak." Ana laughs.

"Thanks, God Girl." I salute her.

I look around the parking lot and realize that changing is not going to be so easy. The bell is going to ring any minute, and people are swarming in the parking lot. "Cover the windows. Quick."

They all hop out and stand by the windows as I duck way down in the seat and change as quickly as possible into my T-shirt. It's way too big and the lettering is on a slant, but it's perfect. I get out of the car and double-check twice that I've locked all the doors and hug all the girls for good measure.

There's a little bounce in my step as I head toward first period. Maybe there is hope for us after all.

12

So how's the driving going?" Ms. Moore says.

"Fine. Haven't killed anyone yet, though this morning I think my bumper was checking out Ashley Anderson's butt." I will the minute hand of the clock to move faster. I think Ms. Moore believes we've made what she would call progress today. The truth is I slipped up and told her that Candace and Emma moved in and how they made this huge nauseating birthday breakfast for me, and Ms. Moore nearly swooned. I never talk about home, so she was positively elated, but now I'm regretting it.

"You know, I'm supposed to report threats of violence like that." She lifts an eyebrow at me.

"Don't bother." I look at the clock again. Hurry up, space-time continuum. "My aim's not that good yet. Her butt is big, sure, but I couldn't promise I'd hit it."

"Is there something interesting on the wall behind me?"

"It's nothing personal."

I start drumming my fingers. I think Ms. Moore would be really disappointed if she knew why I'm anxious to leave. I haven't seen Andrew anywhere, and tracking him down is absolutely vital. He was supposed to see my T-shirt and, I don't know, do something dramatic, like kiss me, or show up with a surprise present because Riley told him it was my birthday. Something. Anything.

"Fine." Ms. Moore stands up and begins to pack up her things. "Off you go, then."

I pop out of my chair. "Really?"

She tilts her head to me. "Yes, really. Happy birthday, Christine."

I grab my stuff and dodge a few stacks of books on the floor as I make my way to the door.

"But think about what I said about Candace."

I freeze, holding the round, brass doorknob. Ms. Moore's lesson of the day #345 was: Try to judge people by their intentions, not by their actions. Her theory is that Candace is trying and that should count for something, but my point is that she's trying to take my mom's place, and therefore she must be stopped.

"Cool." I turn back.

She gives me a slow wave, studying my face. I shake off her piercing stare, open the door, then peal out into the front office hallway and walk toward the exit. I probably have just enough time to stop by the gym to get a soda before art class, aka see if Andrew is hanging out in that horrible little sweatbox.

I hear a familiar laugh, look up, and my heart instantly begins to slam. It's him. Andrew.

"Yeah, they put you in this machine, and you have to be totally still." He runs his fingers through his hair. I love the way he does that.

I slow my approach, trying to formulate a plan to talk to him, but his back is to me, which is a huge problem. Short of pretending to trip and falling into him, he's not going to see me pass by, and there are office workers buzzing around the halls, meaning that I can't very well stand still and wait for him to stop chatting with the registrar.

Andrew pushes something across the counter. "Here's my official note."

The registrar slides her glasses down her nose and smiles at him like a long-lost grandson. "Oh dear. I hope everything is all right. You won't miss the big homecoming dance, will you?"

As he explains his knee troubles, I am just five feet away. Can I tap him on the shoulder as I pass? Okay, yes. That's what I'll do.

"It may impair my dancing, but it was never very good anyway." He laughs. "The doctors said everything will be fine. I just need to take it easy until the spring season." He keeps talking as I approach his side, and if I touch him now, I'll interrupt him. It will be so awkward. I can't.

I crawl past him slower than a slug and drag my feet until I get outside. In the breezeway, I slam my back against the brick wall.

"Stupid, stupid, stupid." I bang the back of my head on the wall. How could I have done that? I blew it. He was right there, and I could have said hi. I stare up at the breezeway's cracked, stained concrete ceiling and bang my head more for good measure.

"Don't tell me you're getting into head banging now."

I freeze. I don't even want to see who it is. I mean, I know who it is, but how much more embarrassing can I be?

I look at Andrew, my ears burning. "Just a little. Some light head banging, more like head bumping really."

He laughs. "Hey, wait a minute."

I smile from ear to ear. He's seen the T-shirt. I could kiss the Miracle Girls.

"Okay, twirl for me."

I spin around, happy to oblige so that he knows I'm not wearing some stupid sappy shirt that any old girl might have. No, this shirt is *me*.

He laughs. "I wish I had known it was your birthday." He loops an arm around my shoulder as if it's no big deal and my spine feels like Jell-O. "I'll walk you to class to make up for it."

I turn my head to talk to him but realize that when I do our faces are so close I can almost feel the heat off his. My stomach does flips.

"Cool." I focus on not tripping. Should I put my arm around him? No, too personal. Right now this is still pretty buddy-like. Who knows what he means?

"Cool," he says and smiles.

For a moment, we walk in awkward silence, and I panic because I don't want to be that shy girl who's boring to be around. His knee. I should talk about his knee. That's a good topic. "So your knee is okay? You'll still be able to make it to the homecoming dance? I know some cheerleaders who would be terribly upset if you couldn't." Riley and her peppy cohorts have been littering the school with posters for the big game and dance. I tried to bet the other Miracle Girls, half the people in my art class, and some kids in my gym class that Riley will win Sophomore Homecoming Princess, but no one was willing to bet against her. She's the unstoppable Riley McGee.

Andrew laughs. "Believe it or not, I don't go out of my way to attend dances." I try not to smile, but the idea of him not going to the dance makes me very happy.

"But seriously, your knee? You're okay?"

Andrew starts telling me all about the MRI machine and how badly he wanted to sneeze the moment they put him in there, but the bell rings, and almost immediately the courtyard fills with people changing classes, and he jiggles his arm a little. For a second I think he might move it away so no one at Marina Vista will realize he likes me, or that he even knows me, but much to my relief his arm stays put. The stares I feel as we weave through the crowds make me want to sing.

"Well, here we are." Andrew finally moves his arm and sweeps it over the art building.

We're here? We can't be here yet. Can I pretend I left something in my car? "Um, right." I kick at something imaginary on the floor.

"Shall we go in?" He grins at me. Does he know how much I want to stay exactly where we are?

"I guess so."

He grins sheepishly. "Listen, I don't suppose you'd want to get together sometime . . ."

"I—"

"My youth group is doing this stupid seventies bowling night thing next weekend, and I thought, you know, it might be your kind of thing."

My kind of thing? I hate youth group. Why did he think I would—? Ohhh . . . it's because I hang out with the Miracle Girls. He thinks I'm a . . .

"But you *have* to dress up because I found this amazing old suit in my dad's closet, and I don't want to be the only one."

Should I tell him I hate church? That I'm not what he thinks?

He shakes his silky blond hair out of his blue eyes, and I worry that I might swoon like a lady in an old-fashioned movie.

"Yes," I say. "Cool. It sounds... really awesome."

13

Oooh." I lean back into the couch and hold my stomach gingerly. I've never eaten so much cake in my life. Emma is jumping up and down in front of me, doing wonders for my nausea. Sugar makes me sick, but it's her fuel.

"Sometimes Sylvie and I like to take cake and ice cream and mash it all together." She starts hopping on two feet, like a bunny.

"Christine?" Dad calls from the kitchen.

"She's not here," I yell back.

Dad and Candace come in beaming at each other. At this rate, I'm going to have another sibling exactly nine months after the wedding.

"Come on." Dad pulls at my arms. "Candace had a nice idea. Let's all go outside and take a picture on the steps together before the sun goes down."

"My dad has a photography lab in his new house," Emma says to no one in particular as Dad pulls his camera off the counter and begins to shove me out the door. "He built it himself, and he can develop his own film."

"Emma," Candace says and gives her daughter a look.

Emma plays dumb. "What?"

Dad pushes me right up to the front door. "No more cake," I moan. "No more ice cream."

"Yeah, yeah." He opens the door and shoves me out. I walk into the yard, notice something different, and freeze.

"*Happy Birthday!*" Emma screams so close to my ear that it starts to ring. She grabs me in a hug.

"Do you like it?" Dad wrinkles his brow.

I realize that I'm standing completely still, staring at the car in our driveway with a blank face. A car? A car!

I jump into his arms and hold him tight. "I love it, I love it, I love it!" I push him away and run to check out the old beater, a boxy Volvo from the early nineties. I run my fingers along the worn paint job and admire the dent in the front. "It's so perfect! I never thought…and then I thought if you did that it would be something brand-new and cheesy."

Dad laughs. "Well, I guess I'll take that as a compliment." He takes Candace's hand and pulls her into a hug. "And I have to give credit where credit is due." Emma runs over, jumps into the passenger seat, and buckles herself in. I open the door and admire the fuzzy interior and inhale the great worn smell.

"I almost bought you the newest Audi convertible but—"

"An Audi?!" I freeze. "Oh, that would have been horrible."

Candace laughs. "You see, James. I told you so."

I stand dead still, squinting at Candace, then at my Dad.

"Candace said the Audi was all wrong for you." He turns to her and smiles. "She convinced me to skip it and then helped me find this car for you."

Candace gives me a weak smile. I turn away and climb into the car, then shut the door behind me.

"Does this movie ever end?" Ana asks for the millionth time. "How long can they possibly make us look at sand?"

"This movie won a ton of Academy Awards when it came out." I toss a handful of popcorn into my mouth.

"They must not have had much else going on back then." She puts her feet up on the back of the chair in front of her.

"No wonder there was no line at the snack bar," Zoe says as she takes a sip of her Dr. Pepper.

"I'm sure the end makes it all worth it." I'm trying to remain optimistic. So far this movie seems perfect for insomniacs, but there must be a reason people liked it so much back in the day.

"I'm not going to make it to the end." Ana throws a piece of popcorn at the screen just as the camera cuts to a shot of camels trekking across the desert—again.

I've always wanted to catch a film at the old movie house on the outskirts of town, and it seemed like an appropriately grown-up thing to do to celebrate my birthday. But apparently they only show old artsy flicks here, and after sitting through two and a half hours of *Lawrence of Arabia* with no end in sight, it's starting to make sense why we are the only four people in the theater.

"I wonder if I could convince Ed to get me a pet camel," Zoe says.

"Am I the only one watching this thing?" Riley asks.

"Yes," the rest of us say in unison.

"If you can't beat 'em, join 'em." Riley slouches down in her chair. "Can you pass the Skittles?" I sling the jumbo-size bag at her.

To be honest, it's not really bothering me that this is apparently the most boring movie ever made. I'm sixteen, I got asked on a real date, I got the coolest car ever for my birthday, and all of my favorite girls are present and accounted for. I could die happy.

"Hey, Riley, what did you get on the trig test?" Ana pulls a compact out of her purse and makes sure she doesn't have anything in her teeth. Luckily, this place is totally low-budget and the sound isn't nearly as deafening as it is in most theaters. We don't even have to talk loudly to be heard over the sound of camels walking and sand blowing.

"Ugh." Riley shudders and tosses a handful of Skittles into her mouth. "Cosines are still haunting me in my sleep. Let's talk about something other than school." She swallows a big glob. "I have an announcement, actually. I, uh—" She coughs a little. "I think I have a boyfriend."

Normally this would elicit screams and cheers from us, but our row of seats is silent. I glance at Ana, who is pursing her lips. Zoe is gripping her hands in her lap. Are they as afraid as I am that this means we'll see less of Riley?

"Oh," I say, trying to make my voice sound bright. "Tom, right?"

Riley looks around and blinks. She seems a little puzzled at our lack of response. "Yeah. I want you guys to hang out with him soon." Her tongue is black from all the Skittles she ate. "I think you'll really like him."

Ana shrugs. "Okay, maybe we can all hang out, like at

church or something." She flashes a smile, but her taut lips make it seem a little forced. "I'm not really supposed to meet boys other places."

"That would be fun," Zoe says, a little too loudly. "You should have him come next Sunday. Even Christine's going to come, right, Christine?"

"Actually"—Riley clears her throat before I can break it to Zoe that there is no way I'm coming next week—"he's not really religious so..."

"What?!" Ana almost chokes on a piece of popcorn.

Zoe shoves a handful of Skittles into her mouth and begins to chew furiously.

"Plus, since he lives in San Francisco, it would be hard for him to get down here on a school night." Riley's voice wavers a little.

"Well, I'm sure we can all hang out another time," I say quickly. There. Saved him and me.

"Look," Ana says and puts a hand on Riley's knee. "I say this in love." Ana squares her shoulders. "Dump him."

"What?!" Riley shakes her head. She turns to me, her eyes wide. "I'm not going to do that."

"It's for your own good. The Bible says not to date non-Christians." Ana makes a sympathetic face, but I wonder if there's more than care for a friend going on.

Riley presses her palms to her face. "I don't think it does say that exactly. That's what people always tell you, but that's not really in there anywhere. I looked."

Ana points at me. "You don't see Christine dating non-Christians. She's with Andrew." Ana smiles at me.

"I'm not really with Andrew. We're just going to a—"

"And even Zoe has Marcus."

"I don't have Marcus," Zoe says, leaning forward. "Take it back. We're not together. I don't even like him."

"But still," Ana says, shaking her head. "I'm worried about you, Riley. What if he gets you involved in...bad things?" Tom seems okay to me, but Ana might have a point. We've never asked what goes on at the parties Riley goes to with her popular friends, and maybe that's because we're afraid to hear her answer. I suppose we all feel a little protective of her.

Riley looks at her lap. "I didn't plan it. It just sort of happened, and we're only going out and having fun right now." Riley studies her nails for a moment. "It feels...okay. He's a really great guy."

Ana bites her lip. "I don't know how I'd survive without Dave's support."

"Tom's a good person, Ana."

Ana looks like she's going to say more but then stops herself, and soon the voices on the silver screen are the only sounds in the theater. My thoughts drift from Tom and Riley to my own problems. I'd wondered what the Miracle Girls would think if they found out that I don't really believe in God, and I suppose now I know.

Zoe clears her throat and breaks the awkward silence. "Um, did I tell you guys what Marcus did?"

I smile at Zoe. She can't bear to see us fight and is willing to do just about anything to change the subject, including throwing herself under the bus.

"You won't believe it." Zoe wiggles her eyebrows, egging us on. She knows we live for details about the bizarre Farcus family.

I decide to play along, hoping to reestablish peace. "What?"

"He came over with a picture of my favorite tree and—"

"You have a favorite tree?" Ana turns back and seems to forget about her spat with Riley. "How does that work? Is it the one with the...best leaves or something?" Ana cracks up.

Zoe shrugs. "It was on the land we sold to the Farcuses. I mentioned to Marcus one day after he'd been following me around for hours and getting on my nerves that he was just about to clear my favorite tree for the stupid pool they're putting in."

"But what was so special about it?" I rack my brain to see if I remember any special tree on that property. I've drawn a lot of stuff at Zoe's house, but I don't remember an unusual tree.

Zoe blushes a little. "It was kind of a loner. There were no other trees around it, and yet it stood tall and straight and proud." She seems to lose her train of thought while she stares vacantly at the screen. "And it had this hollow in the trunk, where my dolls would sometimes live when I was little." She shakes her head and turns back to us. "Anyway, it was stupid. But he saved my tree."

"What?!" I lean forward and look at her. "They're not putting in a pool after all?"

"I guess he talked his parents into making the pool around the tree somehow. Or moving the pool. I'm not sure. But he saved my tree."

"Woooooooowwwwww." Ana nudges Zoe. "That's a really big gesture, Zo."

Zoe smiles in spite of herself. "I told you guys he was nice."

I catch Ana's eye, and we smirk at each other.

"I mean, wait. No. No, I mean, not like that."

"Sure," Ana says, nodding. "We believe you."

"I swear," Zoe says. "He's not as bad as I thought at first, but I'm not like you guys. I don't like the idea of dating yet. I'm not ready." Something in Zoe's voice sounds panicked, but Ana doesn't seem to notice.

I put an arm on her shoulder. "That's cool." Then I glance at Riley, but she's still staring at the screen. The light from the movie dances across her face, and for a moment I think I can see a tear sliding down her cheek, but I'm not sure.

14

"Do you have everything you need? Your phone? Money?" Candace hovers behind me in the bathroom doorway as I finish getting ready. She's blocking the door, so I can't slam it shut, but I am sorely tempted.

"I'm all set." I take one last glance in the mirror. I put a special rinse on my hair to make it extra shiny, and I slicked a light coat of lip gloss on. I don't love the outfit, but Candace's old flowy paisley tunic was the most seventies thing I could find. My jeans are flared at the bottom, and though they're not really bell-bottoms, they'll do. I have to at least get points for trying.

"Call if you need anything. I'll be here." She claps her hands a little. It's kind of weird how excited she is about my date, or maybe she's just glad to get me out of the house.

"When's my dad coming home?" I turn off the bathroom light and step into the hallway. She moves so I can get around her to my bedroom.

"Late." She sighs. "His meeting in Sacramento won't be done until eight, and it depends on traffic from there." She reaches into her pocket and pulls out a slim camera. "But he asked me to take a picture before you go out on your first real date."

Okay, first of all, it's not exactly my first date. Tyler and I went to that gallery this summer, so that makes this my first date that Candace knows about. And second, there's no way my dad asked her to take a picture of it. He hasn't thought of breaking out the camera since my first day of kindergarten. She wants something.

"My dad asked you to do that?"

She flashes her straight white teeth, but I stare at her, and she eventually crumbles. "Okay, fine. You'll thank me someday. Your first date is a big deal, Christine."

Someday? Clearly this lady doesn't suspect that I'm going to break up her and my dad and there won't be any "someday."

"Sure." I paste a cheesy smile on my face and twirl my index finger. "A date. Woo." She rushes to snap the photo and catches my eyes half closed. That'll be one for the books. I dash into my room and grab my sweatshirt off the bed.

"Thank you." She sees the shot and frowns. "Now before you go—" She puts the camera back in her pocket and laughs a bit. "I know you're almost a *woman* now and...I just want to make sure you know how important it is not to... get carried away in the moment." She blots imaginary sweat from her brow.

"Uh..." I stop and study her for a moment. She can't be.

"You have your whole life in front of you, and I'd hate to see you...have to give up your dreams if you...Has your dad ever talked to you, um, about all of this? About how important it is *not* to?"

There it is in the room now, and I feel nauseated. She nearly said it. S-E-X. Why does she have to be such an idiot? Does she have absolutely no idea who I am at all? And seriously, she's pretty much living with my dad, so who is she to talk?

I hold my head for a moment and wonder if I should run, but the room feels like it's spinning. "I..." She waits, biting her lip a little. I can't even look at her. "I've got it under control." What does she think I'm going to do? It's a youth group event, for goodness' sake, and it's me. I couldn't even talk to Tyler on my first date, much less hold his hand.

I brush past her, hiding my face.

"Christine, don't storm off."

I push my arms into my sweatshirt and stomp down the hall.

"You're not a little girl. It's okay to talk about these things." She crosses her arms over her chest, but I ignore her and head to the kitchen to get my car keys. Andrew couldn't get his mom's car tonight, so I'm driving to his house to meet him, and then he'll drive my car to the event since he's had his license for over a year. He's in my grade, but he was held back in kindergarten. So far having a license takes a lot of planning. I reach for my keys hanging on the little hook Candace installed next to the sink.

"You can ignore me, but I have to do this. It's part of my job as a parent."

"Oh please." I turn and face her. "You of all people are lecturing me about this? It's a little ridiculous, don't you think?"

She doesn't flinch. In fact, it's like she doesn't even hear me. She crosses her arms over her chest and follows me as I slip the keys into my pocket and head toward the door.

"I know you like to think no one cares or pays attention to you, but you're wrong." Her voice is remarkably calm, and

I turn around in spite of myself. She's standing in the dark hallway, watching me evenly, one eyebrow raised. I shake my head, then yank the door open. The cool, moist air feels good against my face, and I step outside.

"I'm not trying to be your mom, Christine. But you need to know that someone cares." I slam the door, and her voice goes dead.

MacArthur Lanes, a run-down joint at the edge of an old strip mall, smells like stale beer and sweat. It's dark inside, but the trophy cases gleam and the lights from the arcade cast a hopeful glow over the long, loud main room. The carpet is worn and the turquoise and maroon walls look like they've seen better days, but there's actually something kind of beautifully sad about the place. Even ugly stuff looks cool when it's falling apart.

"Your turn, Cutty," Jake, the loud-mouthed senior with acne-pitted cheeks, calls as he struts back to the curved fiberglass bench. Jake and Ben, Andrew's good friends, are our bowling partners. Apparently the three of them have been in church together since they were in diapers, and they have a lot of inside jokes, including calling Andrew "Cutty."

Andrew stands up, sighs dramatically, then stretches and flexes a bit as he walks to the ball return. He's wearing a tight white three-piece suit with bell-bottom pants and a white vest. It's really stunningly ugly in such a perfect way, and the other guys have gone all out too. I actually look ridiculous in my plain old jeans.

"You want some more soda, Christine?" Ben reaches into

his pocket and pulls out his wallet. He rifles through it and finds a couple of bills. Ben is the quietest member of this threesome and bears a striking resemblance to that stork on the pickle jars. He even has the wire-rim glasses.

"No thanks." I lift my plastic cup, still half-full of Sprite, from the table to show that I'm good.

"Quit trying to impress Christine," Andrew says as he walks back toward us. I look up at the scoreboard and see that he got a spare. Ben chuckles and walks off, his long hippie vest swinging, while Andrew sits down next to me on the bench.

I've been studying the three guys all night. They remind me of Goldilocks's three bears. Jake is short and stout. He's the life of the party, and yet he's a little too loud and brash. Ben, on the other hand, looms high over my head, and sometimes talks so quietly that I can't hear what he's saying. But Andrew is just right. He's a solid foot taller than me, outgoing but a good listener, generous, and hilarious to spend time with.

The lanes all around us are filled with teenagers in their best tacky seventies garb, and there's even seventies music playing over the loudspeakers. Andrew, the preacher's son, is even more popular in this crowd than he is at school. When ABBA's "Dancing Queen" came on, he did an amazing rendition of the dance scene from *Saturday Night Fever*.

Ben gets back with his soda as my turn comes up. I reach for my ball, then stare down the lane. I try to concentrate. There's no way I'm going to win this game, but I can at least make a decent showing. I take a few steps and hold my mottled blue ball up. I swing my arm and let it go, then watch it roll down the lane. It crashes into the pins with a satisfying smack. Eight down. Not bad.

I hear Jake booing and turn to see him laughing. Ben smiles at me, but Andrew isn't on the bench. I look around and see him sitting in front of the scoring console in the lane next to us, playing with the screen. Three girls there are screeching as their fourth throws another gutter ball. The electronic scoreboard shows it's her fifth of the game. I shake my head and reach for my ball again. I bet I can get the last two pins this time.

"Hey!" a thin blonde girl screeches from the next lane, and I realize all of a sudden I know where I've seen her before. She's Kayleen—one of the people Riley was talking to at the coffee shop the other day. Kayleen showed up tonight wearing a short skirt and go-go boots, though they made her exchange the boots for bowling shoes. She points at the screen above her head. "Cutty!"

Andrew cracks up, and though she's pretending to be mad, the delight on her face shows she's really not. Her friends are staring at the screen above their lane, which no longer says her name at all. Apparently Julie, Michelle, and Trystan are now bowling with Dancing Queen.

Dancing Queen—I mean Kayleen—starts hitting Andrew playfully, and he curls up into a ball to protect himself. "Stop...stop...," he gasps, rolling onto the floor to deflect her blows.

"I'll change it back!" he says, ducking her arms.

She stomps back to her lane, but Andrew doesn't follow her and instead just saunters back over to us. The way she's twittering with her friends indicates that she doesn't really want him to change her name back anyway.

"I've known her since first grade," Andrew says, shrugging at me. I nod, unsure what else to do. "She's like a sister to me."

During my next turn, Andrew changes my screen to Wonder Woman. I make a good show of protesting, like Kayleen did, but it's not really the same.

It almost bothers me that my name doesn't really feel all that original. Dancing Queen was at least thematic, but what does Wonder Woman have to do with anything? On the other hand, Wonder Woman has a magical lasso and can fly and save the world. As Andrew bowls a spare and gives me a high five so enthusiastic that my hand stings, I try to convince myself that it might be the best name of all. He thinks I'm a wonder.

It's time to stop overanalyzing everything. I'm with Andrew Cutchins and that's what matters.

15

After two rounds of bowling and an Oreo Overload sundae at the Cold Stone Creamery across from MacArthur Lanes, we climb back into my car. When there's no sermon and no cheesy worship songs, and, well, no church, youth group isn't so bad.

Andrew and I chat a little as he carefully steers the car toward his house. We've been joking around all night, talking about everything, but now, in the dark quiet of the car, it's different. His voice is deep and serious as he tells me about growing up as a pastor's kid.

"You feel like a monkey at the zoo, you know?" He fidgets with the radio stations and shakes his head. I fight the urge to tell him to keep his eyes on the road. "It's like, you have to be perfect because everyone is always watching. I can't just grow up and make mistakes like a normal kid because everyone judges the pastor by his family. They never say that straight out, of course, but that's how it is." The stoplight a good distance in front of us turns yellow, and I push my feet down on the floor of the car in a panic. Andrew eventually presses his foot against the brake, and we glide to a stop with at least two car lengths between us and the car in front of us.

Andrew seems so perfect that I doubt anyone has ever thought anything but the world of his parents. I'm sure my dad's advisors, on the other hand, are constantly counseling him to hide me at home because the politician's daughter shouldn't have a nose ring or pink hair or mommy issues.

"How about you? Are your parents cool?"

Cool wouldn't be the word I would use, but I can't think of any other, so I just nod. I hadn't anticipated how private it would feel inside the car and now that we're here, I realize I've never really been alone with a guy. Even when Tyler and I went to the gallery, the owner was there. I almost feel like I'm in my pajamas or something, like he can see everything. The high squeal of a radio ad against the low hum of the engine is the only sound as we navigate the dark streets.

"Yeah. They're..." I start, but stop myself. They're what? They're not a *they*. They're a *him* and an absence—actually, he's kind of an absence too. "My dad is okay," I finally say, and Andrew nods. "He's not around much." I must be talking quietly again because Andrew reaches for the knob and turns the radio down. "My mom is dead."

I wish I could take it back the second I say it. How did that slip out? At first I don't think Andrew heard me, but then I feel a light touch on my knee and realize it's his hand. He rests it there without saying anything. The muscles in my leg twitch for a moment but finally relax. It's comforting and refreshing in a way. Everyone always feels the need to say how sorry they are or how great she was, but Andrew might be the first person to actually say nothing.

He keeps his hand resting on my leg the rest of the way to his house. Relief washes over me as he pulls into the driveway, and he turns to me.

"You're different, Christine. I like that." He looks like he's going to say more, so I wait.

In the movies, this would be the part where he walks me to the door, but we're at *his* house. The light from his stoop casts shadows across his face, and even in the darkness I can sense that he feels as awkward as I do. I can't very well walk him to the door. This is horrible. Is he going to kiss me? I think I have Sprite breath. Is it too late to pop in a piece of gum? I think so, but what if he goes for it and I taste terrible and he tells everyone at school that I taste like puke and garbage and a bowling alley all rolled together?

Andrew reaches out toward me. I sit very still and bore my eyes into my lap so I won't frighten him away. His hand hangs in the air for a moment too long, unsure of what to do, and finally he puts it on the side of my head and runs it down my hair slowly.

"You have the softest hair," he whispers in the quiet. The car feels like it's about to burst into flames, and while 95 percent of me can't bear to tear my eyes away from my lap because I'm so afraid he both will and will not kiss me, the curious 5 percent of me wins out and I peek up at him. When my gaze lands on his lips, I think I might faint. My vision has adjusted to the dim lighting, and I can easily make out his blue eyes. We stare at each other for a moment, and I can hear his breathing. Is this it? Is he going to go for it? I begin to pray without realizing it, which is silly since I don't go in for all of that anymore.

But then there's a flash of light, and we both turn. The neighbor, the stupid, stupid, completely inconsiderate neighbor, is parking his car in the driveway next door, and it's enough to ruin everything.

Andrew chuckles a little. He takes his hand off my hair and reaches for the door. He stops, leans back, and pecks my cheek, then climbs out. "You want to have lunch on Monday?" He ducks his head inside the door to see my reaction.

"Uh," I start. Lunch. It seems like such a foreign word after being so close to my first kiss. It's too mundane to process. Lunch. Lunch. Lunch. I usually eat with the Miracle Girls, but I guess I can miss a day. "Yeah, I could do lunch."

"Good." He smiles, then straightens up and pushes the door closed. I watch as he walks up the cement walkway toward his house and disappears inside.

I tiptoe into my room. No, scratch that. *Our* room. Emma is asleep in the single bed where my dresser used to be. We had to rearrange all my furniture when she moved in. We got rid of my desk and put her dresser in the closet so now even Joe's bowl fits somehow, but it turns out that Emma is way better than me at remembering to feed him.

I toss my sweatshirt onto the floor, then change into my boxers and T-shirt and slip into bed, replaying the car ride home in my mind. Why is it so easy to talk to him? I never mention my mom, even to the Miracle Girls. Maybe it's because he's an artist too and sees the world in a different way, just like me. I hope the girls understand about our lunch on Monday.

I pull my sheet up and wiggle around to get my position just right. I adjust my pillow and close my eyes. Andrew's face floats in my mind.

"Hey, Christine?"

I sit straight up. What the...oh.

"Yes, Emma?" Great. I'm probably about to hear all about what happened on *The Hills* or the lyrics to Miley Cyrus's new song. If God really was good, Emma would be asleep tonight of all nights.

"Did you have a nice time?" Her voice is low, and in the moonlight from the open window I can see she's lying on her bed, staring straight up at the ceiling. The stuffed bear her dad gave her when she was a baby is tucked under her right arm.

"Yeah." I sigh. "I did."

"I'm glad."

I lie back down on my bed slowly and wait for more, but she doesn't say anything else. Her deep, even breaths are the only sound from her side of the room.

"Why are you awake, Emma?" I readjust my position and try to get comfortable again.

"I don't know. Couldn't fall asleep."

I try to focus my thoughts back on Andrew, but now I can't get the image of Emma, lying there on her bed, out of my head. She looks so small, and some strange part of me wants to reach out and touch her.

"Emma?" I don't really know what I'm saying, but the silence is too much.

"Yeah?"

"Do you ever miss your dad?" I roll onto my right side, trying to get comfortable.

"All the time." Her voice wavers a bit.

"Yeah." I raise my head and fluff up my pillow, then lay my head back down slowly. "Me too."

16

Zoe and Ana are standing at the edge of Riley's driveway talking when I pull up. I park in front of the McGees' house, which is strung with a huge banner that says "Happy Birthday, Michael!" It's Michael's fourteenth birthday, and Riley's family is throwing him a party this afternoon. Most fourteen-year-old boys wouldn't want their sister's friends crashing their party, or a polka-dotted banner for that matter, but Michael is different. Also, he's not exactly Mr. Congeniality, so it would be a tiny affair without us here.

I stroll over to the girls, who are in mid-conversation.

"This morning he came over to see if I wanted to practice our new band piece together," Zoe says, shaking her head. She turns to me. "Marcus." She rolls her eyes. "He wouldn't leave."

"So did you? Practice the new piece with him?" I ask.

"Yes, but only because I had to do it anyway." Zoe's cheeks turn pink, and we're silent for a minute.

"You guys, I'm worried about Riley," Ana says suddenly. "Tom's going to be at this thing, right?" She gestures toward the house.

Zoe nods. "It could be a good chance to talk to him and get to know him a bit."

Ana unwraps a piece of gum and pops it into her mouth.

"I don't want her to get hurt." I glance at her, jawing away at her gum. I love Ana, but I kind of doubt that this is her whole reason for opposing Tom. I suspect there's something far more complex going on here. She's always kind of looking for a chink in Riley's beautiful blonde armor.

"I'm going to see what I can do about it." Ana starts heading up the walkway toward the house.

"Welcome!" Mrs. McGee opens the door and ushers us into the living room. I count exactly one person I don't know: a pale, reedy boy about Michael's age, wearing a dark blue tracksuit. He and Michael are playing Wii bowling, swinging their controllers around spastically.

Riley waves from the kitchen. She's wearing an apron, and her hands are covered in flour. We put our gift—we all chipped in on a star chart since Michael loves astronomy—on the table. Zoe picks a chip out of a bowl on the table and pops it into her mouth.

"Michael, say hi to your guests," Mrs. McGee says.

"Hi," Michael says without turning around, while he swings the controller and sends the ball straight into the gutter. "Eighty-eight."

"And that's Alexei," Mrs. McGee points at the other boy. "He's a nice boy. Just moved here from Russia a few months ago, so his English isn't very good." I smile. Riley once told us that most of Michael's friends come from the international club at school, which was formed to give new immigrants a place to connect, but Michael hangs out there because the kids are nicer to him.

We all watch as Alexei uses his controller to bowl. He knocks over five pins and gives Michael a high five.

"Ninety-seven." I realize Michael is calling out the score after each round. If I know him, that's not the only thing he's counting. If I asked him right now, he could probably also tell me how many chips Zoe has eaten, how many times his father has laughed, and exactly how many tiles are on the kitchen floor, both including and not including the pantry. He's sort of like a counting superhero.

"Hey, guys," Riley says as she stamps cookie cutters into a thin piece of dough. "Come here and meet Tom." We trudge into the top-of-the-line kitchen, and Mrs. McGee disappears into another room. I hear talking and a little laughter in the dining room.

"Aunts and uncles," Riley says, nodding in her mother's direction. "Mom's so excited that she's running all over the house."

Tom, dressed in tan pants and a blue polo shirt, stands next to Riley, pulling the cut cookies off the cutting board and laying them gently on a pan. I'd forgotten how tall he is. He wipes his hands on a kitchen towel, then holds out his right hand to me.

"Christine. Nice to see you again." He gives me an easy smile, and I take his hand grudgingly. He is quite handsome. I'll give her that.

"And this is Zoe and Ana," Riley says, nodding at each of them. She uses her arm to brush a piece of hair out of her face.

"One hundred and five."

"Delighted to meet you," Tom says smoothly, smiling as if he doesn't notice the scowl on Ana's face. He seems comfortable, like he's spent a lot of time here.

"So what are you guys making?" Zoe says quickly. "Cookies?" Her eyes light up.

"One hundred and seven."

Riley bites her lip. "Yep. We're all going to decorate them later. Christine, you will be expected to produce a masterpiece." She laughs, but no one else does.

Suddenly high-pitched shrieking emanates from the living room. Alexei is jumping up and down, his tracksuit rustling. Michael throws his controller down and stomps his foot, then begins to wail. He does this screaming thing that will drive you bananas, and it looks like he's about to launch into it here at his own party.

"*Michael!*" Mr. McGee appears in the doorway, but Tom gestures to him to stay, striding through the living room. Mr. McGee takes a step back, as if he's deferring to Tom. Alexei looks confused and toys with the strap of the controller in his hand.

"Michael," Tom says, taking the birthday boy by the shoulders. He looks into Michael's face. Michael looks around, not meeting his eye, but Tom just waits. Slowly Michael begins to quiet down, and soon his whimpering stops.

I look from the scene in the living room to Riley, who smiles. "Tom's mom is a psychiatrist at the UCSF medical school. She specializes in autism, and Tom has helped her out at the clinic since he was a kid," she says quietly. Zoe looks like she wants to give Tom a big hug.

"Would you like to play again?" Tom asks, and Michael nods. "Okay. Pick up the controller." Michael obeys Tom's calm instructions. "Alexei, may I use your controller?" The small Russian boy nods and hands over his controller.

"Thank you." Tom puts his hand through the safety loop and pushes a button to go to the main menu. He selects his character—a tiny little digital version of Tom—and begins the game.

"You guys want to use the cookie cutters?" Riley asks, gesturing to the pile of metal shapes on the counter next to her.

"Actually," Ana says, "it's a nice day for a walk, don't you think?" She takes a step toward the door, then looks back, urging us to follow her.

Riley looks uncertainly out the window at the gray afternoon. It's November and thus not a nice day for a walk, but Ana goes right out the front door, and the rest of us don't have any choice but to follow her. Riley takes off her apron and lays it on the counter, and we all chase after Ana.

"What's going on?" Riley asks, her smile fading a bit. In the pit of my stomach I feel a rock forming. Maybe it's the foggy, damp weather, but I have an eerie feeling all of a sudden. The hair on my arms stands up.

"This is an intervention," Ana says calmly.

"No, it's—," I start, but Ana cuts me off.

"I'm worried that Tom isn't right for you. He's older, he lives too far away, and he's not good for you spiritually. And isn't he going away to college next year?" Ana crosses her arms across her chest and suddenly looks exactly like her own mother. "You're going to get hurt, and I'm worried."

Riley stares at Ana, incredulous. "You didn't even give him a chance. Not even a little bit." She takes a step toward Ana, her fists balled, then turns to us. "Is that what you guys think too?" Zoe shakes her head vigorously, and I make some sort of noncommittal gesture. I don't mind Tom exactly, but I do think we have a growing problem here. What happened to the girls who would back each other up, no matter what? The girls who could spend all day helping Zoe's dad with some weird project in the garden? Where did our easy friendship go?

"Everyone loves him. My parents love him. Michael loves him. No one else has a problem with this. What's the big deal?" She takes another step toward Ana, who stiffens her shoulders and stands firm.

"We just don't think this is right. You're going to get hurt, and—"

"Okay, Ana. *You* don't like Tom. I get it." Riley points her finger at Ana. "But why? What's the big deal? What is this really about?"

Zoe goes into panic mode, shaking her head. "You *guys*."

"Is this about the trig test you got a C on?" The moment the words leave Riley's mouth I have the urge to duck for cover. It's no secret that Ana struggles with math.

"What?" Ana rears her head back. "No. This isn't about school at all. This isn't about me. It's about—"

"Please, please don't do this. You need each other." Zoe wrings her hands.

"Zoe's right." I put my hand on Zoe's shoulder. "Stop it."

"Of course it's about you. It's *always* about you." Riley says, rolling her eyes. "You and Princeton. You and Dave. You and God. All you ever think about is you." Riley seems surprised by her own outburst, and she stops and clears her throat.

Ana looks like Riley has thrown cold water in her face. For a moment, there's a spark in her eyes, as if she's mustering the words to fight back, but then it passes, and tears start to pool.

"I see," she says slowly. Fighting back sobs, she begins to walk away, down the lawn toward the street. I don't know where she's going, since she doesn't have a ride or a phone to call anybody to come get her, but she holds her head up and doesn't look back. Zoe covers her face with her palm for a second, then chases after Ana.

I watch them go, then reach out my arms and pull Riley into a hug. I'm not really a touchy-feely person, but I make do, and soon Riley's body is shaking. Over her shoulder, I can see Ana throwing her hands in the air, and Zoe trying to calm her down.

I think Ana really is trying to do what she thinks is right. She believes that Riley needs to hear our reservations about Tom, but what I'm learning, what I wouldn't have the first clue how to tell her, is that sometimes what we actually need isn't really that important. Sometimes just being there for each other is enough.

I know in my heart that things have been said today that cannot be taken back. What we had was special... Now it's all messed up.

17

walk into the living room wearing jeans, a plaid shirt rolled up at the elbows, and a gold hoop in my nose. This is phase two of my brilliant plan. If Candace doesn't slap me on the face or curse a blue streak, I'll give up painting forever. Dad is going to be so angry when he sees how she treats me.

"Christine?" Dad stares at my outfit, his eyes bulging out. "We don't have time for this tonight." My dad's angry tone of voice is followed quickly by the sound of someone running down the hallway in heels, then Candace appears in the living room. Dad stands up and pushes his chair back from the kitchen table where he was looking over a stack of papers.

Dad's district covers the area from San Francisco down the coast, including Half Moon Bay. It's not like being the governor, but it's bigger than being president of the Rotary Club. It's somewhere in between, kind of like being a congressman but just for the state of California, so his staff felt that he needed to have a huge, nauseating engagement party at the Ritz, as if just being in the same room with my dad and Candace isn't nauseating enough. The gala is officially being thrown by the mayor of Half Moon Bay, but a lot of bigwigs are attending it. And I am not.

I spin around so they don't miss the fact that I am wearing my favorite black Chuck Taylors too. Candace's face is utterly calm, but I can almost see her internal temperature rising as my plan starts to work. "If your friends can't accept me the way I am, that's their problem."

Emma, who is waiting quietly on the couch, dolled up in a pink dress, her silky chestnut hair falling down her back, lets her mouth drop to the floor.

My dad is pretty pale normally, but suddenly his face is as red as the sun. It looks like steam might shoot out of his ears at any moment. Fine. As long as Candace yells at me and Dad lets me stay home tonight, I don't care. No way am I going to prance around at an engagement party and act like I'm excited about this ridiculous marriage. Besides, I promised Zoe I'd call her so we can strategize about how to resolve this horrible fight.

"Put something else on now! *Now!*" He points at my bedroom.

I cross my arms over my chest and raise my chin. "No. I'm an adult. I was invited. I can wear what I want." I give him a saccharine smile, and out of the corner of my eye, I see Emma still gaping at me. "Unless, of course, you're ashamed of your own daughter."

Dad clears his throat and takes a step toward me, but Candace raises her arm to indicate he should stop. Here it comes. She's going to kill me, and hopefully she'll get so angry that they'll call off not only the party but the whole stupid wedding.

"James? A word?" She drags him down the hall to his office where I can hear them hissing at each other. I try to listen in, but even though the walls are paper-thin in our little house, they're just out of earshot. She's probably trying to convince him that it would be easier to leave me home and tell everyone I have a cold or that she knows a nice boarding school in North Dakota that does a great job with troublesome stepdaughters like me.

"You'd better thank me when you're in high school," I say to Emma, who finally closes her mouth. "You're going to have it so easy. I paved the road for you."

"I think you look pretty," she says quietly.

My dad comes back into the room, his nostrils flared, with Candace on his heels. "Okay." He opens and closes his hands into fists, and Candace gently touches his back. This makes him stop doing the fist thing, and he mutters quietly. "Get in the car everyone. We're leaving."

They bustle around me, Candace digging in her purse for her keys, Emma doing one last spin in her dress, my dad patting his coat, looking for his wallet, while I stand completely still. Wait. They're going to let me go like this? Why isn't Candace seething at me, threatening to do me bodily harm?

"Come on, girls," Candace says and smiles warmly at me. It's not even one of her Kool-Aid-laced fake smiles. Her heels click on the wooden floor as she walks toward the front door, and Emma stands up obediently. I glance down at my outfit. They're not really going to let me go in jeans. What kind of trick is this?

"But—"

"We have to get going or we're going to be late," Dad says through his teeth. Candace gestures for me to hurry, and I realize they're serious. "Come on, Christine."

I look down at my jeans and notice there's a hole in the right knee.

"One second." I dash back to my room, swap the plaid shirt for a feminine top with a scooped neck, shove my feet into ballet flats, and change my nose ring to a simple diamond stud. I'm still wearing jeans, but at least I no longer look like Johnny Depp. Even I have more pride than that.

They're all buckled into their seats waiting for me when I trudge to the car.

Maybe they're going to drop me off at a home for wayward girls, I think as we cruise down the quiet streets of Half Moon Bay, but as we near the hotel, I realize they're serious. We're really going.

When we pull up to the uniformed valets in front of the Ritz-Carlton, I admit defeat.

The Ritz-Carlton is perched on an emerald green cliff, high above the Pacific Ocean. When you look out the windows, you can see straight into the moody abyss. Not that I've been doing that or anything.

"Did you see the fish eggs?" Emma squeals as she comes up behind me.

"I'll pay you twenty bucks to try them."

She claps her hands over her mouth. "Not for a million dollars." She grabs my hand and begins to pull. "But come look at this."

I allow myself to be dragged to the chocolate fountain.

"Look, they have donuts, and strawberries, and raspberries, and even marshmallows!" She skewers a marshmallow on a wooden stick, plunges it into the fountain, and devours it in one bite.

This must be one of the benefits of having a little sister: you're never alone at these kinds of things. That doesn't really make up for having to share my room and put up with her mom, but at least it's something.

For the next two hours, Emma and I sneak through the crowd unnoticed. I catch a few people staring at my outfit, but I hold my head up and pretend it doesn't bother me. We sample the full offering of hors d'oeuvres and stalk the waiters carrying the best selections. Plus, we make friends with the guy at the bar, and he gives us more soda whenever we want it without waiting in the line. And every five minutes Emma hits the chocolate fountain like a serious addict.

And not once does either my dad or her mom utter even a syllable to us. In fact, they don't even glance our way. It's almost like we're invisible, even when I wear old beat-up jeans and a nose ring, even when everyone else seems to stare at us.

A few couples are starting to hit the dance floor when Emma grabs my arm.

"Christine." Emma's lip quivers as she clutches at her stomach. "I, um, don't feel so good." Her skin is a lovely shade of green.

I grab her by the shoulders and steer her quickly through the crowd. "It's okay. Hold on." I make a beeline for the bathroom, knocking into a few people on the way. At least the carpet has a busy floral pattern. If we don't make it, the stains won't show too much.

I shove the heavy door open with my shoulder and sigh in relief when I realize the ornate bathroom is vacant. I swing open the door to the handicap stall and pull up the seat, and immediately Emma empties the chocolate contents of her stomach.

I rub her back and try to remember what my mom did when I was sick. A rag! She'd get a cool rag. I leave the stall and grab a towel from the stack folded in a basket on the bank of sinks. Only at the Ritz would they have real towels to dry your hands. I run the towel under the cool water and try to ignore the puking noises behind me. It's a good thing I don't have a weak stomach. I'll bet Zoe would be puking in the next stall over if she heard this.

I walk back to the stall, shut the door, flush the brown chocolate and marshmallow mess, and plop down next to Emma on the cool marble floor. It would be gross in any other bathroom in the world, but it feels like you could eat dinner off the floor here.

I put the rag to her head. "Thank you," she mumbles. I shrug because really it's no big deal. Anyone in my place would have done the same. Emma tries to laugh. "I don't want to eat chocolate for a year."

"Yeah right."

She begins to push herself up, but the bathroom door bursts open, and high-pitched voices invade our little sanctuary. Heels click on the smooth marble, and we both fall quiet. I don't want to embarrass the poor kid. It's pretty humiliating to throw up at your first fancy party.

"All I know is that Naomi must be turning over in her grave."

My ears prick at the sound of my mother's name. They must think they're alone.

"Really," a different voice says. "I don't know what James can be thinking. That Candace seems a bit common, right?"

I push myself up, trying to hear better, but I don't recognize the voices. I should burst out of this stall right now and rain down a flood of curse words on them so vicious and nasty that they'll be ashamed of themselves for the rest of their lives, but morbid curiosity keeps me quiet and still.

"If I had known he was available, I would have bumped into him around town, if you know what I mean."

I look down. The floor isn't really as bright white as I thought. It's actually kind of beige.

The women giggle, and I can hear one peeing while another seems to be doing her makeup. I hear the sound of a compact opening and closing.

"He's very good looking."

Beige with interesting swirls and bumps in it. Marble is actually quite beautiful if you really look at it.

"Definitely." The woman coughs a little. "But I was going to give him a year to grieve. I thought it'd take him longer than this to recover."

How dare they talk about my mom like that? And my dad for that matter? He isn't over my mom! Can't they see that?! That's what this stupid Candace thing is all about. I should come out now and give it to them.

I hear a toilet flushing; then a stall door opens and a faucet turns on. "Well, that Candace is smarter than I gave her credit for."

Emma reaches out and puts a hand on my arm, but I don't turn. I never realized how cold and hard marble is.

"May I use that? I left my lipstick at home."

"Sure."

There's a pause as one of them applies a new coat of paint. "Yeah, she seems like a real airhead, but she's the one who got the assemblyman and never has to work again."

One of them laughs a low throaty guffaw. "You're right. She's the smartest pageant queen I've ever seen."

The other one snorts as their voices move toward the door. "But she's still cheap and tacky." They both cackle in delight and push out into the hallway.

I wait, but the only noise is a faint sniffling.

I turn around and see Emma still on the floor, but she's covering her face and crying into her hands. I replay the conversation in my head, remembering all the awful things they said about her mom. I may not like her mom very much, but Emma is her daughter.

I slip my arm around her shoulder and pull her back from the toilet. We lean against the wall, holding each other, and I take the rag out of her hand and press it to her forehead again. She buries her head in my shoulder.

"Christine?" She takes ragged gasps of breath. "My mom is a good person. You know that, right?"

I blot her forehead and frown, considering this. Is she? "Of course I do, Em."

Emma's beautiful blue eyes well up with tears.

"I just don't think our parents are right for each other." I pull her close. "Do you?"

Big tears roll down her perfect pink face and drop onto her dress. She tries in vain to wipe them off. "No. I want my mom and dad to be together again."

I smile and breathe a sigh of relief. This kid is really okay. I put my hands on her shoulders. "We'll always be sisters, okay?"

Emma gives me a big hug, and for a while we just hold each other on the bathroom floor.

18

bend one knee and prop the sole of my shoe up on the rough brick behind me, trying to look cool leaning against this wall, which isn't the easiest thing to do. Andrew said he'd meet me right here, and I meant to tell the Miracle Girls that I couldn't come to lunch with them today, but... okay, I chickened out. Ana and Riley would probably just use it as an opportunity to pull out their claws and dig into one another, and I don't need that drama today.

I glance over at our usual broken wooden picnic table, but no one has arrived yet. I realize they might not be coming to lunch after all, given how rocky things got at Michael's party on Saturday, and the thought depresses me. Zoe and I have to come up with a new plan to bring the Miracle Girls together, but lately she's been hanging out with Marcus and the band kids a lot and I increasingly find myself alone, leaning against walls like an idiot. How do we bounce back from Ana telling Riley to dump her new boyfriend and Riley telling Ana that she's, well, a little jealous of her?

I hear people coming from the J wing and look up hopefully, but Andrew isn't in their group.

I really thought he might kiss me Friday night, and then I could finally take one step closer to being a normal teenager, but maybe it was in my head. Unfortunately, since my friends aren't really talking to each other right now, I can't exactly get their perspective on this. I was going to bring it up at Michael's birthday party but then...

And to make matters even worse, my mom keeps showing up in my dreams, meaning that I haven't been sleeping well. I can feel a headache coming on...A little hammer in my head, just behind my right eye, begins to pound. At least the sun isn't out today. The fog is shrouding the trees, and the air feels wet and heavy.

"Hey, Christine." It's a guy from my gym class. "Holding up that wall?"

I shrug. "It's performance art."

He looks confused and walks away, just as a flash of red catches my eye. It's Zoe. I wave at her, but she doesn't see me as she barrels over to our table. The lunch hordes have arrived now, and I can barely make her out through the occasional parting of the teenage sea. She takes a seat at our little picnic table all alone and dumps the contents of her lunch sack out. She glances over both shoulders, and I swear it looks like she's about to cry. I start to walk over to her. I'll just say hi, explain what I'm doing—well, if there is a way to explain waiting for a guy who is much too popular to even notice you and who is obviously standing you up at this very moment—and then come back to my position on the wall.

"Christine!" A familiar voice behind me makes me stop and turn around. Andrew jogs up to me, and my heart thumps with his every bounce. "Wait up."

I walk back to the wall, checking an imaginary watch on

my wrist. "Listen, I have places to go, people to see. I can't be made to wait all day."

Andrew runs his fingers through his hair. "You're right. I'm sorry. I got held after history class for a lecture." He sizes up the lunch crowd in the courtyard, everyone bundled up in sweatshirts and knit hats. "It seems I wasn't giving Queen Victoria the proper respect. I got caught talking again. It's been my problem since kindergarten." He grabs my elbow, and my hand throbs in jealousy. Elbow-holding is for friends; hand-holding is for a girlfriend. "C'mon. Kayleen is saving seats for us."

I'm thankful he walks in front of me so he can't see my face fall at the mention of little miss Dancing Queen.

"Thanks," Andrew says to Kayleen as he plops down on the bench next to her. There isn't quite enough room for me at the table so I stand there, shifting my weight from one foot to another, panicking and looking like an idiot. Why don't they scoot over?

I toss a glance over my shoulder and see Zoe walking away, her head hung low. I kick myself for not getting to her in time to explain. She looks so small and sad, but...I'm kind of trapped here.

"Oh!" Andrew pops up again. "Sorry, Christine. Everyone, this is Christine." He gestures at a table of people I recognize but don't really know since they all orbit a planet of popularity I'm not allowed to visit. "Christine, this is everyone." The guy on my right reluctantly slides down a little so that I can lean on the bench next to Andrew, but Kayleen doesn't budge an inch.

"How long did Mrs. Mortimer keep you after class?" Kayleen giggles.

Andrew rustles her hair. "Oh sure, gloat, why don't you? You're the reason I got in trouble."

I clear my throat. I am still here, right? I haven't disappeared entirely?

Andrew turns to me. "Kayleen is the reason I was late to get you. She asked me a question about basketball, and Mrs. Mortimer jumped all over me." He shakes his head and pulls a lunch out of his backpack. "Goody-two-shoes Kayleen didn't get in trouble at all, of course." Kayleen wrinkles her lightly freckled nose, and suddenly my yogurt doesn't look so good.

The sound of two plastic trays hitting the table turns my focus from Kayleen. It's . . . oh no. I nearly fall backward onto the courtyard lawn when I see that it's Ashley Anderson and Zach Abramo, everyone's favorite A-list couple. Barf. A few people at the other end of the table scoot over to make room for them.

I guess I should have realized that Andrew ran in this circle, but how am I supposed to sit across from the guy who left Riley to die and the ex-best friend who betrayed her? I need to make an excuse and get out of here. The last thing I want to do is have one of my flip-outs. Ms. Moore will make me talk about it for months.

I tap Andrew on the shoulder. "Listen, maybe we should just hang out another time."

"If it isn't Marina Vista's favorite alterna-teen." Ashley's sticky sweet voice drips across the table to me. I stare at her for a moment, then look at Zach, who won't meet my eye. At least he's ashamed of himself. "Christine Lee. Well, I never thought I'd see the day. Don't you have a nostril to pierce right now?" Ashley beams at me.

I lean across the table. "I can't believe you'd even—" I feel Andrew take my balled up fist into his hand, and it startles me.

"I begged Christine to have lunch with me today." Andrew's voice is calm and stern. Ashley starts to protest but instead bites her lip, slides down into her seat, and looks away without a word. My anger drains away just as quickly as it bubbled up, and I feel a calm wash over me.

Everyone at the table stares in my direction, making my cheeks burn, and I have to ignore a small part of me that wants to stand up and shout, "Ha! In your face!" at each and every one of them. Christine Lee is not some circus freak. She just so happens to be Andrew Cutchins's crush.

It's quiet for a second, but soon everyone is talking about what they're doing for Thanksgiving and the table returns to a normal hum. As Zach explains how his mother is insisting that he bring Ashley to his grandmother's house, I lean in to Andrew.

"Thank you," I mumble. It's hard for me to be sincere because I don't get a lot of practice.

He tugs gently on my hair. "It was my pleasure. She made me cry in first grade when she told everyone I was wearing Spider-Man Underoos, which I was not." He laughs. "I've never really forgiven her."

"You got the last laugh, Mr. Basketball Star." I raise my green tea bottle in a toast to him. "My only shot at getting the last laugh is if I grow up and become a famous painter."

Most people would assume I'm kidding, but I suspect Andrew knows this is as close to a career path as I've got.

He shakes his head. "They're jealous of you." He rubs my thumb with his, and my whole body comes alive when I realize he's still holding my hand. How does he do that? "You've already got the last laugh."

My insides feel warm and gooey, and it's a small miracle that I don't liquefy into a puddle right now and pool underneath the bench. I dig my foot into the soft grass under the picnic table, then notice something I recognize. Shoes. I know those shoes.

"Riley?"

"Um, hey," she says, sizing up my present company. I drop Andrew's hand as if I've been caught doing something wrong. "I stopped by the table, but no one was there."

"Well, as I live and breathe." Ashley laughs. "This day is just full of surprises. How *have* you been?"

"I gotta go," Riley mumbles as she walks away.

"Wait," I say to her back, but she doesn't stop. Andrew, oblivious to what's going on, starts joking with Zach about who will win the Stanford-Cal game, and Ashley's high-pitched giggle pierces my eardrums.

What am I doing at this table? That's it. I'm going to go. I'll catch Riley and try to explain that I didn't know I'd be sitting with her two mortal enemies, but as I gather up my things, I feel Andrew's hand on my knee again.

Riley's blonde hair fades as she walks down the breezeway, her head slightly bowed. I swallow. Maybe I can catch up with her after school. She'll understand.

19

"hmigosh. Here she comes. Don't forget what to say." Zoe bolts to the door and peeks through the peephole as Riley walks up the walkway.

"Cool." I'm just playing along here. I figure when Riley and Ana realize that we've had to resort to lying to get them to come together and work out their differences, they'll feel so guilty they won't even be mad at us. This feud has gone far enough.

Riley knocks on the door, and Zoe opens it so quickly that Riley looks confused. "Zo, were you waiting by the door?" Riley steps in and freezes. "Oh," she says. "Christine." She appears to be trying to process my presence. "I thought..."

Zoe walks around her, wringing her hands. "Yeah, ha ha ha. Um, Christine said she couldn't make it, but at the last moment, um..." Zoe looks like she might cry. She's the worst liar ever.

Neither of them has mentioned lunch on Monday. We've all been kind of doing our own thing all week, and it seems safer not to bring it up, so I've been pretending nothing is weird, even though things are definitely weird. And on Tuesday, only Zoe and I and this quiet freshman girl Tracy showed up for the Earth First meeting at lunch. Sure, Riley had told us she had a Key Club meeting and couldn't make it, but Ana didn't even bother to make an excuse. She's avoiding all of us.

That's when Zoe and I cooked up this plan. We decided to invite both Riley and Ana over for a movie night and sort of, I don't know, throw them together and see if we could broker a peace deal between them. We figured out that Zoe should tell each girl that I couldn't make it so they wouldn't suspect anything. She invited Riley for 6:45 and Ana for 7:00 so they wouldn't see each other as they came in. We couldn't have the two of them meeting before the big confrontation.

But now, in the heat of the moment, Zoe is having a hard time keeping up the ruse, and I'm wondering how to step in. I'm no professional like Ana, but I'm still way better at lying than Zoe.

I roll my eyes. "It's The Bimbo's fault. She said I had to watch Emma. Then her stupid Yogilates class got canceled so all of a sudden I could come over." I make myself comfortable on Zoe's couch. "I hope you don't mind that I crashed your hang-out time."

Riley shrugs, totally oblivious to what we're pulling. "'Course not. So what are we watching for our movie night?"

Zoe clears her throat and shrugs. We weren't really prepared for this question and didn't even try to actually rent something. I say the first thing that comes to mind.

"*Transformers*."

Riley's brow creases. "Really? Um, I already saw that with Michael."

I spring up from the couch and dive for Zoe's entertainment center. "Ha ha ha. No, I'm just kidding. We're not watching that." I yank the door open. Inside I find old VCR tapes of *Love Story*, *Doctor Zhivago*, and something called *Jesus Christ Superstar*. What kind of movie collection is this?!

Riley laughs awkwardly. "Whew, good. I hated it."

Zoe joins me on her knees and pulls out a tape. "Yeah, I was thinking of this one, but if you guys—"

The doorbell rings, and I hear Zoe gulp. I nudge her because she seems to be frozen in place.

"Oh, right." She jumps to her feet. "I wonder who that could be?" She sounds like an actress in a bad local theater group. She takes a deep breath, then opens the door. Ana is standing there.

I wave at Ana like a maniac.

"Christine? I thought you couldn't make it." Ana strolls into the room.

Riley bolts upright, grabs her coat off the couch, and begins to hurry to the door.

Ana whips around and glares at me. "You guys planned this." She shakes her head at us.

Great. Now she hates us all. Maybe this was the wrong thing to do. In fact, I'm pretty sure it was as Riley tries to brush past me and I move to block her.

"Ana, I'm sorry I tricked you, but I had to do something. I couldn't take it." Zoe's voice is squeaky. "The Miracle Girls are special. Different. We have to stick together."

I attempt a smile for Ana, but she shakes her head.

Riley steps forward. "Ana, I'm...I'm sorry." She says it quietly, and Ana's face doesn't change. "I am. But you need to give me the space to make my own decisions."

Ana shakes her head. "Don't you see?" She shrugs. "I said

that stuff about Tom because I care about you. These two are too concerned with keeping the peace to stand up to you and tell you what you need to hear."

Riley doesn't say anything as she pulls out her phone and calls her mom to come pick her up.

20

Zoe hasn't stopped wringing her hands since Riley left. We messed it all up.

None of us was really in the mood to watch a movie after Riley went home, so after a few minutes of awkward conversation, I decide to take off too. Ana called her parents, and even though they're at some event and can't leave yet, they're going to swing by and get her on their way home.

"I'm sorry," Zoe says for the thousandth time as she walks us to the door. In retrospect, it does seem like kind of a dumb plan.

Ana shakes her head. "It's not your fault," she says again. She takes her jean jacket off the coat rack and slips it around her shoulders. "It's..." She sighs. "I just want what's best for her, you know?" She sounds like she's trying a little too hard to convince herself, but I don't dare point that out.

"I know. We all do," Zoe says quietly.

I don't have the energy to have this conversation any longer. I just want to go home and hide out in my—my heart sinks. I can't even hide in my own room, or in the studio. "I'm going to go."

Zoe waves from the door as we make our way down the path to my little car. Thank goodness for my car. Maybe I'll drive around all night so I won't have to face anyone.

I climb in. The air inside is cold. I rub my hands together and then slip my key into the ignition and turn.

Nothing happens.

I turn it again, but the engine stays silent.

I take the key out and examine it. It's the right key. I try it again. Silence. I try it a few more times. Nothing works.

I think I read something about batteries being involved in starting the car. I pull the lever to open the hood and walk around to take a look. Yep. There's the battery right there. My car knowledge exhausted, I continue to stare down at the bumps and coils snaking around under the hood with no idea of what I'm looking at.

I sigh and pull out my phone. It rings through to my dad's voicemail as I walk back to the door.

Zoe's face lights up as she lets me back inside, and within minutes Zoe's dad, Ed, is hunched over the open hood with a flashlight while I try calling my dad again, but he's not picking up. He's supposed to be on his way back from Sacramento tonight. Ana and Zoe are sitting awkwardly on the couch.

"It looks like a fuse," Ed says as he walks back in the front door, takes his plaid jacket off, and hangs it on the coat tree. "I'm afraid I can't do much about that. I thought it might be the battery. I could have given you a jump, but I think you're gonna have to take it in to the shop." He adjusts his baseball cap and gives us a sympathetic smile, revealing his crooked front tooth.

"I can drive you home, if you like," Ed says, gesturing at his car. "Or you're welcome to stay here as long as you need. We've got plenty of room if you want to spend the night."

I love Zoe and everything, but all I really want to do is go home and climb into my own bed right about now. I force a smile and try my dad again.

Ed nods, then walks into the kitchen and turns on the water. It sounds like he's washing his hands.

"My parents are at a party for one of my dad's clients," Ana says, shaking her head. "There's no way they'll leave early, but you can come home with me when they get here." Ana's parents are overachievers too. They won't leave a work event just because Ana wants to go home.

"We could watch *Love Story*," Zoe says. "It's like the original chick flick. I swear it's good."

Ana sighs. I dial my dad's cell one more time. When it goes to voice mail again, I shake my head and take a deep breath. I'm frustrated, but I'm surprised this doesn't bother me more than it does. Maybe I'm getting used to it. I sigh and punch in a different number.

Fifteen minutes later, Candace walks in the door. Her smile is too wide, and her hair is too big, and she makes annoying small talk with Zoe's parents when all I want to do is get going, but somehow I almost don't really mind too much. In any other circumstance, I'd probably make fun of how thrilled she sounded when she picked up the phone, but...she's here and that counts for something.

21

When I walk into her office on Tuesday, Ms. Moore is wearing her jacket, one of those black peacoats people from the East Coast always wear. Something weird is going on. "Cold?"

"Not yet." She stands up and ushers me back out the door. "We're going on a field trip today."

"Ooh, like to the zoo? How about tidepooling? I love tidepooling. Our class went tidepooling in fourth grade, and Melissa Harris fell into one of the pools. Do I need a permission slip?"

She pulls the door closed behind her and steps into the hallway. As we pass Ms. Lovchuck, Ms. Moore tosses a careless wave at her, but she doesn't look up, and Ms. Moore doesn't seem to notice. She leads me out into the courtyard.

"What did I do to deserve such a treat?" I zip up my hoodie.

"It's time for a change of scenery, don't you think?"

I cough a little, but she smiles as if she's unaware that she's freaking me out, which is totally bogus. She walks down the cement breezeway toward the language classrooms, her footsteps echoing. It's not too late to run back inside, but she doesn't stop, and she doesn't look around to see whether or not I'm following her. It's like she doesn't care what I choose to do. I give in and jog a little to catch up with her.

"It's a lovely day, isn't it?" She takes a deep breath and lets it out slowly. I squint up at the sun. Huh. I guess it is kind of nice actually. I hadn't even noticed the sun was out, and it's chilly, but in a brisk, invigorating way, not a freeze your gizzard kind of way.

"Sure."

"Did you do anything fun this weekend?" she asks as we walk out of the courtyard and onto the long, sloping lawn where the stoners hang out.

"My car died." I let my steps fall into rhythm with hers as I walk next to her.

"What?" She turns her head a bit but doesn't stop walking.

"It's in the shop now. Turns out old cars have old problems."

"What happened?" We're passing by a small grove of evergreen trees, and their sweet smell reminds me of Zoe's backyard. I recount the evening, and Ms. Moore listens without interrupting, but when I mention the part about my dad not showing up, she demands every single detail, then sets her mouth in a firm line.

We move along the edge of the parking lot, and for a moment I think we might actually go on a real field trip, but Ms. Moore doesn't break toward any of the cars. I pick out my normal parking spot, near the corner of the student parking area under the trees. I sigh and keep walking.

"Where are we going?"

"I don't know." Ms. Moore sounds as if she's considering the question for the first time. "Any place you'd like to go in particular?"

Is she serious? She smiles and turns her face up to the sun like she's loving every moment of this.

"Not really."

"I was thinking it might be nice to check out the pool."

"I usually leave the swimming to Joe."

"He's still alive?"

"At my house, you have to be a survivor."

She smiles. "How's the wedding planning going?"

"Well, let's see. They reserved a cathedral. A simple church wasn't good enough for Candace. It's in San Francisco. I guess it's famous or something." I imagine the horrible service, me standing up there, dressed like a pastel birthday present with bows from head to toe. "I don't really know why they want to get married in a church anyway. It's not like either of them goes to church."

"Churches are nice." She leads me past the gym, pulls out a little key and unlocks a metal gate, then swings it open to reveal the pool deck. The high walls of the gym and locker rooms surround the cement deck on three sides, but the fence on the fourth side keeps the riffraff out while providing a nice view of a grove of cypress trees.

"Sure, churches are probably nice if you *go* to church. But it's kind of hypocritical to make a big deal about getting married in a church if you don't attend any other time."

In the middle of the deck is the long shallow lap pool, its surface smooth and calm, a beautiful shade of turquoise. Next to it, separated by a low metal railing, is the smaller, deeper diving pool, dark and shadowy, with two low boards and one high board. When the swim team gets here, this place is loud and chaotic, but when there's no one else here, it's quiet and feels peaceful in a way.

"I don't know." Ms. Moore pulls the gate shut but doesn't

lock it, then walks down a few cement stairs to get to the deck. "It must mean something to them. Even if they don't go regularly, getting married in a church is a statement of some kind."

She walks along the edge of the lap pool, and I follow. The water is four feet deep here, according to the little black number on the edge of the pool, but it seems much shallower than that from this angle. It looks like I could reach down and touch the smooth white bottom with my hand.

"Don't you think God would rather have them show up on special occasions than not at all?" She stops at the lifeguard stand and turns to watch my reaction.

Tiny wisps of steam curl up from the surface of the smooth water. It resembles glass, and I have the sudden urge to jump in just to disturb the perfect surface.

"I don't think God cares."

"I don't believe that." She starts walking again, toward the diving pool. "I suspect you think God cares more than you're willing to admit, even to yourself."

I follow her, unsure of what else to do. She skirts the edge of the deep, blue depths of the diving pool, her footsteps sounding in this cavernous space, and puts her hand on the silver rail of one of the low diving boards. She steps up onto the thin white board, and it dips under her weight. She bounces lightly on the end a few times, and I suck in my breath. She's finally lost it. She's going to do a swan dive in her clothes.

Thankfully, she bends her knees to stop the board from bouncing, then stands at the edge and looks into the blue abyss before carefully lowering herself down to a sitting position. The board curves toward the water, and she bounces up and down a few times, then gestures at the other diving board. I shrug, scramble onto it, and slowly edge my way out to the end. We bob up and down silently for a minute.

The surface of the pool is almost hypnotic.

"I used to dive." Ms. Moore raps her fingers against the rough fiberglass board.

"You did?"

"In high school." She laughs, a low, quiet laugh.

"Why did you stop?" I move a little, and the board bounces again. The bottoms of my Chucks just barely touch the surface of the water.

"It was fun, but I knew I couldn't ever be really good because I refused to compete on the high dive." She nods at the tall board next to us. "I did a little three meter work, but there was this big tower with these huge cement platforms, and the coach wanted me to dive off those. I told him the day he made me do it was the day I would quit diving."

"Why?"

"I was afraid of heights." She stares into the depths of the pool and frowns. "Diving is tough. Most of the time you're falling blindly through the air and you can't see the board behind you or the water under you. You have to be willing to throw yourself into the air and trust that physics will work like it's supposed to."

"And you couldn't handle that." I concentrate on keeping the bottoms of my shoes at the surface of the water. I point my right toe and feel a little water creep into my sock.

"I've always regretted that." She nods. "What would have been the worst that could happen?"

"You could have croaked."

"True. Occasionally someone will hit their head on the cement or land wrong and sustain internal bleeding. But almost never. Usually people figure out how to let go and conquer their fear. They get over it, they get better at it, and they end up doing beautiful things."

"I'm not joining the diving team."

"Tell me about the accident."

If I slipped under the surface of the water, I could stay beneath for a while. The water would deaden sound, and I could let myself drift off into blessed unconsciousness.

"Christine?"

"It was raining." I bite my lip and stare down at the water. The sun glints off the surface in a thousand different pin-pricks of light. "We were arguing." I swallow and keep my eyes trained on the water. "She—" I lie back on the board, feeling the hard fiberglass press into my spine, but it feels good, gritty. The sky is clear and cloudless, a deep blue almost the same color as the pool.

Here, in this strangely beautiful place, I almost want to tell her about that day, but the smarter part of me knows better. If I open up now, I may never be able to stop.

I wish I could slip into the pool and study the world through the water's surface, watch everything swirl, warp, and melt into itself.

"That's okay," Ms. Moore says finally. She leans back on her board too, then pulls her feet up so they rest on the edge. "It's a start."

22

The magazines say that if a guy asks you out with less than two days' notice, you should say no and act like you already have plans. That shows him you're not sitting around waiting for him to call.

Has anyone ever actually taken that advice? Who in her right mind would say no when Andrew Cutchins calls on Saturday to ask if you want to hang out? You say yes. You say yes even if you don't know what he means by "hang out" and even if you're not sure if it's a date or not.

Andrew just found out he could get his mom's car for the night, and he's picking me up in a few hours, but the late invite means that I don't have enough time to fix one major problem: a big red zit, right between my eyes. It's like a bull's-eye, and I need to do something about it. I lean back and squint at myself in the mirror, but it doesn't get any better.

A pot crashes to the floor in the other room, and I grimace. Candace is attempting to make dinner. God help us all.

The obvious thing here would be to ask Candace what to do because she must have lotions and creams that can make any kind of imperfection vanish, or at least some thick makeup to cover it up. But I have a little pride, and I'm not going to go begging from her.

I guess I'll have to make a trip to the store. I pull open the bathroom door carefully, peek my head out, and look up and down the hallway. Clear. I run to my room, grab my sweatshirt, and then make a dash for the kitchen to get my keys. I got my car back yesterday, thank goodness. The TV is blaring some Disney show in the other room.

"Christine!" Candace beams at me from behind the stove, wearing a calico apron as if she's Betty Crocker. "Where are you off to?"

I need to find another place to keep my keys, far away from prying eyes.

"The store."

"Oh, so's your dad!" She gestures to the other room. "I need more flour and some eggs, so I'm sending him on an emergency run." She laughs. "Why don't you go with him? Save on gas?"

"Uh..." I didn't even realize my dad was home, and she has no idea what store I was planning to go to.

"Come on, Christine," Dad says from the hallway, slipping his feet into black loafers. "We'll go together." Argh.

"Um..." I cannot think of anything more humiliating than going to the store to buy makeup with my dad, especially if he finds out I need it for a date. They both look at me. "Okay."

On the way to the store, Dad tells me about his latest round of legislative meetings, and I nod along, but I'm really constructing my game plan. I'll act casual until we get there, then run off to the cosmetics section and pick out some cover-up quickly. Dad will still be wandering helplessly around the produce section looking for the flour by the time

I'm through the register line and have my purchase safely bagged in my pocket.

The glass doors slide open as we step toward them, and when Dad stops to examine the list Candace gave him, I make a beeline for the cosmetics.

Okay...wow. There are a lot of different kinds. I narrow in on a brand I've heard of and begin to examine the little colored bits of plastic they put out to display the colors. I place ten different shades against my wrist. They have names like "Fair" and "Porcelain." I flare my nostrils, catching a glimpse of my nose ring. I guess they aren't going to have one that's called "Half-Vietnamese, Half-Chinese." I settle on Fair and grab some matching powder. I even snag a tube of colored lip gloss for good measure. Okay, now I just have to make it to the cash register without running into my dad.

I walk to the end of the aisle and duck down the row toward the registers. So far, so good. But—wait. Oh no. I jump into the closest aisle and stand completely still, holding my breath. What are the odds that Ms. Moore would feel the need to come to this very store right now?

I peek over to the cash registers again. I don't think she saw me. Let's just hope she doesn't need any...I look around me...paper cups. I wait for a minute. Okay, surely she's disappeared down the wheat germ aisle or whatever it is she eats.

I'm about to make a dash for it when I hear her.

"Well, hello there, Mr. Lee." I freeze. They're on the next aisle. What is she doing talking to my dad? Dad doesn't say anything for a moment, and I imagine him trying to place this strange woman in front of him. My dad's a politician.

He meets people all the time, everywhere, and they always remember him, but he very rarely knows who they are the next day. "Natalie Moore." I hear a rustling that sounds like maybe she's holding out her hand to him. "Christine's teacher?"

"Yes, of course." Dad sounds relieved, though he's trying to play it off like he knew. "How are you? Christine talks about you all the time."

Can Ms. Moore tell this is a lie? I pretty much don't talk to my dad about anything.

"She talks about you a lot too." Ms. Moore says smoothly. "In our weekly counseling sessions?"

My dad coughs. "Of course."

"I'm delighted to run into you." A haggard-looking woman pushes an overloaded cart down the paper goods aisle, and the squeak of the wheels makes it difficult to hear, so I lean in closer to the row of cups. "I was hoping to talk to you about Christine's progress. I've called your home several times, actually." She has? She clears her throat. "And your office as well. But I never seem to get an answer."

"I've been away a lot recently, but I'm sure my secretary has those messages for me." He coughs again. "Sorry about that."

"I know." I hear a clang, as if she's putting something into her cart. "That's kind of the problem."

"What?" My dad sounds confused.

"You're never around," Ms. Moore says this calmly, but I can picture the shock on my dad's face. No one talks to James Lee like this. "You're never home. Your daughter has been crying out to you for attention, and you're not even around to notice."

"I'm sure I don't know—"

"The hair? The nose ring? What do you think that's about?" She sighs. "You weren't there the night Riley fell off the cliff." Her voice gets louder with each word. "You weren't there to pick her up from the Pumpkin Festival. You weren't there the night her car died. You *aren't* there. She just wants you to be around, to be present, but you're not."

I'm a little horrified and a lot embarrassed for my dad but, in kind of a sick way, also a little pleased that she's sticking up for me. No one sticks up for me.

"I work in Sacramento," my dad says quietly. His voice is shaky, and a bit confused. "But my fiancée—"

"Is no substitute for her father. She wants *you*." I feel my cheeks get hot. It's like she's seen my darkest thoughts, the ones I haven't shared with her or anybody.

"I..." Still, my heart kind of goes out to my poor father, ambushed in the soup aisle. "I'm sorry. I didn't know."

For a moment, I think Ms. Moore is going to let it go, let my dad finish his shopping with a shred of dignity intact, but to my delight, and horror, she goes in for the kill.

"Have you heard her talk about her mother since the accident?" All I hear is a low conversation about beef from the butcher's stand, and I know my dad is shaking his head. "Neither have I. Don't you think that's problematic?"

"I..." Dad starts, then changes tactics, his voice louder. "I can't believe this. How dare you?"

"I'd love to have you come in for a parent-teacher conference," Ms. Moore says. "Why don't you give the school a call to arrange a time?" I don't hear an answer, but soon a shopping cart is rolling down the aisle toward the back of the store, and I turn and walk the other way, my head down. I didn't hear any of it. I have to pretend I didn't hear any of it.

I don't run into anyone as I get to the checkout lines. I choose the shortest one, and moments later I'm waiting by the door, examining the junk in the gumball machines to kill time. A girl in my math class has the whole collection of Homies. How many quarters does it take before you manage to collect them all?

"You ready to go, sweetie?" I turn to see my dad with grocery bags in his hands, smiling like a maniac. Okay, he's going the fake cheerfulness route. I can play along with that, even though he's never called me sweetie in my life.

"Aye-aye." I give him a little salute and smile, but I'm careful not to meet his eye. He keeps the smile pasted on his face as we walk toward the car, but he moves his hands so much I can tell he's agitated.

"Did you find everything you needed?" He doesn't take his eyes off the pavement.

"Sure did. Thanks." I look out the window the whole way home.

23

hold my breath a little and dab the spot very carefully. If I get this zit covered, I'll feel like Michelangelo when he completed the Sistine Chapel. I lean back and stare at my face. That's probably the best I can do. You can still see it, but it kind of blends in if you squint.

The doorbell rings, and I dab matching powder on the rest of my face and swipe lip gloss on. Then I tear down the hallway to my bedroom as my dad answers the door.

"Oh," Dad says. I can hear the surprise in his voice. These old houses are insulated with tissue paper or something. You can hear people breathing two rooms over. I slip my sweatpants off and grab my favorite pair of jeans.

"I'm Andrew Cutchins." I zip up my jeans as the pause in their conversation tells me they're shaking hands. "I'm here to pick up Christine." I grab a shirt from the closet.

"Yes," Dad says, sounding bewildered, though it's not exactly his fault. I told Dad I was hanging out with a friend this evening, and that's true. He just didn't ask enough questions to find out that that friend was a guy.

"Annnnndrrrreeewwww," Candace sings. "I'm Candace. I'm Christine's soon-to-be evil stepmom." She laughs at her joke as I pull on my socks as fast as possible. Now, where are my Chucks? I find one in my half of the closet.

"And this is Emma, my daughter."

"How tall are you?" Emma asks. I crawl over to her bed and peek under Emma's frilly white lace bed skirt.

"Gotcha." I pull the shoe out and cram it on my foot. Hold on just a little longer Andrew. I'm coming.

"Do you like Christine?" Emma says.

For a moment, I wonder if I should call the whole thing off because going out there now would be too embarrassing, but I picture Andrew's gorgeous face and know I can't resist.

"*Emma,*" Candace says. "That's not nice. You know better than that. Andrew, may I get you a glass of water?"

I'll have to tell him that Emma's crazy or something. I stand up, grab my bag, and take one last look at myself in the mirror. "Wish me luck, Joe."

"Hi, Andrew," I call from down the hall, interrupting his speech about his family and his church. I walk into the living room and mouth "I'm sorry" at him, and he laughs like a good sport.

My dad and Candace are hovering awkwardly, and Emma is so excited she's practically hopping around the living room.

"I think we're going to head out." I nod over to the door, and Andrew stands up.

"Wait," Candace says quickly. "Um." She nudges my dad, who doesn't seem to be processing what's going on. Candace shakes her head at him. "Where are you guys going?" Her voice is a little hard, so she smiles to make up for it.

I bend down to retie my shoelaces, which are already

in perfect bows, because I don't know how to answer this. Andrew only said we were going to hang out. We might be taking a private jet to New York for all I know.

Andrew clears his throat. "We're just going to hang out..." He obviously doesn't want to say more.

"Good-bye," I say firmly, then stare hard at Candace. This time she kicks my dad, who still doesn't get it, so I walk to the door.

"It was very nice to meet you all," Andrew says and shakes my stunned Dad's hand one more time before joining me.

"Bye, Dad," I say over my shoulder. The door slams, and we head over to Andrew's car.

He runs his hand through his hair. "Why didn't you tell them I was coming over?"

I feign shock. "I told them you were coming over." I weave around the mailbox to get to his car. "I told them my friend was coming over and that we were going to hang out."

"Your friend, huh?" He opens the passenger-side door of his mom's car. I slide into the worn upholstery and smile as he walks past the windshield.

I shrug. That was kind of genius, nearly Riley-level boy intelligence. Now I wait to see if he denies that we're just friends. I hold my breath as he opens his door, sits down, and fastens his seat belt, but instead of denying our friends status, he turns the key in the ignition and tunes the radio to a top 40 station.

"I'm not entirely sure if my plan is going to work. That's why I wasn't sure what to tell your parents—"

"They're not my parents," I blurt out. It sounds a little mean, and I immediately regret it. We stop at a light, and I laugh at nothing, trying to lighten the mood. "I mean, that lady, she's..."

Andrew is blushing at his slip. He knows more about my mom than anyone, but it's an easy thing to say by accident.

"No big deal." I punch him gently in the shoulder.

He pulls forward and starts heading down Main Street. Are we going to Half Moon Bay Coffee Company? The record store? That would be awesome.

"Well, anyway, I really hope my little plan works out." Andrew drives the car past the coffee shop, and I bite my lip. He takes a right. Wait a minute...

"We're not going to school, are we?"

His face breaks into a huge grin.

"You realize it's Saturday?" He nods. "Plus, I'm severely allergic to school." He laughs a little as he pulls into the school parking lot. "No, really. I am. My throat closes up, and I didn't bring my epinephrine pen."

As he parks his mom's car in the vacant lot, I pretend I can't breathe. He shuts the car off and puts the keys in his pocket. "Don't you trust me, Christine?"

He gets out of the car quickly, then walks around and opens my door. Normally I wouldn't be that into all of this chivalry, but my jeans feel sewn to the seat. He's taking me on a date to school? Pardon me, he's taking me to hang out at school. Okay, he's definitely not into me. Maybe I can fake like my dad is calling me and I need to go home. This is too embarrassing.

He gives me his hand, and I take it because there seems nothing else to do. He pulls me from the car, and I barely remember to grab my purse. "Follow me."

We walk across the black asphalt as the wind cuts through my clothes. Christmas will be here in just a few weeks, and it's really getting cold now. I clench my arms and follow him at a slow pace down the breezeway. Where could we be going that would be in any way fun? Or, for that matter, open?

"Is this how it all ends for me? People will say, 'Christine? I think I remember her. Didn't they find her body in a locker in the J wing?'"

Andrew laughs loudly. "That's why I like you. You're so funny."

He turns left down the B wing, and I know immediately where we must be going. He walks up to the art room and hesitates for a moment, then tries the handle. The doorknob turns, and he laughs.

Was he always this tall? It strikes me as a little funny that I would end up dating...or whatever this is...a basketball player. I hope this doesn't mean I'm going to have to start going to his games.

"I'd always heard that Mr. Dumas 'forgets' to lock his classroom so people can come here on the weekends, but I was never really sure if it was true or not." We walk into the studio and flip on the lights. They flicker on, and the low hum of the fluorescent bulbs fills the room. This is my favorite place at school, but now that it's empty it feels almost holy. I run my hand over the smooth, cold surface of the long table.

"I caught you smiling, Christine Lee. Looks like you should have trusted me on this one." Andrew stands close to me, and we smile at each other for a moment. He shakes his head a little, then walks over to the cubbyholes where the

works in progress are stored and pulls out the canvas he's
been working on.

"The truth is, I need your help." He puts the canvas on
an easel, and I walk over to inspect his work. He's painting a
man in front of a box. That's about all I can tell. "I can't get
my dad's hands right." He hands me a snapshot of a young,
hippie-looking guy standing at a podium. He has long strag-
gly hair, he's wearing a shirt with a huge embroidered collar,
and he's rail thin.

I snicker a little. "This is your dad? The same one you have
now?" I met Andrew's family briefly the night we went bowling, and his dad looks like a guy in a Sears catalog: normal
clothes, slightly out of shape, sensible haircut.

"Yeah, I love this picture. It's when he first got out of sem-
inary. He was going to change the world."

For a while we discuss what Andrew's doing wrong
with his dad's hands. His perspective is off, and I show him
where I would make changes and eventually leave him to
work on my own stuff, feeling like I might have actually
helped him.

I find my canvas and shake my head. This is not my best
work, but since I don't really have anywhere to paint at home
anymore, I'm kind of losing my edge. Or maybe it's the subject matter I chose.

I plop my canvas on an easel across the room and pull
some tubes of paint out of the drawer. I sort of wonder if I
should move closer to Andrew, but painting is such a private
thing. I can't have anyone—even Andrew—look over my
shoulder or I won't get anything done.

I begin to dab at my work here and there. I'm having a

hard time getting the light right. It's supposed to be reflecting, but the highlights look like a big white blob.

The window by the door is dark, and my soul feels light and happy. For the longest time, neither of us speaks as we both become engrossed in our work. There's something really intimate about being together without talking. With Andrew, I don't have to say anything. He gets me.

The highlight is a little too yellow. Maybe that's the problem. I dab a touch of blue into the paint and smooth a bit onto my canvas. That's a little better. It should feel like it's blinding you.

I'm concentrating so hard that I don't hear Andrew come over. The next thing I know, he's slipped his hands around my waist, and, as if this has happened a thousand times before, as if I'm the kind of girl who dates a lot, I lean back into him a little.

"Hi," he whispers and slowly rubs his cheek against mine as a million fireflies take flight in my body.

"Hi," I say. *Stay, stay, stay,* I chant in my head. With his arms around me, the world has melted away.

"What is this?"

I swallow, unsure whether I still have the ability to speak. I start slowly, dazed. "It's a study." I draw a long breath. "It's breaking glass, with the sun hitting it."

He lets his chin drop to my shoulder. "It's amazing." He brushes his lips across my cheek and I feel light-headed, then he leans in and places a light kiss on my brow.

24

There's a knock at my door. "Your stuff is all over the room. You don't have to knock anymore." It's a boring Wednesday night, and I'm doing my usual— sketching instead of studying.

Dad peeks his head through the doorway. "Um."

"Oh." I drop my pencil. "I thought you were Emma." I sit up, hoping he doesn't actually come in my room because that would be weird. He hasn't come in here since I was...a long time ago.

Dad pushes the door open but doesn't step inside. "I wondered if..." He puts one foot in, then steps back out. He sighs. "You busy?"

"No." The moment I say it, I regret it. He's up to something, maybe something Candace put him up to, and I should have said I was busy to save us both the embarrassment.

"Good, then." He motions to the hallway. "C'mon. I need your help." He flees my room quickly.

Help? Well, that's probably a good sign. I'll bet he wants advice on what to get Candace for Christmas, and I know just what to tell him: a life. Ooh! Or maybe a brain. No, no, no. I know. A clue. Now that would be awesome. I toss my sketchbook aside and head out.

"Grab your heavy coat."

Dad won't tell me where we're going. We're riding along with our windows a little cracked, dressed up like a couple of snowmen. This really can't be good.

"So, I—" His voice fails him and ends in a squeak. He takes a sip from the water bottle in the cup holder, and I die a little inside for him. He's almost in physical pain when he's alone with me. "I wanted to talk about...Andrew."

Curveball! Curveball! Maintain calm, Christine. "Oh?" Didn't he hear that Candace already gave me her version of "the talk"?

The light turns green, and he accelerates the car onto the highway. "In the future, I want to know if a boy is coming over."

I scowl. Now he wants to play Dad? After all this time? "Why?"

"Because I'm your father and I get to know where you're going, who you're going with, and what he's like. I don't even know this kid."

I cross my arms over my chest. "He's not a kid."

Dad grips the steering wheel tightly, keeping his eyes on the road. "I'm sorry. I didn't mean to..."

We pass fallow fields where artichokes, lettuce, tomatoes, and all sorts of berries will grow in the spring. Now the upturned dirt just looks sloppy and hopeless.

"I'm sorry. I didn't go about that right." Dad rolls in his bottom lip. "But I would like to meet your...the guys... who are your friends."

I pick a fuzz ball off my black mittens, then roll my window down a little more, hoping to let the awkwardness leak out of the car. I can't believe we have to talk about Andrew. "Okay," I mumble, hoping he heard it because I don't know if I can say it again.

Dad's shoulders relax. "Okay." He fidgets with the radio dial. "Good." He finds a talk radio station and sits back. "He seemed very nice. I think I know who his father is."

I nod. There's got to be a way to change the subject. Let's see. Candace. There's got to be something I can say about Candace.

"Are you at all worried about Candace's ex-husband?" I blurt out. I'm kind of proud of myself, actually. This might be just the thing to raise doubts. "They were married for a long time. Are you sure she's ready for this whole marriage thing again?"

"I'm not worried." Dad shakes his head. "Are you?"

"I don't know. They got married pretty young. She must have loved him a lot." I study his face to see how he reacts. Maybe I'm onto something here.

Dad gives me a shy smile. "We've had plenty of long talks about this, and aside from Emma, they don't have anything in common anymore. There's no need to be concerned." He bobs his head a little bit. "Don't worry. She's not going anywhere."

His smile is so genuine that...He thought I was actually worried she might leave! Is he that dense? How can this man be genetically related to me?

As I'm sputtering, trying to come up with a response, Dad takes a sharp exit off the highway and we careen down the frontage road, turning onto a small dirt path between two fields. Unlike most of the fields around our town, which are empty in the winter, these fields are bursting with green trees in neat rows.

"We're here." Dad sounds about as uncomfortable as I feel.

"What is this place?" Outside my window, cheery people decked out in flannel are stomping around in a muddy field. "Isn't this where Cabbage Patch Kids are born or something?"

"No," he coughs. "It's a Christmas tree farm."

I turn to my dad and see that his face is filled with hope.

"We need a tree, and I thought it'd be fun to cut our own this year." He musses my hair, and somewhere deep inside my memory bank I recall him doing that years ago.

He waits for a moment to see how I will react. I could run, end this ridiculous outing now. Or I could grab the keys and wrestle my way into the driver's seat. He's watching me carefully, and I sigh. Okay, if he's going to try, I guess I have to try too.

"Let's go kill a tree."

We climb out of the car and stroll over to a guy wearing one of those big Elmer Fudd-looking hunting caps and a name tag that reads Buddy.

"Hi, we'd like to get a Christmas tree."

Buddy eyes my dad's expensive haircut, manicured nails, and wool coat. "The precut trees are right behind me," he says through a wad of something in his cheek and gestures over his shoulder.

"We want to squeeze the life out of it all by ourselves." I mimic chopping it down.

My dad laughs quietly, but Buddy is not exactly into the

holiday spirit. His nostrils flare. "Cut yer own trees are right there." He turns around behind him and grabs a saw from a rack. "Here's your saw."

Dad reaches for the saw slowly, as if Buddy might try to bite his hand, then we hightail it out of there.

"What is his deal?" Dad says, nearly tripping over a hole in the ground. His use of slang sounds so foreign that it makes me laugh.

"I think he was a disgruntled Santa's helper."

We walk over to a field with long rows of Christmas trees in all shapes and sizes. Dad wanders through the closest row, running his hands over the needles. "They look kind of funny like this, don't they? I've only ever seen them after they've been domesticated." This is about as close to roughing it as the Lees get.

I kick the trunk of a big Scotch pine. "Ow! They're vicious in the wild." He smiles, and I begin to relax. This isn't so bad. We wander up and down the aisles, hunting for the perfect tree. At one point, he stands behind a particularly small tree and frowns. But once he pronounces it "Tiny Tim" and gets a dirty look from another cranky worker, I know he must really be related to me. It's funny, I look like my mom, and my dad couldn't even draw a stick figure, but I guess I am like him in some ways.

"What about this beaut?" I slap my hands together and puff out my chest like a logger.

Dad leaves a particularly sad evergreen specimen and comes over to inspect my tree. He nods and strokes his chin thoughtfully, as if appraising it carefully.

I run my hand over it like Vanna White. "It's tall, green,

and, um, I think it's straight, and"—I lean in and take a huge whiff—"it smells piney."

Dad shrugs, making me worry about that saw in his hand getting a little too close to his knee. "Works for me."

"Then let's chop this sucker down."

Dad pretends to crack his knuckles and loosen up his neck. "Okay, I'm going in." He hands me the saw, lowers himself very slowly, and then says to me, "Scalpel!" I give the tool back to him.

It takes him quite a while to saw through the trunk of our tree. I watch many families pass us, their fathers shouldering their trees or showing off by helping the workers tie them to the top of their SUVs, but Dad does eventually get our tree to fall over. Well, he sort of pushes it over, but I cheer anyway.

25

"On your mark." Fritz wiggles his eyebrows. "Get set. Sculpt!"

At the sound of his voice, thirty teenagers squeal in delight and begin to cover paper plates with piles of whipped cream. On my left, Ana is carefully squirting the whipped cream into precise spots. Riley, on my right, is going for a tall tower of cream and sculpting it with her hands.

When Ana invited me to the big youth group Christmas party, I kind of put her off. Things are still weird with all of us. I've seen Ana and I've seen Riley, but this is the first time I've seen them together since the big spat over Tom, or school, or whatever their problem really is. They haven't said a word to each other all night.

When Fritz told us we'd be sculpting winterscapes out of whipped cream, I wasn't even surprised. Every time I darken the doors of this place, Jell-O, whipped cream, marshmallows, or eggs are involved. I'm just glad nothing is being squirted on me tonight.

"There's a huge prize at stake." Fritz walks through the rows of competitors and tries to act like this is a serious event. He looks down at my blank red plate as he approaches us. "Christine, not into dairy?"

"I'm lactose intolerant."

Fritz chuckles and walks over to inspect Zoe's piece. "Is that a stable?"

"I'm trying to do a whole manger scene," she says, sculpting a fairly impressive cow.

I take the cold can of whipped cream and draw a smiley face on my plate. I set the can down, then sit back and squint at it.

At least Three Car Garage is singing cheesy Christmas classics for us. Dave is wearing a bright red necktie and an amazing Santa sweater that made Ana laugh hysterically, so that alone has made my time here worth it.

"Okay, five minutes left." Judy, Fritz's wife and partner in crime, is taking notes on a clipboard.

Next to Andrew, Tyler seems like such a cheese ball. I don't know how I ever thought he was so wonderful. It's funny how crushes blur your sense of judgment.

"And, *stop!*" Fritz screams as the timer on Judy's watch beeps.

"Okay, I want to see all hands on the tabletop as Judy and I come around to score your masterpieces." Fritz and Judy whisper to each other and make notes on their boards, trying to act very serious, as they walk down the line, judging each "sculpture."

"Hey, Ana. Christine." We turn to the sound of Riley's voice, and I see something white flying through the air. I duck, but a tiny glob of whipped cream lands on Ana's hand, and Riley howls in delight.

I stand up, grab my can of whipped cream, and give it a good shake. "That was really stupid, Riley." I point at my mostly empty plate. "As you can see, I have the fullest can here."

I hold the can over her head, wiggling my finger over the trigger. "I wonder how you'd look with a nice hat?" I shake the can again.

Riley looks up. "Don't do it! I'll get you back!"

While she's distracted, Ana seizes the opportunity and shoots whipped cream toward Riley. It lands on her face, and people around us hush and stare. I back away, slowly. Riley grabs a wad of napkins and runs them over her face, then tosses the napkins down.

"I can't believe you did that!" She grabs her own can, but hesitates.

Ana cocks her head to the side. "You going to cry about it, cheerleader?" She puts her finger on the nozzle of her can. "Can't take a joke?"

Uh-oh. Wait. *Was* that a joke?

"Oh, I can take a joke," Riley says, laughing. She keeps a smile pasted on her face as she calmly makes a Z across Ana's fancy Banana Republic top.

Ana looks down in horror, then lifts her head carefully, and a slow smile spreads across her face. "It's on."

"Guys?"

Zoe is at my side in a moment, but she's too late. Ana and Riley are spraying each other with whipped cream as everyone else in the gym runs for cover. Ana and Riley are screaming stuff at one another, but I can't quite make out what they're saying, and I can't tell whether they're joking or serious. Maybe a little of both.

They fall to the ground in one wet mass and begin to roll

around, spraying each other with whipped cream, and Zoe and I step farther away. I'm happy to stop them from killing each other, but not if they're covered in whipped cream. There is a line.

"Ladies, ladies!" Fritz shouts above them, but they don't seem to hear him. Ana screams, and Riley fills her mouth with whipped cream. Fritz walks around to the other side of them. "Stop it!"

And then an ear-splitting whistle peals through the gym. The girls stop rolling around and look up. Judy has her arms crossed. "That's enough."

Riley seems stunned that everyone is watching them. She laughs a little and stands up, then helps Ana up awkwardly.

"How about a hug?" Ana says quietly. Riley eyes her skeptically, but they embrace, getting more whipped cream all over each other. I can't tell if they're smiling or not.

I never knew you could take a bath with nothing more than a little hand soap, paper towels, and a sink, but Ana and Riley have managed to do just that. They're still eyeing each other warily, but at least they're not throwing things at each other. Maybe that means they got the tension out with their little stunt. Maybe this whole crazy thing was just good ol' fun. Right? I mean, that's what it has to be about.

We locked the door, so it's only the four of us in this tiny little church bathroom that smells like diapers. Riley just peeled her shirt off and stuck it under the faucet, and now she's drying it with the hand dryer.

I clear my throat to break the silence, trying to think of

something to say. Ana glances at me, then turns back to her shirt. I meet Zoe's eye, and she grimaces.

Well...this is kind of the perfect opportunity to get their take on Andrew. With all this other weirdness going on, I haven't really had a chance to ask them about it. Should I bring it up?

I hesitate, and Zoe jumps in. Bless her.

"Guys?" Zoe is boring her eyes into the industrial-grade tile floor as if there were a hole opening up in it. "I have to tell you something."

Ana waits expectantly, and Riley smiles. "You okay, Zo?"

Zoe gives her a dopey grin. "Maybe?" She takes a deep breath. "Marcus tried to kiss me."

"What?!" Ana screams.

Zoe glows red from head to toe. "And I kind of let him."

"You did?!" My own loud voice startles me.

"I didn't really mean to. And it was just a peck on the lips. It doesn't really count."

Ana claps her hand over her mouth, and Riley swoops in to hug Zoe. They fall on her with a hundred questions while I stay perfectly still.

Zoe got her first kiss?

Great. Now I'm officially the only Miracle Girl who's never been kissed. I swallow back the urge to tell them about Andrew. It's too embarrassing now.

The cheese stands alone again.

26

The house is dark and blissfully quiet. I adjust the cushion behind my head, lean back on the couch, and sigh. It's so peaceful when no one else is here. Candace went out to the studio hours ago, and Dad and Emma have been quiet for long enough that I know they must be asleep. The only light in the house comes from the white lights Candace strung up on the Christmas tree, and the room smells like fresh pine. Everything else is in the shadows, and familiar pieces of furniture look foreign and new. It's funny how things you've seen every day of your life can change when you look at them differently.

It's 1:00 a.m. Andrew and I have been talking for four hours. I'll be tired tomorrow, but I don't care. And maybe because it's late, or because of the strange lighting, or because he's worn me down, somehow, a little while ago, when he asked me about my mom, I forgot to stop myself from telling him about her. I told him about how she would disappear into her studio for hours and come back into the house with paint all over her hands, and I could tell what she'd been working on based on the colors smeared across her clothes.

And I told him about how much she loved Christmas,

and how she would hang wreaths and fresh greenery all over the house, and how she loved to play Christmas carols while she painted.

"Yeah, Christmas is a big deal at the pastor's house too," Andrew laughs quietly. "It's show time. It's when you fill the seats with all those people who don't have time for God all year long. You play a few sappy songs, make 'em cry, and they give money—then you're set for the year. It's a sacred tradition."

Being a pastor's son has warped Andrew in a lot of ways. Things that normal people cherish—weddings, funerals, religious holidays—are part of his everyday world and only mean that his father will be working harder than usual. It's weird to realize that the pastor has a family he's neglecting when he's attending to you.

"Oh come on. Even you can't be so cynical that you don't like Christmas music." I pull a crocheted blanket that Mom made for me during her hippie phase up around my neck. I can only assume Dad hasn't gotten rid of it because of its functionality and warmth. Does he even know where to buy blankets?

"I do like Christmas music! I'm not Scrooge. I just don't like the kind of sappy stuff that puts butts in the pews on Christmas Eve." Andrew sings a few bars of "The Little Drummer Boy." "I like the old stuff."

"Ooh, you're so retro and original, what with being misunderstood and all."

"No, really. 'Silent Night' makes me want to vomit. But there's a lot of great stuff out there. In fact," he says, a jingle in his voice, "that's why I called."

"You had a point four hours ago?" This phone call marks

some kind of personal record for me—never have I talked for so long.

"I did, as a matter of fact."

"Do tell."

"My whole family is going to see the *Messiah* on Saturday night in San Francisco. My parents said I could invite someone, and I wondered if you want to go."

"The *Messiah*?" Wow, his family really does like Jesus. I always assumed pastors took their families to R-rated movies and Hooters and stuff when no one was looking, but Andrew's family goes to hear people sing about God. I should just say no now. This family is way too holy for me.

"Yeah. It's by this guy Handel, and it's performed by a huge choir every year in the opera house."

"Hey, I know what the *Messiah* is. My dad's not a pastor, but I'm not a Satan worshipper either. My mom loved the *Messiah*." There's this famous chorus she liked to play over and over. I loved sitting in her studio with her, watching her paint with the music playing in the background.

"Seriously?"

"Yeah." I let out a long breath. "She was pretty religious actually."

"So you'll come?"

"Saturday?" I don't have anything going on, but . . .

"It's at the San Francisco Opera, so wear a dress. My mom is making me wear a tie."

"With your family?" How's he going to kiss me in front of his family?

"I can't wait for you to get to know them. Can you be at my house at six?"

"Um…" A dressy night with his family. Is that a date? It's not *not* a date. Hanging out with the family is a serious step that you'd only bring a girlfriend along for. "Sure."

"Good." He lets out a long, deep yawn, and I snuggle down under my mom's blanket. Saturday night. My stomach flips a little. "I'm beat."

"Yeah, I should probably go to bed too." I'm not going to bed. I'll never be able to fall asleep now, but I pretend to yawn anyway.

"Cool. See you at school tomorrow. And don't forget about Saturday." The line goes dead. As if I could forget about Saturday.

The *Messiah*. My eyes travel out the big sliding glass door toward the studio. In the darkness there are no signs of life, and it looks exactly the same as the last day I saw her. If I squint a little, it might be two years ago.

I roll onto my side and adjust the pillow under my head. It's late and I should get to bed, but I'm kind of mesmerized by the tree. Candace's lights really do make it look nice. Maybe I'll stay here a little while longer. There's something so strange about being awake in the middle of the night. It feels like this living room is all that's real—like there's no one else in the world. I try to pretend I'm an adult living in Manhattan all by myself.

The lights in the studio flick on and catch my eye. I lean back against the pillow again. Candace is up too.

For some reason, this annoys me. I liked being the only one in the world. Leave it to her to make me feel ordinary again.

With a sigh, I push myself up. Might as well go to bed now.

27

Andrew's family is amazing. I was practically trembling when I drove over to his house this evening, but his mom, dressed to the nines in a red sequined jacket, wrapped me in a hug, and his twelve-year-old sister, Angela, and her friend Rebecca have been chattering away and asking me questions all evening. They kind of remind me of Emma, only they're not annoying.

And Andrew—well, I nearly choked when I saw him all dressed up in a suit. Men should seriously wear suits every day, like in the black-and-white movies Zoe loves so much. Everyone looks better dressed up. He introduced me as his "friend Christine," but I guess that's the kind of thing you say in front of your parents. Girlfriend would be way too embarrassing.

"Andrew tells me you like classical music," Mr. Cutchins says as we make our way through the crowd in the enormous lobby of the San Francisco Opera. He's wearing a dark gray suit with a conservative necktie. I shoot a panicked glance at Andrew, who shrugs and looks away as if he hasn't heard anything. Is it a mortal sin to lie to a minister?

"Sure." I nod, praying he doesn't ask me anything else because I don't know an alto from an oboe.

"It's a shame more people your age don't appreciate it. We

tried to raise our kids with a deep love of all kinds of music."
We start up a staircase covered with rich red carpet.

I glare at Andrew, remembering his comment about
"Silent Night." He's cracking up. "Who's your favorite com-
poser?" Mr. Cutchins continues.

"Hey, Dad, where are our seats?" Angela reaches to grab
the tickets from her father's hand, and I could hug her. She
and her father confer, then Mrs. Cutchins takes the tickets
to an usher in a fancy uniform who points us to our seats.
We're in a huge room with three levels of velvet seats and
enormous velvet curtains.

Andrew takes my hand as we walk up the steeply pitched
steps to row H. His parents file in, then Rebecca and Angela
follow, and Andrew and I sit on the end. By the time the
lights in the theater dim, I'm practically giddy with excitement. Andrew keeps his hand on mine, and as the huge
choir takes the stage, he rubs my hand softly.

Finally, the funny-looking conductor swings his stick.
They all start singing, and I feel like I'm supposed to do
something. Do we really just sit here and watch? I look
around uncertainly, and everyone else seems to be sitting
and watching, so I begin to relax and enjoy the moment.

The music is beautiful. There must be three hundred people on stage, and they're all singing different parts, but it
somehow comes together to form one amazing sound. A big
sound. For the first few songs, it seems like the music is in a
different language because the words are all broken up and
sung strangely and repeated over and over, but as I listen
more closely, I begin to pick out phrases, and soon the words
make sense if I concentrate hard enough.

I try to block out everything going on around me and absorb the music. Hearing these familiar notes, even in this overwhelming space, is oddly comforting. The first part is about the birth of Christ, which I guess is why people always listen to it at Christmas, but when I close my eyes, I don't see lonely travelers and a baby. I see a cramped little studio, warm and humid, and an overstuffed couch, and paints strewn all around. I see my mother humming along to the music. We never talked while she worked, but I liked being in the same room with her. She always said that Jesus' coming to earth as a little baby reminded her that God was good.

Suddenly the audience stands up. Is it over? No one is moving toward the exits. They're just standing. I rise to my feet too. Oh right. This is that chorus part. I look down the row and see Andrew's dad bobbing his head with the music and Rebecca texting. But Mrs. Cutchins is standing perfectly still, staring straight at the stage, with tears in her eyes. Andrew catches my eye and squeezes my hand, and I smile at him, then look back at the stage.

Somehow everyone knows when to sit back down. The choir goes on singing as the conductor waves his arms around wildly, and I lean forward and strain to discern the words. This is the part that doesn't make sense. The baby in a manger thing I can understand, but now they're singing about death being overturned, even though it isn't true that someone could die and come back again. That cannot happen no matter how much you hope and wish and pray that it could.

A tear runs down my cheek as I try to remember her face. I can only picture it in distant memories these days. I can't

call up her face at will. I have to think of a day and then let
the memory play forward like a movie in my mind. Andrew
interlaces his fingers with mine. I take a deep breath, then
let it out slowly and try to smile.

I catch a whiff of something, a smell that is foreign to
this place and yet so familiar to me. I take a long sniff and
recognize it: oil paints. The warm, woody, greasy smell of oil
paints is wafting through the auditorium. I look around to
see where it's coming from, but no one's broken out a canvas
or anything.

"What's that smell?" I whisper, leaning toward Andrew.

He sniffs. "I don't smell anything." He pulls my arm into
his lap. I let him take it, but I keep looking around. No one
else is sniffing, trying to identify the scent. No one else
seems to even notice it. I train my eyes back on the stage.

I know she's not here. That's stupid. She's dead. I lean into
Andrew's shoulder. But I'm here, enjoying something she
loved, so maybe she's not totally gone either.

28

always wondered what kind of people don't decorate their Christmas trees until Christmas Eve, and now I know. Apparently it's a Bimbo family tradition. Woo.

Candace put the lights and the tinsel up as soon as Dad and I brought the tree home last week, but apparently they always wait to hang the ornaments on Christmas Eve. Candace went on and on about being a new family and blending traditions—blah, blah, blah. We used to go to church, but we don't do that anymore, so Dad and I don't really have any traditions to throw into the old melting pot.

But that's okay. Candace can do her worst tonight and it's not going to affect me because Andrew officially likes me. After Saturday, I'm sure of it. I touch my pocket to make sure I have my phone. He'll probably call me to say merry Christmas soon.

Candace took the liberty of putting together a party mix for the evening's festivities and so far "Jingle Bell Rock," "Rocking around the Christmas Tree," and a jazzy version of "I'm Dreaming of a White Christmas" have featured prominently. It's like she thinks we're in a movie where the sound track tells you how you're supposed to feel, and apparently we're supposed to be upbeat.

Emma is bouncing around the living room on a sugar

high, trying to avoid stepping on the presents piled under the tree. I keep thinking she's going to bop herself too close to the blazing fireplace, but so far no horrific accidents. She keeps coming over and showing me her ornaments, which her mom dug out of a box in the garage yesterday. Hers are all shaped like angels because her grandmother gives her a new angel ornament every year. Somehow it never occurred to me that she had grandparents.

"See this one, Christine?" She holds up a crystal angel with a silver halo. It dangles precariously from a narrow string in her hand. "I got this one when I was ten. I helped my grandma pick it out at this craft fair we went to in Santa Cruz, and then I forgot all about it until Christmas, when I opened up the box and there it was." She shrugs, waiting for me to acknowledge her story. I nod. It's kind of cute how excited she is about all this. It's her first Christmas away from the house she grew up in, but she seems to be holding up well. She'll head to her dad's place first thing in the morning.

Candace walks into the living room with a plate of cookies. They're slice and bake and a little too crispy around the edges, but I take two anyway and settle back down into the armchair to watch the spaz go at it.

"Christine, where are all your ornaments?"

I gesture toward the back of the tree, where I very carefully hung all of my ornaments facing the wall. They're just the ones I made in kindergarten and stuff. Dad packed away most of the ones that were actually meaningful when he purged the house last year and hid everything in boxes in the attic.

Candace shakes her head and puts the cookies down on a side table, then lowers herself onto the couch next to my dad. She leans in and puts her head on his shoulder. Dad puts his arm around her. Candace only kept a few ornaments from her old house, and she had already hung all of hers up. She has an American flag theme.

"And see this one, Christine?" Emma holds up a pink angel with a skirt that looks like it's made out of spun sugar. "This was from last year." She cocks her head. "I don't know where she got it. Mom, do you know where Grandma got this ornament?"

"No idea."

"Well, I don't know where it came from, but I like it." She hangs it on a branch by the stereo and takes a step back to examine its placement. She nods and moves on to the next ornament.

"These chocolates are good," Candace says, popping one into her mouth. "Ana made them herself?"

"Yep." Ana came by with a plate full of homemade chocolates shaped like candy canes and holly leaves today. She and Dave made them to bring to the old people they always visit at the nursing home, and they had a bunch left over, so they decided to spread the holiday cheer. This was maybe the first time that seeing them together didn't make me gag. I sort of get it now, how you can like someone so much that you turn into a complete dope, and it made me happy for Ana.

"She's quite the overachiever, isn't she?"

"And then some." I roll my eyes, and Candace laughs.

"This is one my dad made for me." Emma holds up a small, framed photograph with a red ribbon on top and hangs it on a low branch. It's a black-and-white shot of Emma, probably taken a few years ago, with her dad. I squint at it. I don't think I've ever seen a picture of her dad before. He kind of looks like Billy Ray Cyrus.

I go back to my seat on the armchair. I don't know how I feel about having her dad on my tree. I know it's her ornament and all, but...something about it feels really weird. I glance at my dad, but he's making goo-goo eyes at Candace and doesn't seem to be noticing much of anything.

I've just gotten comfortable in my chair again when the doorbell rings.

Dad, Candace, and I look at each other because no one wants to get up. My heart starts to race. Could it be? I touch the phone in my pocket.

"Maybe it's Santa," Candace says, looking hopefully at Emma.

"Mom, you're so lame." Emma rolls her eyes and places an angel onto a branch, then walks toward the door. "I'll go let 'Santa' in."

I stand up and glance at the mirror above the couch. My mascara is smudged beneath my left eye, so I frantically try to wipe it away, then grab the ponytail holder from my wrist and pull my disheveled hair back.

Candace shrugs. "A few years ago she would have believed me."

"I heard that," Emma calls from the hallway.

She swings the door open and starts squealing. A few seconds later, Emma reappears in the living room with Riley at her heels.

"Look who's here!"

"Hey." Riley comes into the living room and sets her purse

down on the floor carefully. "Am I interrupting?" She smiles at my dad and Candace, who waves her into the room.

"Not at all. We were just hanging out. You're more than welcome."

"Thanks." She looks at me uncertainly.

"You wanna help me hang my ornaments?" Emma hands her a silver angel without waiting for an answer. Emma loves Riley because she's exactly who you dream of growing up to be when you're in middle school. Riley's tall and beautiful and popular and funny... No little twerp ever dreamed of being a freak with a pierced nose when she grew up.

"Sure." Riley shrugs and takes the angel from Emma's hands.

"Aren't you supposed to be at church?" I reach for another cookie. Maybe Candace has resorted to lacing her cooking with addictive chemicals to make up for other shortcomings.

"We just got home. Michael was having a meltdown. I had to get out. I hope it's okay..."

"Of course." I nod. "You want to go into my room?"

"Chris-*tine*," Emma whines. "You can't go hide out in the room on *Christmas Eve*. You have to stay with us."

"That's okay. I want to help decorate the tree anyway." Riley smiles at Emma, who beams back. She hunts around for a minute, looking for the perfect spot for the angel, and hangs it next to a glittery snowman. Emma hands her the next one, and Riley obediently looks for a place to hang it.

"Hey, how'd you get here?" I call from the chair. Riley has her learner's permit, but she can't drive herself. "Did someone drop you off?"

She glances at Dad and Candace, then shoots me a panicked look.

"I'm going to get some apple cider," I say quickly. "Anyone else want any?" Riley gives me a grateful smile.

"Me! Me! You want some help?" Emma calls, bouncing up and down.

"Riley will help me." I gesture for her to follow me into the kitchen.

As soon as we're safely in the kitchen and out of earshot, I turn to her. "What's going on?"

"I took the car. I had to get out of there, Christine."

"You *what*?"

"They'll never notice anyway." She shakes her head.

I eye her carefully. "Let's hope." I turn and pull the refrigerator door open and take the jug of cider out. "So what happened?"

"Michael wants Tom, and he flipped out when we told him Tom couldn't come."

"Where is he?" I take a pot off the hanging rack, pour half the jug of cider into it, and put it on the stove.

"Mexico." Riley winces.

"Excuse me?"

"He's surfing there. He had the time off school so..." She shrugs.

"Wow. I didn't know he was going away. When did he leave?"

"Well...I guess if I'm honest I kind of didn't really know he was going away either. He texted me yesterday to tell me." She leans back against the counter. "And then he left with his older cousins. He didn't call me."

"Whoa." Genius response, Christine.

Riley sighs. "I mean, don't you call your girlfriend before you leave for the week?" Her beautiful face is pinched and pale as she crosses her arms over her chest. "And he hasn't called since he's been there. I know the phone lines are bad and stuff, but…" She looks at me hopefully, no doubt wanting me to reassure her.

"Yeah. Probably just the phone lines," I say quickly. "Or maybe he hasn't had time." I stir the cider, willing it to heat up.

"Yeah." She bites her lip. "But the thing is, now I'm kind of wondering if maybe you guys were right." Riley's cheeks are pink, and she doesn't meet my eyes.

My nostrils flare. Tom isn't that bad. It was Ana who thought he spelled bad news, but if he hurts Riley I'll…

"No. I'm sure he's really busy." I think white lies are probably okay on Christmas.

"Yeah." She sighs. "So there's that. And then Michael was inconsolable when we told him Tom wasn't coming over tonight. He pitched this huge screaming fit in church. It was mortifying. I just couldn't deal with it. As soon as we got home, I took off. And I thought if anyone would understand, you would."

"Seriously. Welcome to the freak show. A boyfriend in Mexico and an Asperger's tantrum don't have anything on this mess of a family."

"Emma's really sweet." Riley laughs a little.

"She's growing on me." I dip my finger into the cider and decide it's warm enough. I lift the pot and start pouring it carefully into mugs.

"I remember last summer when you said you were going

to break your dad and The Bimbo up. I'm so glad you're over that now."

"What? I'm not over it." I pour some cider into a mug with a grinning reindeer on the side. "I'm just...regrouping. She's harder to get rid of than I imagined. I need a new plan of attack."

"Oh." Riley moves the reindeer mug and puts a Mrs. Claus mug in its place. "I haven't heard you talk about it in a while. And you and Emma seem to be getting along so well. I thought..."

"No, definitely still in breakup mode. Emma agrees. She wants her parents back together, so she's going to help." I yank another mug off the shelf. "Do you think I want the rest of my life to be like this?"

"Well." Riley looks out the doorway into the other room, where Emma is currently sprawling out across the couch, resting her feet on her mom's lap. The fire casts a cheerful glow over the room, and the tree is dripping with lights and ornaments. They're all laughing and singing along to the music. "No. I..." She swallows, then looks back at me. "I guess not."

29

She burned the eggs. How do you burn eggs? I didn't even know that was possible, but we were all in a rush this morning because Emma was supposed to be at her dad's place by nine, and I guess she kind of forgot about them for a while. For an *hour*. Candace set an alarm (talk about crazy) and got us all up at seven so we could rush through opening presents before shipping Emma off.

Here's the thing about rushing through Christmas morning: once it's over, there's not really much else to do. I hung up the new car scent air freshener and fuzzy dice Emma got me, put away the clothes Candace picked out, pocketed the cash from Dad, and that was that. Now Dad is off making an appearance at some Christmas event in town, and Emma is at her dad's, and it's too quiet. This place is a tomb.

Candace is in the kitchen making her mother's famous lasagna for Christmas dinner—another tradition, and from what I understand from Emma, the only thing her mother can successfully cook—and I'm lying on my bed, staring up at the ceiling.

It's only 10:00 a.m. What am I going to do with the rest of today?

I try to brainstorm new ways to start a rift between my dad and Candace, but I don't come up with anything so I reach for my phone. No message from Andrew. Maybe Riley's around. But her phone rings and rings, then goes to voice mail. No one answers her parents' landline either. I try Zoe because she never goes anywhere.

Zoe picks it up on the fifth ring. "Hullo...?" She sounds half asleep, but she's home. You can always depend on Zo.

"Zo? Are you still in bed?"

"Christine?" She moans. "What time is it?"

"It's Christmas morning, and you're still asleep?"

"I was."

"Where are Dreamy and Ed?" Zoe only calls her parents by their first names. They're kind of hippies, not that that makes it seem any less weird.

"I don't know. Sleeping, probably."

"Don't you guys do some big Christmas thing or anything?"

"Usually, but we were up late. My dad did some landscaping work for this guy across town who couldn't pay him, so instead he gave us a hot tub."

"What? You have a Jacuzzi now?"

Zoe yawns loudly. "It's purple. It's from the eighties or something. We were up late sitting in it."

"Okay, that's weird, but whatever. You want to come over?"

"Can't." The phone gets muffled, like she's covered the mouthpiece, then it clears up. "We're having an early dinner with the Farcuses, and I'm supposed to help my mom make vegan carob cake." Zoe gags. "And I have to shower and stuff."

"Oh. Okay." She'll get up for Marcus Farcus but not for Christmas presents? Zoe may be worse off than she lets on.

"Well, uh, have a good Christmas, I guess. Call if you get bored."

"Sure. You too."

I flop back on the bed and dial Ana's house. She isn't allowed to have a cell phone, which is really inconvenient because we have to call her house, and if her dad answers it's really uncomfortable because he's not the friendliest guy. But luckily this time Ana answers. Only she's speaking Spanish. What the...

"Ana?"

"Christine! Sorry. I thought you were my grandma calling from Mexico. Hey, can I call you back? I'm on the other line with Maria."

"Oh. Sure." Maria is Ana's old housekeeper who moved back to Mexico earlier this year. Maria basically raised her, and I know Ana misses her a lot.

"It might be a while because my grandma may call. Ooh, but guess what? I got a laptop! It's so cute. Did you get anything fun?"

A laptop? Cute? She already has a desktop computer in her bedroom. Why does she need a laptop?

"No, not really."

"Oh. Look, I'll call you later, okay?"

"Yeah. Later. Bye." I hang up and let my phone fall onto my bedspread.

Great. What do I do now?

Would it be weird if I called Andrew? I guess not, right? I think back to the night we spent on the phone together. We're bonded now. I could call him, but then, he'll probably call later. I'll just wait.

I glance over at Emma's empty bed, then walk over to check on Joe. He swims to the top of the water, thinking I'm going to feed him. "Are you a pig or a fish?" He looks at me like he's famished, and I toss in a few flakes that he attacks with vigor. After he eats them all he swims back to his little cave and hides. Even my fish doesn't want to hang out with me. I'm so bored.

I pad down the hall in my socks and walk into the kitchen. Candace is standing behind the counter, spreading lasagna noodles across the bottom of a pan. There's so much tomato sauce on the counter that I actually think she might be bleeding at first, which, frankly, is a distinct possibility when she's in the kitchen with all those knives. She lifts her head when I come into the room, looking tired.

"Hey there." That isn't her normal pageant queen smile. She almost seems to be forcing herself to try. "Thanks for this." She points to the kitchen timer I gave her this morning. "It's coming in handy already."

I shrug. I feel a little bad about that. She actually spent a lot of time picking out clothes that she knew I'd like from the vintage store, but I got her a kitchen timer because her cooking stinks. I thought it would keep her from burning water. She was very sweet about it, making a big show out of trying out all the features, but still I could see she was a little hurt. Maybe I should have put a little more thought into it.

"Need any help?"

"I'm almost done." She smiles weakly, and I notice that her skin looks dry and sallow. "Thanks though."

I pull out one of the kitchen chairs and take a seat. "Lasagna. Odd choice."

"Yeah. My mother taught me. It's Emma's favorite." The crease in her brow deepens. "Not that that matters today. But it's something we've done for years." She spreads cheese over the noodles, then adds a layer of meat.

There's a bowl of nuts in the center of the table. I grab a handful and toss a salty cashew into my mouth.

"She wanted to be here on Christmas Eve to hang out with you." She smiles and pours tomato sauce over the meat. "I guess we could have had something more festive for dinner since she won't be around, but this just feels like Christmas to me."

"I like lasagna."

"What did your mom usually make?" Candace watches me carefully.

A part of me wants to scream at her that she has no business asking about my mom, but another part of me knows she's trying to be nice and that it's Christmas and she misses her daughter and I should give her a break. And then there's the part that can't actually remember what my mom made for Christmas dinner. Did we even have a traditional meal? I'm not sure.

"I don't know." I shrug. "Whatever." I reach into my pocket and check my phone. No messages. Silence echoes throughout the kitchen.

"Do you have any big plans for the day?" Candace puts a final layer of cheese on the lasagna and brushes her hands off.

"Not really." I type a text to Riley.

Call me. I'm so bored.

"Well in that case, I was thinking—" Oh no. She wants to bond. I need to invent some plans, stat.

"Actually I —"

" —how you have all these art supplies, but I haven't seen you paint in a while. And I thought I might throw it out there that you're welcome to use the studio if you want to paint in there."

"What?"

"It was very nice of you to share your room with Emma. I want you to still have a space to go and paint and ... just, you know, if you want to. If you don't, that's fine too." She unrolls some tin foil and rips a piece off in one clean motion.

"Oh."

"I'll be out of the studio soon enough. Then it will be yours again. I know it's special to you. And I want you to keep painting."

"Cool." Painting. Huh. I stand up slowly and push my chair in, scraping it across the linoleum. "Thanks." I walk slowly down the hall toward my room because I don't know what else to do.

30

"Oh my goodness. Would you look at this gravy boat?" Candace holds it out like she's found the Holy Grail. "Do you like it? In the lace pattern? Or do you prefer this basket weave one?" Candace holds up another mysterious piece of china. This one has a red criss-cross pattern. What could it be for? Is there a separate dish for...potatoes?

"Um, gosh." I eye the registry gun in Candace's hand, an idea forming. A smile spreads across my face. Well, yes. Why didn't I think of it before? I'm really falling down on my job of being the evil stepdaughter. "Go with the lace. It'll work for any occasion."

Candace looks relieved. "You're so right about that." She puts the funny looking basket weave pot back on the display table. "Do you think your dad will like the lace?" She picks up a teacup so ostentatious and dainty it would make the Queen Mum blush.

"He doesn't care what you get, as long as you're happy. You know Dad."

"You're right." Candace flips the gravy boat over and zaps it with the bar-code gun.

Wait. Where's Emma? I look around the crowded Bloomingdale's floor and spy her slumped over in a chair that's clearly meant to hold bored husbands. I decide to leave Candace to it. She's frantically gunning every single piece of obscure and useless china in the Wedgwood Vera Wang Lace collection, so she won't miss me if I sneak off for a moment. I weave my way through the post-holiday-sales hordes to Emma.

I touch the back pocket of my jeans, making sure I remembered to bring along my phone. I used to always know where my phone was because it would, you know, ring, but now I keep losing it because this week it's been silent, mocking me with its utter lack of good tidings from my friends and, more importantly, from Andrew. Thankfully, late last night I remembered that Andrew had said something about going to his grandmother's for Christmas. She must not live around here, which would explain everything. Families never let you get away to make phone calls. He's tied up, it's the holidays, and he'll call soon. I can't believe I'm so bored I agreed to go to Bloomingdale's.

I kick Emma's shoe. "What are you doing?"

She opens one eyelid, then shuts it again. I don't think she slept a wink at her dad's place. "Nap."

I kick her shoe again. "C'mon. I have an idea."

She sighs. "What? I want to stay here and nap. Is Mom looking for me yet?"

I crane my neck in Candace's direction. She's conferring with a Bloomingdale's employee about china. "No. She's in the zone."

Emma yawns.

I grab her hands and pull her up. "I need your help, pip-squeak, so move it." Once I have her on her feet, she gives her head a good shake and seems to wake up a little. I take her elbow and drag her downstairs.

"Where are we going?"

"You want to break up my dad and your mom, right?" I step on the escalator and drag her on behind me. She nearly trips but catches herself on the motorized railing.

"Well..." Her voice is quiet. She must be really tired. "I don't know."

I glare at her. "What?!"

The escalator stairs flatten, and I pull her over to the side, away from the stampeding crowds of shoppers.

Putting my hands on her shoulders, I lean over so we're eye to eye. "What are you talking about? Don't you see? This is the only way to get your parents back together again."

"My mom's so happy, though." Emma bites her lip.

I drop my hands from her shoulders. I can't really argue with that. Her mom does seem a little happier each day we inch closer to the wedding. Unfortunately our happiness levels are inversely proportional. Ooohhhh...I think that was a math joke. And Mr. Mackey thinks I'm unteachable.

"Em, you've got to help me." I put an arm around her, putting out of my mind that I'm being a little manipulative. But who's going to look like a hero when her mom and dad get back together again? "Please? For me?"

"Fine." She sighs, and before she can rethink her decision, I usher her over to the registry check-in desk.

"There! That's it!" I run over to the Godiva chocolate display. "Give me the gun." Emma squeals, hands me the bar-code gun, and I register for four of everything on the whole stand. People are going to think Candace has a chocolate obsession.

I don't know if I'm surprised that the dim-witted registry lady gave Emma another gun or not. On the one hand, when we checked in with her this morning, she didn't look like this job was her life's ambition. On the other hand, Emma is a terrible liar. But I was proud of her. She marched right up to the registry director and said her mother had sent her for another gun so she could help. Plausible enough. Kids like to be involved. The lady promptly handed the gun over, and since then we've been running wild in Bloomingdale's, gunning down every single bizarre treasure, trying to one-up each other. So far we've registered Candace for a sausage maker, a spa footbath, another engagement ring (my idea), two hideous elephant lamps, and a lifetime's supply of Godiva truffles.

Emma cocks her hip and holds out her hand for the gun. "Chocolate? I can do better than that. Gimme that gun." She takes off down an aisle, and I have to sprint to keep up with her as she disappears near a display of robes. I follow but somehow lose her. Panting and standing on my tiptoes, I try to spot her short frame among the tall racks, but that's when I hear it. Well, I hear two things.

The first noise that registers is so beautiful that for a moment I assume I must be hearing things. But on the second ring, I know: it's my phone. As I reach for it, I also hear Emma's telltale laugh in the lingerie section behind me, but I block it out. He's calling me; he's finally calling me. My heart slams in my chest. I have to remember to not sound like I was waiting for him to call.

I pull my phone out of my pocket, and my heart sinks when I see the picture of Zoe across the screen. I stand in the middle of a busy path, holding my phone in front of me as if I'm from 1975 and don't know what a cell phone is or how to answer it. I notice a few shoppers staring at me. Finally, the call goes to voice mail and I frown.

"Christine!" Emma pulls on my arm.

"Ow! Jeez!" I yank my arm away. I can't believe it wasn't him. What's going on here? Doesn't he know that New Year's Eve is tomorrow? Doesn't he know he's supposed to arrange something? How am I going to get a kiss at midnight if he doesn't call?

"I found the most awesome thing. Wait till you see it." I check my phone again to make sure I saw that right. Yep. My worst fears are confirmed. It was Zoe.

"Come on!" Emma moves behind me and begins to push me forward. Maybe I missed a call sometime? I punch buttons...

"Stop it, Em!" My yell silences the frantic shoppers for a moment. At least one woman gives us a look clearly meant for naughty children.

Emma wilts before my eyes. "Sorry," she mumbles quietly.

Oh no. Too harsh. Okay, I need to refocus on our mission here.

"Sorry, Em." Let's see. What would a good big sister do? I decide to sling my arm around her shoulder and grab her in a headlock. "Picking on your elders? Huh? Huh?" I give her a gentle noogie.

Emma wriggles free, a smile back on her face. "Okay, seriously, Christine. You've got to come see what I registered for." She takes my hand, and I let her pull me away.

It's not too late. There's still plenty of time to set something up for tomorrow night. I put my phone to my ear and listen to Zoe's rambling voice mail as I cruise through the hosiery department. Who says hosiery anymore anyway? Zoe is inviting us all over to sit in her new hot tub tomorrow night. Too bad I'll be out with Andrew.

Emma drags me into the lingerie department, past all the slinky silk and lace numbers over to a section with a huge sign that says, "The Silver Collection."

"What in the..." I spin slowly. I didn't know they made such ginormous, hideous bras and panties. Most of them resemble tents.

Emma walks to the end of a long row of bras and reaches high over her head. She can't quite touch the one she wants, so she jumps. After a few tries, she pulls it off the rack.

"Can you believe this?!" She slips her rail thin arms through the loops. Each boob holder—probably not the technical term—is the size of Emma's entire head.

I start to laugh, unable to hold it in. "You—I can't..."

Emma struts back and forth in the space between the racks as if she's a supermodel working the runway.

"Emma..." I try to stifle my laughter. It's too much to watch her in such a giant bra.

She stops in front of me and snaps her fingers in the air like a diva. "Vogue, vogue, vogue, vogue."

I lose it entirely and have to lean over my knees to catch my breath because I'm laughing so hard.

"I registered for ten. Do you think that's enough?"

I nod. "I think that'll do just fine."

31

C hristine, get in." Zoe splashes my leg a little. "You've got to be freezing."

"Splash me again and I'll pummel you, Red." I told Zoe and Ana that I'd only hang my feet in the hot tub tonight. I can't very well boil in a tub all night *and* monitor my phone. I decide to deflect attention from myself.

"What's your appendage doing tonight, Ana?"

Dreamy and Ed put their new hot tub on the deck outside their back door, which means we're surrounded by a thick forest. The cold, clammy night air smells like the pungent eucalyptus trees in Zoe's backyard.

Ana rolls her eyes at me because she hates that joke, but come on—she earned it fair and square. "Mom and Papá said this holiday was too mature, and they didn't want us to spend it together."

This isn't exactly how I envisioned New Year's Eve either. In my dreams, I'm not here, I'm out somewhere with Andrew, but I could at least be okay with this if Riley were here. Our little group feels incomplete without her. The empty fourth side of the hideous purple hot tub seems to mock us, reminding us that our tight little group is no more, that Riley is out with her cool friends tonight. She said she'd already accepted Kayleen's invitation before Zoe called and she couldn't back out, but I don't buy it. Even if it's true, that's not what's really going on here. None of us has even mentioned her tonight.

I grimace. Ana throws her hands up in the air, getting a few droplets of water on my baggy khaki shorts. "I know. They're crazy. It's accepted fact. But next year I'll be off probation and really allowed to date, so the worst will be over soon. Plus, they did let Dave come to family dinner tonight before I came over." Her eyes go glassy, and she looks away for a moment.

I take a sip of the sparkling cider Zoe's parents gave us, but it's flat and dull.

At least with Ana's chattering, no one seems to notice my funk. I study the bottle's gold label with long, lilting silver writing and a picture of an apple tree. For a moment, I imagine a New Year's Eve in Manhattan. Andrew would look so dashing, the black of his tuxedo setting off silky, honey-colored hair. We'd dance to orchestra music, and at midnight there would be champagne and a kiss.

I pull my phone out of my pocket and punch the side button to see the time. 10:21. He's not going to call. It's too late to call. Well, really it was too late to call when the sun set yesterday, and yet I still held out foolish hope, but finally now, at the very edge of a brand-new year, I know that he's really and truly not going to call.

I hop off the edge of the hot tub and shimmy out of my shorts numbly. Behind me the girls laugh and sip their cider while tears sting my eyes. I don't get it. How could he not call after the concert? It felt so real that night. He kissed my forehead as we left the opera house. He held my hand.

I had some vague idea that I might get their take on the

situation tonight, but without Riley, it just feels weird. She's the one who knows all about guys. Ana has only gone out with Dave, which is the weirdest pseudorelationship I've ever seen, and the day I take dating advice from Zoe is the day I retire from dating. Better to just keep it to myself.

I pull my shirt over my head and blot my eyes secretly so that Ana and Zoe won't notice I'm crying. I know it's horrible, but I wish I hadn't come at all. Being here is twice as depressing. I want to be with him. Or I want to go back to happier times when we were all here, laughing and hanging out, no one talking about their boyfriends, or their grades, or their other friends. A chill runs through me. It's bad luck to greet a new year like this.

I look up at the dark sky, festooned with tiny sparkling lights, looking for help, but the heavens don't answer.

We've just finished pouring the last of the sparkling cider when Zoe gasps.

"What was that? Did you guys hear that?" She stands up in the hot tub and stares into the dark December night. Zoe's backyard fronts acres and acres of old-growth forest, and it's like being in the middle of the woods. We can't see anything past the deck railing.

"Do you think it's an ax murderer?" I grab one of Zoe's feet under the water and make her jump.

"Ah! Don't do that!" She makes a face at me. "These woods are freaky at night."

She dips back into the water, shivering.

"Hey, Christine," Ana screams at the top of her lungs. Ana has spent most of the last hour submerged in the hot water with just her face poking out. This means she can't hear, so she's really loud. "Go get your phone. See what time it is again."

I pull her shoulders up until her ears are out of the water. "You're going to wake up Dreamy and Ed."

She nods and then goes back under.

I reach for my phone resting on the edge of the hot tub and try to keep it from slipping into the bubbling water.

"There!" Zoe points at something in the yard. "You must have heard that."

Zoe and I peer into the backyard. Beyond the deck is miles and miles of dark black nothingness. Ana is still hovering under the water with only her face poking out.

I pull her back up. "There's only one minute left in this year. Why don't you enjoy it above the surface? You're making me feel like I'm hanging out with my goldfish."

"Fine," Ana says, reaching for her glass on the side of the hot tub.

"Okay, I'll tell you when it changes to midnight." I pick my phone up, and the light from the screen is the only light except the stars. I hold it up in the air and then bring it down. "It's not exactly the ball dropping, is it?"

Ana goes under but keeps her hand with the glass flute in the air. She comes up sputtering. I press the side button of my phone and it glows blue again. Wow. If you just sit there waiting on it, a minute takes a long time to pass.

"Okay." I wave my phone, and Zoe begins to clap. "It's midnight! Happy New Year!"

Then I hear it. It sounds like someone is walking through the yard near the deck.

I twist so my body is facing the railing. "What the—"

"*Aaah!*" Zoe shrieks and scrunches as low as she can in the water.

"Wait! Listen. It's that old song." Ana stands up and turns her head toward the sound. She looks at us, then leans toward the yard. I move toward the railing and squint to see what she's looking at. There are people playing shiny instruments in the yard, and they're coming toward us.

"What in the world?" Why is there a marching band coming through the forest in the middle of the night? I judge the distance from here to the door. If we run now, we can probably make it. Zoe stands up slowly and leans toward the railing too. She watches silently as the flashes of brass meld into real instruments.

"It's that New Year's song," Ana says, her eyes wide. "The one they always play in sappy romance movies. Old Lang something or other."

I grab for my phone. "What—"

"Oh no." Zoe's jaw hangs open. "Marcus?"

The shadows give way as the players keep advancing toward us through the trees. Soon it's easy to tell that it's Marcus and three other guys. Two of them are playing trumpets, a skinny freshman I recognize from math class is playing the French horn, and Marcus keeps squeaking notes on his trombone. They look oddly grim, coming out of the darkness like that, playing this out-of-tune song.

"Marcus? What are you doing?" Zoe slips back under the

water. Poor Zoe. I don't think she wants Marcus to see her in her swimsuit.

The guys stop, and Marcus marches up the wooden stairs toward us. Zoe's cheeks are bright red by the time he makes it to the edge of the hot tub. "Happy New Year, Zoe." He tosses a handful of confetti in the air, and it rains down on us. Then he leans forward, his mouth puckered up like a fish, and shuts his eyes. Zoe stares at him in horror.

Marcus opens his eyes and smiles, undeterred. I glance at Ana, who looks as stunned as I feel. Did Marcus really organize this whole crazy stunt for Zoe?

"You look beautiful." He smiles at her hopefully, but she shakes her head and sinks her shoulders under the bubbles, her eyes wide.

Marcus sighs, gives a slow wave, and turns back toward the stairs. Zoe watches him go. When he gets to the bottom of the stairs, the ragtag band starts playing again and marches off.

"You guys, that was so embarrassing," Zoe squeals, but I'd swear there's a hint of delight in her voice.

Ana and I stay silent as they disappear into the woods. The last few notes vanish into the night, and I can't help but wonder if Zoe knows more about guys than I give her credit for.

32

The fact that I don't see Andrew until my final class on Monday is proof that God enjoys watching us suffer. Not only have I not heard from him since we went to the concert together, I still have to wait the entire day to find out what the deal is. The only upside is that this long, excruciating day gives me time to form a plan.

I pull open the door to Mr. Dumas's classroom and relax a little when I see that I'm the first one here.

"Well, well, well," Mr. Dumas says, not even looking up from a stack of papers on his desk. How does he do that? "Someone is punctual today. Looking forward to art class, I assume?" The way he says "art class" I know he means "Andrew Cutchins." He's relishing watching our relationship, or whatever this is, unfold.

I ignore him and slide into my usual seat. Normally I wouldn't ignore a teacher, but Mr. Dumas is not normal. I sling my backpack up on the table into the space next to me and pretend to dig for something deep in the bottom, something I can't quite find. People begin to file in, laughing and talking, filling the awkward silence in the room.

I have to know that I didn't make this whole relationship thing up. When you write down all the facts on a piece of paper, it doesn't amount to much, and I don't want to be flirting and hanging all over a guy who doesn't like me back, so I realized that the only way to handle this Andrew situation is to throw the ball back in his court, to use a basketball metaphor. He has to choose where he's sitting today. If he sits by me, well then, it's open season on flirting. I'll make sure he knows how much I like him, and if he doesn't respond...I'll have my answer. But at lunch today it occurred to me that there was another possible scenario. Someone could sit next to me before Andrew arrives and then my data will be inconclusive, so I decided that I would have to make it look like I was holding it for him...or maybe I lost my pencil in the bottom of my bag. And so far, my plan is working.

Finally almost everyone has arrived. I find my phone in the bottom of my bag and check the screen for the time. He has one more minute. Oh no! What if he's not even in school today? That's a scenario I hadn't even thought of. My heart races. He has to be in school today. I can't stand waiting even thirty more seconds.

And then, like an apparition, he appears in the doorway. It's been so long since I've seen his gorgeous face that I'm stunned. This is who I thought would call me? Get real, Christine. He looks like a model.

Andrew's eyes sweep the room, and I smile and try to look inviting. Ever since that first day he sat by me, he's always taken the chair next to me, but the seats aren't assigned in Mr. Dumas's class, and there are more than enough spots to go around. He could sit anywhere.

He avoids my eye as he weaves his way down the first row, and I realize I'm not breathing as I watch him step over Susan Cahn's giant backpack to get to the empty seat by her.

It's not even a matter of plopping down in the first seat he saw. He had to work to get to that seat. I hear a few people bustle.

"Mr. Cutchins. Welcome back." Mr. Dumas says, but even he seems shocked. Instead of his usual sarcastic tone, his voice is faltering. Andrew shrugs, and Mr. Dumas shakes his head a little. "Right. Well, today I'm going to bore you with my lofty intellect and rapier wit..." Everyone but me groans. The best days in art class are the ones where we get to create, but occasionally Mr. Dumas lectures us on certain movements, techniques, or famous artists.

Mr. Dumas clicks on the ancient slide projector and points it toward the screen at the front. He begins to drone on about *chiaroscuro*, some Italian word that means light and dark. I try to listen, but only snippets of his lecture seep through my brain.

Light is Andrew's hair. Dark is mine. Light is how he used to make me feel; now my heart is pumping thick, black oil through my veins. Maybe he's forgotten me. Maybe there never was a "we." Maybe I misread the shadows and shadings of our relationship. Was it a friendship? Am I nothing more than some needy girl who made it all up? Can he not see all the ways he has shed light on my dark little life?

For what feels like an eternity, Mr. Dumas snaps one slide after another of the freakiest art you've ever seen. There's an angel that looks like it might devour people, a manger scene that is oddly menacing, a woman smiling like a joker. I almost feel dizzy at the parade of paintings, but finally after a feverish hour of hand-wringing and fretting, the bell rings. I've never been so happy to hear it.

Andrew begins to pack up his bag. He's joking with Susan Cahn, seemingly unaware of the spell he's put me under. He's going to stroll right out of here, and nothing will get resolved. At the thought of spending another evening torturing myself, I force myself to act.

"Andrew," I say, springing to my feet. "Wait up."

He turns around and grins at me.

I keep my face stony and calm. His smile disappears, but he stops packing up his bag and his shoulders slump a little.

I put my notepad in my backpack. I didn't take a single note while Mr. Dumas was talking, but I can't worry about that now. What should I say to Andrew? I stall, pretending yet again that I can't find something at the bottom of my bag, letting everyone else leave. Even Mr. Dumas steps out of the room, chasing after another teacher, and suddenly, we're all alone.

I clear my throat. "So, um, where have you been?"

Andrew shrugs. "Went to see my grandmother on Christmas day." He slings his bag onto his back. "Other than that, I just hung around the house driving my mom crazy."

I know I'm supposed to laugh at this, so I don't. "Why didn't you call me?" I walk toward the front of the classroom. "Your phone lines were all down due to a freak storm that only hit your house, and the dog ate your cell phone?"

Andrew guffaws as if he's in on the joke. "Just busy." He pulls on a strand of my hair and winks at me. "Why didn't *you* call *me*?"

I glare at him. He's going to make this hard. I'd at least hoped he would own up to liking me, even if he had to admit that his feelings had changed. Instead he's acting like nothing happened.

"You said you would call me."

Andrew runs his fingers through his hair. "Listen, Christine..."

I wait.

His mood seems to turn. "Look." He purses his lips. "I like hanging out with you." He shakes his head dramatically, as if he pities me. "But I have *a lot* of friends." He looks into my eyes like I do with Emma sometimes. "I like being... *friendly*. I didn't realize that you—," he glances at the floor, "were taking it so seriously."

I feel like I've been punched in the gut. I manage to make some kind of squeak before I turn on my heel. The door slams shut behind me, and as my footsteps echo in the breezeway, I try to convince myself that I didn't make this up. He led me on. He made me believe he liked me. He made me feel like the only girl, and he did it on purpose.

I nearly run into Mr. Dumas as I storm down the hallway. He cocks his eyebrow.

"Hell hath no fury like a painter scorned."

I open my mouth, but just walk away.

33

S o it's been ten days, and I'm officially giving up hope."
Riley sounds defeated over the phone line. I hold my
cell phone with my left hand and steer the car toward
my house with my right, even though I swore I would never
do this. Talking on the phone while driving is dangerous and
illegal and really stupid, especially on such a gray, misty day,
but when I saw it was Riley calling me, the allure of a friendly
voice was too appealing to pass up.

"He still hasn't called?" I push the brake pedal down
slowly, even though the red light is almost a full block ahead.
I'm driving really slowly anyway to make up for the phone
thing, and it takes about a second to bring the car to a stop.

"No." I hear metal banging on her end of the line.

"Has anyone heard from him? Maybe he's hurt or
something."

"I called his house yesterday." She sighs. "His mom
answered. Talk about mortifying. They got a postcard he
sent a few days ago."

"So he's alive and kicking." I pull the car to a slow stop
about a mile behind the car ahead of me. I thought I'd get
more comfortable behind the wheel, but so far, it hasn't
happened.

"So it would seem. Which basically means he's over me."
There's another clang right by Riley's phone.

"Where are you?"

"The locker room. Practice starts in a few minutes." She
sighs. "I'm not exactly in the mood to cheer."

"Sounds like someone needs a nice long drink of the
Kool-Aid."

"Shut up." She laughs a little. "Look, I have to run, but I
was calling to see if you wanted to hang out Friday night.
You know, just us. It'll be like a single girls' night out."

Ugh. Single girls. My least favorite phrase. Two normal words that when combined produce horrific, pathetic
results. No matter how much fun you try to make it sound,
being a single girl isn't very exciting.

"Zoe's technically not dating Marcus." The light turns
green, and I look around to make sure the intersection
is totally clear before I press my foot on the accelerator
cautiously.

"But she might as well be. And it doesn't matter anyway.
He adores her. She can't be in on our pity party when she
has someone dying to be with her. So what about Friday?"

"Friday night? I have to check my busy schedule. Let's
see. I guess I could fit it in between stewing about Andrew
and plotting revenge on Andrew."

"Perfect." A shrill whistle blows from Riley's end of the
line. "We'll be two single girls out on the town."

"Look out, Half Moon Bay." I shake my head. Riley's
always fun, so even if the occasion is pathetic, we'll still have
a good time. "Here we come."

The driveway is empty when I pull up in front of the house. Candace teaches Yogilates today, and Emma went over to Sylvie's house after school to plan some kind of Sadie Hawkins Dance with the rest of the student government, so no one will be back for hours. I head straight to my room, slam the door, and instinctively stay on what's now my side.

I flop onto my bed and slip my headphones into my ears. Closing my eyes, I try to lose myself in the music, but I can't stop thinking about what Andrew said. How could he say we were never more than friends? Did it really all mean nothing to him? A tear works its way out of my eye and slides down the side of my cheek. I turn the music up and try to banish him from my head. Let's see. I'll think about Friday night instead. There are a few movies out I want to see, or maybe we'll drive down to the beach. Lots of people hang out there. Heck, maybe we'll even meet some new guys, guys who have brains and actually care about us.

But as I picture the scene, the only guy I can envision is Andrew.

I need to get up and do something instead of lying here driving myself crazy.

I walk down the hallway and look around in the kitchen. Too bad I'm not one of those Betty Crocker types. I could go for some cookies right now. I grab a handful of chips and wander into the living room.

The Christmas tree is still up, ornaments dangling from every branch. Cleaning up after a holiday is not nearly as fun as getting ready for one. I briefly contemplate taking the ornaments off, but decide it's Candace's mess.

I pop a Dorito into my mouth and walk to the sliding glass door. There's the couch where Andrew and I had our long talk. I was so happy, so hopeful then. I shake my head and look out the door at the backyard, gray and dripping, wrapped in the fog that blankets Half Moon Bay. It feels appropriate today. I run my eyes over the empty flowerbeds Mom used to plant each spring and glance at the studio.

Wait. The studio. Candace said I could use it to paint whenever I wanted. I tap my finger on the glass door. Huh. I turn on my heel and dash to my room, grab my bag of paints, then slide open the door and walk across the yard. My shoes slip on the wet grass, and I yank open the door and look around.

It smells the same. Despite Candace's lotions and perfumes lined up across the top of the oak dresser, it still smells like grease and mold and dust. I inhale deeply. Grandma Ba's couch is now crammed into my dad's office, and this place is covered with Candace's stuff. Looking at it no longer makes me want to retch, so that's progress I guess, but even crowded with her things, this place still reminds me of my mom.

I can set up my easel there by the nightstand. That's not too far from where Mom used to paint, and if I remember correctly...I pull open the door of the closet. Dad shoved Mom's painting stuff in here when she died, and it didn't seem worth it to clean it all out since Candace was only going to live in here for a few months. I reach toward the shelves and pull out a stack of small canvases. They're prestretched, not the kind Mom preferred but good to have on hand for when inspiration strikes. There's a box of solvents and cleaners on the bottom shelf. Some half-used watercolors are jumbled in with paintbrushes and boxes of pastels in the cardboard box on the floor. I push aside a wad of rags to see what else is in here. Just touching her things is comforting. Even if Candace lives here now, this is still my mom's place.

I feel something hard and rectangular at the back of the closet. Pulling it out slowly, I gasp. It's . . . it's the painting she was working on. That day. She washed her brush out and left the canvas on the easel to take me shopping, and she never got to come back and finish it.

I run my fingers over the canvas lightly. If you didn't know better, you'd think the painting was abstract. It's just a brown square at the moment, but I can tell by the grain of the wood and the perspective that it's actually our living room window. What was she going to paint inside the window? Was the viewer supposed to be able to see through it?

I trace the glass pane with my finger. She liked light, loved seeing how it played off different objects, and was fascinated by things that reflected it — mirrors, glass, foil. She liked the symbolism of it all, how light is all around us and we just have to return it —

A jar full of thumbtacks crashes to the ground. I guess I must have knocked it over, though as the tacks sprawl across the wooden floor, I don't really remember touching it. The hair on my arms raises, but I shake it off and collect the tacks back into the jar. I hope Mom doesn't mind me messing with her stuff.

I peer at the surface of the painting in my hands. It's a couple of feet tall and about the same width. It's only just begun, really. I wish I knew what this one was going to be about.

I put the painting down on Candace's daybed, then reach back for the piece of wood on the bottom shelf and pull it out gently. Her easel. Mom had a couple of bigger easels, but this one sets up on a table. I look around the studio. I could take this inside, maybe work on it in my room, but... Candace's dresser might work. I push a row of bottles aside to make room for the easel, then set the painting on it gently. I stand back and scrutinize it. There are all those unused canvases in the closet, but there's something about this one that grabs my attention. It wouldn't be blasphemous to finish her painting, would it?

I dig out the square piece of fiberglass she used as a palette and open her bag of paints, then squirt a tiny little bit of cerulean blue onto the palette. No sense pushing out more than I can use. I coat my brush in it and touch it lightly to the canvas. I bite my lip, squint at it, and relax a little. What I did looks good. It didn't ruin the painting. I smooth the glob out and add another highlight.

Mom had finished a painting of the moon before this one. She loved that it was a giant cosmic mirror, reflecting the light of the sun into the darkness. She always wove references to God into her paintings somehow. Maybe that's how she really saw life.

I wish I had that kind of faith. I want to love what she loved. But every time I start to think that maybe she was right, that maybe there is something more out there, someone comes along and convinces me we're all just a bunch of screwed up people trying to make our way down here in the darkness.

Even the people who are supposed to be all good and stuff turn out to be jerks in the end.

I try to block Andrew's face out of my mind. I hate that even in this sacred space I can't stop thinking of him. I hate that he took my glimmer of hope, made me believe there really might be some bigger plan, someone out there pulling strings we can't see, and then twisted it into something horrible.

I squeeze out a little yellow and mix it with a tiny bit of the blue. I try to picture her face, but the edges are getting blurrier every day.

The light is disappearing from the windows when the studio door opens. Candace looks at me, her eyes wide.

"Oh. Christine." She straightens up and brushes her hands over her face quickly, sniffling a little. Her eyes are red, and though she's trying to hide it from me, it's obvious she's been crying. "I didn't know you were in here."

She steps inside and closes the door softly behind her.

"Yeah." Well, this is awkward. What am I supposed to do? I've never seen Candace cry before, and it's pretty clear she was hoping to get to her room without anyone seeing. "You said I could paint here, so... I thought..."

She nods, tears brimming in her eyes. "I'd actually like to be alone right now, if that's okay."

I look from her to the painting. It's coming along nicely. She wants me to leave now?

"Can I have another fifteen minutes?" I dab my brush at the canvas and try to block her out, closing my eyes to refocus.

"No." My eyes fly open at the hard edge in Candace's

voice. She's staring at me, her legs wide, her hands on her hips. "No, you may not. I'd like you to leave now."

"What?" I am pretty sure I'm staring at her, but I don't really know what else to do. Who is this person?

"This is my room now, Christine. You may use it to paint, but when I need it, this is my room." She takes a step toward me. "And after the stunt you pulled at Bloomingdale's, I don't really want you to be here at the moment."

I set my brush down on the palette.

"I received a notice that someone purchased the fifteen men's belts we registered for. So I went online to see what other treasures 'we' had picked out. I started going through and weeding out the garbage, but it quickly became apparent that it would be easier to scrap the registry and start over." She sits down on the edge of the bed. "Which isn't exactly something I have a lot of time for at the moment, in case you hadn't noticed. And then there's the fact that the entire city council now thinks I wear a size 48 DD bra and secretly want a new engagement ring." She crosses her arms over her chest and stares at me. "And the worst part is, I thought we were doing so well. I really thought we were making progress, you and me, but it turns out you're still the mean-spirited, immature child you always were. Your father and I are getting married, and nothing you do is going to change that."

She throws her hands up in the air, tears streaming down her face. "So, no, Christine, believe it or not, you may not finish up your painting. I want you out of my room, now."

Did I hear her right? I glance at her to make sure she's not about to crack up about the great joke she just pulled, but she's dead serious. I lay the palette down and walk to the door without a word.

As I trudge across the grass back toward the house, I try to figure out what just happened. I can't believe she called me mean. I'm the good guy here. She's the one marrying my father when my mother has only been in the grave a year and a half. *That's* mean.

On the other hand, who cares if she did call me mean? This is a huge victory. It's exactly what I've been working toward all along. A few more fights like this one, and she'll never marry into this family. But if it's such a great feat, why do I feel like crying?

34

Ms. Moore looks up from the papers she's reading and puts her sandwich down on a paper towel when I push open her office door.

"I like the bling," I say. Ms. Moore's style could be described as eccentric on her best days, but the new black horn-rimmed frames, accented with rhinestones at the edges, are a new high—or low, depending on how you look at it. I kind of like that she's never tried to fit into the whole J.Crew aesthetic this town seems to love.

"The better to see you with." Ms. Moore wipes her mouth with paper napkins and runs her fingers together to brush off the crumbs. "Sorry, I was running around at lunch and didn't get a chance to eat. Do you mind?"

I shake my head.

"So, how was your Christmas?" She takes another bite of her sandwich and rolls back a little on her chair's metal wheels.

"Oh, you know." I shrug. "A laugh a minute. You?"

"Lots of snow." Ms. Moore is from Massachusetts, and she went back to spend a week with her family. The phone on her desk rings, but she ignores it.

"Ugh." Half Moon Bay may be cold most of the time, but we never have to deal with the dreaded white stuff.

"It's not so bad. It's kind of a nice change of pace, really. No one bugging me." She glares at the phone as it starts ringing again and takes a sip from the water bottle on her desk as the little voice mail light on her phone goes on.

"So." She leans forward and crosses her arms over her chest. "Did you miss her?"

Nice try, but a sneak attack isn't going to work today. I decide to change the subject. "What do you know about guys?"

She eyes me skeptically and gestures toward her naked left hand. "Apparently not enough. Why?" Ms. Moore moved to Half Moon Bay to flee a broken engagement. She claims to have thrown a dart at a map, but I don't buy it. It's too cinematic, plus I'm sure old Lovchuck threw some money at her and that was that.

"Say a guy takes you out a few times. Say he acts like he likes you. Say he promises to call. Then he doesn't. He acts like it was nothing and implies that you read too much into things. Are you crazy or is he?" I slouch down in my chair and stretch my legs out in front of me. "Or does it mean he doesn't like your nose ring?" I lace my fingers together in my lap. "Hypothetically, of course."

Ms. Moore chuckles. "I'm sure he likes your nose ring just fine." She takes another bite and chews thoughtfully. "Did you miss her?"

I watch the blinking light on her phone.

"Yes." I clear my throat. "So is he a jerk or what? I mean, here he was trying to act like the best Christian in the world, and he turns out to be scum just like everyone else."

"How did your dad deal with it?" She pops a potato chip

into her mouth. It's one of those baked flavorless kinds. What's the point?

"He took me Christmas tree shopping." I glance at her, then quickly look away when I see she's staring at me. She doesn't know I overheard her in the store, and I'm not sure how she'd react if she did. "So, do you think there's any chance he'll call? Or was it all an act?"

Ms. Moore seems to have no trouble following my train of thought. "I don't know." She sighs. "But I think it's pretty telling that you keep talking about Andrew when I'm asking you about your family."

"How did you know who I was—"

"I'm a teacher. I have eyes in the back of my head." She smiles and nibbles on a chip before continuing. "Why are you so fixated on this guy, Christine?"

"Uh…" Is she serious? I mean, I'm sixteen. It's not really rocket science. "Because he's hot? And because he seemed to be interested in me but now he's not?"

"Granted. Your interest in boys is age appropriate." She wipes her fingertips on a paper napkin. "But you're all too ready to talk about him now when I'm asking about your mom, and I've never even heard you mention guys before."

"Maybe I didn't want to talk about them before." I shrug.

"Maybe it's a diversionary tactic." She clears her throat. "Or maybe it indicates something much more."

"Is this one of those weird Freud things?"

"Hardly." She snorts. "But doesn't it seem possible that you're fixated on this guy because it keeps you from having to think about other absences in your life?"

I unlace my fingers and shove my hands under my legs.

What is she talking about? It sounds like she's a little too excited about that psychology degree to me. She does this with English too, reading symbolism that simply isn't there into books. I mean, sometimes a water pump is just a water pump.

I'm opening my mouth to tell her where to put her Freud when the phone bleats out again. She glances down at the number flashing across the screen and sighs.

"I'm sorry. I've got to get this." She shakes her head and holds up a finger to me. "Yes?" She doesn't try to disguise the disgust in her voice. "I understand." She makes a note on the paper in front of her, then writes down a phone number. "Got it." She waits while the person on the other end says something more. "Fine. I have to go." She hangs up the phone quickly. "Sorry." She turns back to me and rolls her eyes. "My lawyer. So. Back to you avoiding my questions."

35

"Christine? How do you want your burger cooked?"

"Bloody." I give Dad a sarcastic grin.

He flares his nostrils for a moment but recovers quickly. "Great! Medium rare it is. Emma?"

Emma's tongue is pressed to her top lip in concentration as little beads of sweat populate her brow. "Huh?"

Candace walks over to the kitchen table. "Do you like your burger pink in the middle? A little underdone?"

Emma puts down the expensive fountain pen and scratches her nose. "Gross. No!" She peers into the kitchen. "I like my burgers really, really flat. And totally done."

Dad bites his lip and turns around. "Okay, I think I can figure that out."

Candace walks over to my side of the table. "How's it going?"

As she looks at the envelope I'm working on—Assemblyman H. J. Goldberg and Mrs. Goldberg—I can tell she's about to swoon, but I'm being punished, so she refrains from complimenting me. Ever since I did calligraphy on Emma's campaign posters, leading her to victory as vice president of the seventh grade class, Candace has been obsessed with my work. "I've done a hundred and four."

She sighs in delight. "Oh my." She goes back into the

kitchen to help Father of the Year with his first ever attempt at cooking dinner.

I can't believe she's rubbing it in like this. They're sending save the date cards to 578 people, and Dad thought addressing all 578 would be a suitable punishment for Emma and me for ruining Candace's wedding registry.

"How many do you have done, Em?" I whisper.

She counts her envelopes, moving her mouth silently. Finally she sets them down and rolls her eyes. "Fifty-two."

I put my head on the table and bang it quietly. Emma doesn't know how to do calligraphy, and her cursive is not the best, so Candace insisted she print very carefully, but printing takes her forever. Emma's eyes are red and there's a blister forming on her middle finger from gripping the pen so hard. "It's okay. I'm moving along pretty quickly. It won't take that much longer." She tries to smile but doesn't seem to be able to muster the strength.

I pick up my list. We decided Emma should take the first 100 and I'd start at guest number 101. Let's see who's left. Malcolm Slocum IV. Miller Franklin Haun and Mrs. Haun-Young. Mallory Louise Bard and Guest. If these people are anything like their names, this should be one snore of a wedding. My eyes scan for "Dominguez"—that should be easy to pick out—but I don't see it. I look on the third page...nothing.

"Hey, Em." I put my list down. "Let me see your list for a second." She hands it to me and slumps down in her chair. Laughter comes from the kitchen, and I roll my eyes.

I carefully check each name. There's no "Ana Dominguez," and I don't see Riley or Zoe either. Okay, that's it. There's only so much a person can take. I walk into the kitchen, clutching Emma's list.

The smell of raw red meat hangs in the air as Dad puts burgers onto the George Foreman grill. He doesn't even know you're supposed to close the top of the stupid thing. Candace has her arms around my dad's waist, and they're giggling and murmuring to each other.

"Ahem," I say, not even pretending to cough.

Candace turns around and beams an evil stepmom grin at me. "Need a glass of water?"

I ignore her and tap my dad on the shoulder. He turns around with ground hamburger bits on his hands. "Where are my friends?"

Dad walks over to the sink to wash up, then shuts off the faucet and dries his hands on his apron. "You can bring a friend." He glances at Candace, and she nods. He raises his voice so that Emma can hear in the next room. "We talked about it and decided you can each bring one friend."

"Yay!" Emma screams, coming back to life a little.

"*One* friend?!" Who would I choose? Riley? No, it would hurt Zoe too much. And heaven forbid I skip Ana—she'd never let me hear the end of it. This is the last thing the Miracle Girls need. "I can't bring *one* friend. I have three friends. You know that." The moment I say it, though, I realize that he probably doesn't know that.

Dad walks over to Candace and turns around. She begins to untie the apron from his neck and says, "Actually, Christine, we thought you might want to bring Andrew."

Dad pulls the apron over his head and tosses it on the counter. "Perfect idea." Candace picks his dirty apron off the counter and wads it into a ball. "Bring Andrew. I really like him. Where's he been anyway?"

I shut my eyes. They can't seriously be asking me this. "Andrew can't come. He's..." I open my right eye, and Candace is giving me her pity face. "I told you he's just a friend. My friend Andrew. I'm not inviting him."

I hold the guest list up. "Do you see this? I am addressing 'save the date' cards to all of these people. The least you could do is allow me to bring my three best friends."

Candace's mouth is a straight line. Dad puts a big hand on my shoulder, covering it entirely.

"Christine, it's our special day. The wedding is about our family coming together. You don't need your pals there."

Pals?! I stifle a laugh. What century is this guy from?

"James," Candace groans under her breath.

"Well, I'm not addressing any more envelopes if I can't even bring..." My family. That's what I want to say. I need my Miracle Girls family there for support. *Our special day.* The phrase rings in my head like a threat.

Candace tries to catch my dad's eye, and it reminds me of when I was little and adults would spell words they thought I shouldn't hear.

"Christine. I'm sorry." He holds his head like it's going to explode. "But no means no. You and Emma can each bring *one* friend."

As I stand there sputtering at the injustice of it all, Emma appears in the doorway. "Mom, can I bring Dad?"

Candace walks over to Emma and grabs her by the arm. They disappear into the back of the house, Candace hissing at her the whole way.

Dad shakes his head at me. "Christine, when Candace and I decide on a punishment, we're going to stick to it."

His words sound rehearsed, like she's been coaching him on how to discipline me. I know she thinks I'm spoiled. Never mind that when Mom was alive we didn't have these sorts of blowups.

"I'm sorry that you can't bring all of your friends. But if we let you bring three people, we'd have to let Emma do the same. And we can't add six people to the guest list at this point. The ballroom only fits so many people. Please try to understand."

And then it dawns on me. Who cares? There's no point in caring about this guest list drama because this bogus wedding isn't actually going to happen. Candace is already about to run for the hills, screaming at the tops of her lungs.

"Whatever," I say under my breath and start to walk away.

"You can see them any other day of the year."

"Sure," I say over my shoulder. I sit back down at the kitchen table and start addressing the next envelope, tears welling up in my eyes.

"I love you, Christine. I really, really do," he whispers. I can feel him hovering a few feet behind me.

Then why are you pushing what's left of my mom as far away as possible? I fight back the tears and intentionally misspell the next name: Kernel Philip Hanley and Mrs. Hanley.

36

I t's too bad being a freak only gets me out of PE one day a week. While I wouldn't exactly say that being grilled by Ms. Moore is any better than dodging the balls that are currently being thrown at my head, at least her office doesn't smell like sweat.

It wouldn't be so bad if every PE class on the planet weren't crammed into this one little gym, but since it's raining, all of us are stuck in here. The squeak of rubber soles on the smooth wooden floor mixed with the thump of bouncing rubber and the occasional yelp or cheer creates a cacophony that echoes across the room.

"All right, let's get started." Ms. Lewis lets out a shrill squeak on her whistle. She looks particularly witchy today, with a long black crepey skirt and a black T-shirt, and she's deathly pale in the harsh fluorescent lights. What kind of PE teacher wears a skirt?

Riley looks at me and shrugs, then walks slowly toward the tape line on the gym floor. My garnet shorts ride up a little as I follow her. Who designed these things, and how is it that Riley looks perfectly normal in her gym clothes while I look like a freakishly skinny oaf?

It doesn't help that my class is stuck playing the lamest sport ever. Wait, does dodgeball even count as a sport? I bet it doesn't. But we're in the middle of our golf unit (come to think of it, golf doesn't really count as a sport either), and since we can't hit balls with little metal lightning rods around outside in the rain, we have to take whatever we can get today.

None of this is ideal, but it wouldn't be the end of the world if... I peek over my shoulder to make sure it's really true. Yep. Andrew Cutchins is over there on the basketball court. He looks my way, then turns when he sees me watching him. Now that it's officially basketball season, I guess he'll be in here a lot more. I love the way the whole school is complicit in this. If you're on a sports team—one that actually wins, unlike our football team—and it's the day before the first game of the season, you're somehow mysteriously allowed out of class to practice. So much for learning. Hooray for America's future.

Thanks to the can-do-no-wrong basketball gods, we're all crammed around the perimeter of the court. That's the way high school works. They'll take any chance they get to remind you how insignificant you are.

Ms. Lewis blows her whistle again, and large red rubber balls start flying at my face.

"So have you figured out what you want to do tonight, Riley?" I duck as a ball whizzes by my left ear. I don't know how I could have made it through this week without the promise of a Friday night out.

I steal another covert glance at the basketball court. Hmph. Guess his stupid knee is all better. One of Andrew's goon friends is staring at me, so I roll my eyes at him and turn around. Great. Now they all probably think I'm stalking him.

Riley grimaces and jumps to the left to avoid a ball coming straight toward her. "Uhh..." She reaches for her short ponytail at the nape of her neck and tightens it up again. "About that..."

"What?" The thump of a rubber ball hitting the ground next to me makes me jump. A loud cheer goes up on the basketball court, and I look in time to see Andrew toss the ball in the hoop. Show-off.

"Yeah." Riley barely turns in time to miss a ball. "Did I mention Tom called?"

"Riley McGee, you will not do this to me."

"They're driving back today. It turns out he was seriously out in the middle of nowhere." She coughs a little. "Like, an hour from a phone." She smiles sheepishly.

"What? What are you talking about?" I can't believe she's actually trying to play this off like it's okay. "He went off and texted you that he was leaving. He didn't call you. It's been two weeks!"

"Well, he tried to call, but like I said, he was out on an island off the coast of Mexico. They didn't really have a phone. But he called as soon as he got back to Baja." She swallows. "And he did send me a postcard, but he had the address wrong, so it just arrived yesterday."

"But what about not warning you he was leaving?" I must sound a little hysterical because people are turning around to stare at me. A stray basketball bounces onto our dodgeball court, and I ignore it.

"O'Neill—" She shrugs at me. "You know, the surfboard company? They called him suddenly. One of the pro surfers they were training for this big competition down in Mexico broke his arm, and they needed a replacement immediately. So he went. His parents said he could go if his cousins went

along. It was a great opportunity. He might get sponsored."
Even in the midst of this monologue, Riley manages to avoid
getting hit by a ball.

"So...you forgave him."

"What else could I do?" She frowns a little.

"And you're canceling on me."

"He gets back tonight." Riley shrugs helplessly. "I was
hoping you'd be willing to reschedule?" Her cheeks are pink,
and her clear blue eyes look at me hopefully. I can tell she's
honestly sorry...And yet can't she see that I need this,
that so much hangs in the balance, that not spending time
together is all we do now?

"But that's not fair to me."

"I know." Her voice is high and strained. She's almost
pleading with me. "I know, I know. But Christine, I need to
talk to him. I miss him, and...I want to see him."

"I—" The wind is knocked out of me, and I stumble
back. A rubber ball hits the ground by my feet—I think it
bounced off my stomach. I take a deep breath and shake my
head. Ms. Lewis is gesturing for me to step toward the outside circle. I throw my hands up. "I hate this game!"

Picking up the ball, I move as slowly as possible to show
everyone exactly how excited I am about being involved in
this ridiculous pseudosport. Riley tries to catch my eye, but I
look away before I have to deal with her sympathy too. Riley
dates some guy who disappears in the middle of the night,
and she gets to cancel our girls' night because her knight in
shining armor sweeps back into town. I try to date a good
Christian guy and grasp for the little bit of faith I have left,
and he breaks my heart.

"Christine, are you going to hold that ball all day?" Ms. Lewis yells across the gym. She looks like she's putting a hex on me from across the floor, and I duck her glare.

And then, before I know what's happening, I'm walking toward him—stalking may be a better word for it. Whatever it is, I'm not really in control of what I'm doing here. Andrew sees me coming and winks.

"What are you staring at?" I try to keep my voice low, but it seems to echo in this giant gym.

"Your mad skills." Andrew cocks his head and laughs. "You're funny to watch."

"What? I'm funny?" His teammates stop playing and gawk at me. I'm kind of standing in the middle of the court where they're trying to play.

Ms. Lewis calls me again, but I couldn't care less. Something has gotten ahold of me, and I need to say it.

"I can't believe you call yourself a Christian."

"What?" Andrew's mouth falls open in shock. The basketball coach is walking toward me, his big bushy mustache waggling.

I feel bad for a moment. Maybe I shouldn't have said it.

But I meant it. It wasn't a nice thing to say, but it's true. How can he treat me like he did and still pretend to be a Christian?

"Christine, I—"

"And I'm a better painter than you." I don't even wait to see his face. I turn on my heel and run to the door of the gym, my polyester shorts swishing. Ms. Lewis is blowing her whistle incessantly behind me, but as I step out into the cool rainy air, I don't even care.

I'll take a detention for it. I can't spend another minute in there with those people.

37

put my backpack on the ground and lie down, propping my head up on it. "Nope, still incredibly uncomfortable."

"Zoe will be here any minute." Ana stands up and dusts off her J.Crew khakis. She peers at her butt to make sure she hasn't gotten her pants dirty. "We can't abandon her."

I study Ana's face. She and Riley never really resolved their fight, but at least they're able to be around each other now. Granted it feels like arctic chills when it happens, but I suppose at least they're not hurling insults at each other.

"What time is it?" Riley asks quietly, looking at me. Why is it every locker in this joint has patches of paint missing? The one across from me looks a bit like Van Gogh's *Starry Night*.

"It's 3:45." I sigh.

I sit up, bruising my tailbone on the hard ground. "Okay, executive decision. If she doesn't get here in ten minutes, we're leaving her a note on the door and calling it a day." When the other members of Earth First saw that Ms. Moore's classroom was locked, they ran to catch their school buses or just started walking home. I wanted to join them, but Ana threatened my life.

Ana sighs. "Fine." She gets a spiral notebook out of her bag, throws it on the floor, then sits carefully on top of it. "I only wanted to wait for her because it would be good to actually have a meeting this month." She gives Riley a wary look, but Riley doesn't meet her eye.

The Earth First meeting was supposed to be right after school today. Ana checked the date with Ms. Moore last week and then sent an e-mail out to all the members. But Ms. Moore hasn't shown her face at school all week. When she had a sub on Monday, I didn't think much of it, but when I stopped by her office for our session on Tuesday and there wasn't even a note, I began to get a little concerned. Now it's Thursday and there's still no sign of her.

"I think something's wrong. It's not like Ms. Moore to miss school." Ana tries to get more comfortable on her notebook.

Riley pulls her head up from the locker she was leaning it against. "Maybe she's sick?"

Ana shrugs. "I've been eavesdropping on my mom's phone calls. Mom's in good with the head of the PTA." That girl is an expert spy. It's almost scary. "I think Ms. Moore made someone powerful angry."

"But how?" Riley shakes her head. "It doesn't make sense."

"I'm not sure." Ana brushes a lock of dark brown hair back behind her ear. "It's hard to know when you're only hearing half of the conversation, but it seems like there was an *incident*."

I sit up again. "An incident? Like she socked someone?" I swallow a lump in my throat. I haven't told anyone about the phone call from Ms. Moore's lawyer. "Whoever it was, they probably deserved it."

Ana sighs. "I love her too, of course. But you know how she can be. She doesn't exactly play by the rules."

"That's why we like her." Riley bites her lip.

Ana looks at her watch. "I know. But I keep hearing about 'the incident.' She's upset someone."

There's a rustling at the end of the hall. I look up to see a flurry of garnet and gold polyester coming our way. "Sorry!" Zoe screams down to us. Her cheeks are red, and Marcus is trailing behind her. He blows Zoe a kiss, then dashes down the hallway. "Sorry, sorry, sorry!" Zoe rushes up to us and comes to a stop in front of Riley. "Band practice was over, but Marcus and I decided to practice our— Why are you guys in the hallway?"

Zoe's cheeks are pink, and her eyes are bright, but maybe that doesn't mean anything. She couldn't have chosen Marcus over us, could she? Riley meets my eye, and I know she feels it too. Zoe, the one who saw what we were when none of the rest of us wanted to acknowledge it, put Marcus before us.

Ana gestures toward our broken picnic table, and we all move over there and settle in. I try to pay attention as Ana drones on about a beach cleanup she wants to organize, but I'm not really listening. I'm thinking about what this means.

"Congratulations, by the way!" Zoe says suddenly.

"Oh, thanks. It's no big deal." Riley digs in her purse and pulls out lip balm, then smoothes it over her lips.

Ana turns to them. "What's this? Are congratulations in order for Cheerleader Girl?" Her voice is thin and tight, and the hair on my arms stands up. What now?

Zoe nudges Riley. "Tell them."

"Naw. It's stupid."

Zoe's mouth drops open. "It is not stupid! Dreamy showed me this morning. The *San Jose Mercury News* made Riley Outstanding Student of the Month for the Bay Area!"

"What?!" Ana screams. For a moment, I hold out hope that it's the kind of scream that could be interpreted as a sound of joy, but the look on her face makes it evident that it's not.

"Ana," I whisper at her through my teeth, "stop it."

She laughs loudly. "Really, Riley. That's so great."

Riley rolls her eyes. "Whatever." She turns back to Zoe. "My parents woke me up with a copy this morning. It was really cute."

"So how did you get nominated?" Ana's voice wavers a bit, but she pastes a smile on her face.

"I don't know. My dad nominated me or something."

Ana smiles in a saccharine way. "Oh, of course."

Riley leans forward. "What do you mean?"

Ana sighs. "It just seems a little convenient that you always get handed awards like this." She shrugs.

Riley stares at the table, her eyes wide.

"I do as well as you in school, but somehow you seem to win all the awards. It's just a little strange, that's all." Ana looks around, as if expecting us all to back her up. I clear my throat.

Riley waits, but no one says anything. Zoe's lip starts to quiver, and I try to make my mouth form words, but nothing is coming out. Finally, Riley lets out a long breath and hoists her backpack onto her shoulder.

"You know, this is why people think you're annoying. There's more to life than school. I've always defended you, but, hey, maybe I was wrong." Riley turns around and walks away, and I see her slipping through our fingers with every step.

"Wait!" I scream, almost not even recognizing my own

voice. Riley stops in her tracks but doesn't turn back. Her shoulders rise and fall quickly, like she's trying to catch her breath. And that's when Ana takes it too far.

"I told you guys she wasn't one of us."

I can't move. Maybe it isn't really happening. Perhaps it's all a bad dream. But when I look at Ana's face, I know it is happening, that she did utter those words out loud. I look from her smug face to the back of Riley's head, and I make a decision.

I walk over to Riley, grab her by the arm, and physically yank her back. She seems to be in shock, but allows herself to be dragged to our table. I give her a gentle push and make her sit across from Ana, next to Zoe, who is now picking at the table's splintering wood.

I walk to the end of the table and put my hands flat on the top. For a second or two, my mind is totally blank. I've never done anything like this before. I don't know if I even can. But then I look around this old broken table, I see all my dreams for the future, the only family I've known since my mom died, and I know that I have to do it. "I will not let this happen. You guys are being idiots."

They both start talking over each other, pointing fingers and accusing. "Shut up!" I scream and they stare at me, mouths hanging open. "We've been falling apart, bickering, losing focus all year." I stare down at the table and notice a few flecks of garnet paint, the same color as the school walls. How did it get here? How did I never notice it before? "It's going to be the death of the Miracle Girls if we keep this up."

My words echo off the walls of the empty courtyard.

"Okay, look." My voice is just a whisper. "We love each

other." I gesture around the barren breezeways. "We're not like the rest of the people at this miserable school. We have something that's deeper than all of this. We may not like each other every day, we might all have faults that drive each other crazy, but we're loyal. We stick together. That's what it means to be a Miracle Girl. You put the other girls first and no one"—I give Riley a knowing glance—"and nothing"—I glare at Ana—"comes between us."

I dust off my hands and take a deep breath, waiting for them to say something, to agree with me, to hug each other and say they're sorry, but nothing happens.

"Fine." I grab my bag and sling it over my shoulder. "Ruin it all, and then we'll have no one." Zoe rises like she's going to stop me, but I ignore her. "You guys were all I had."

38

She's started counting down the days. With each square she crosses off the calendar in the kitchen, I get more panicked. I'm running out of time.

I've been brainstorming for weeks, but so far nothing has worked. She didn't fall apart when I told her I wouldn't wear the stupid green bridesmaid dress she settled on. The theme is officially "Spring Into Spring," and involves an "organic" palette. Candace shrugged and said I was welcome to wear whatever I want.

She didn't scream or cry when I told her I hated the invitations she picked out, and that there was nothing in the world they could do to make me address them for her. She smiled and said she was planning to hire a professional calligrapher anyway.

And she didn't even react when I called the priest who's marrying them and told him I opposed the marriage. He listened politely, and that was the last I ever heard of it. I don't even know if he told her about the call, but I do know the wedding planning is proceeding whether I like it or not.

I look around my bedroom, hoping for inspiration. I have to think of something. There has to be a way to end this stupid thing. Emma's no help. Ever since the save-the-date debacle, she's sworn off being my accomplice, and I actually suspect she might want this wedding to happen now.

Let's see. I begin flipping through my drawers, looking for inspiration. When I come up blank, I wander out into the hallway and then to the kitchen. I could burn the house down. That might work. But that punishes me too.

I could run away. Surely they wouldn't go through with it while they have a kid missing, but where would I go? They'd find me pretty quickly at any of my friends' houses. And what would I live on? It's not like I have any money saved up. Okay, scratch that.

I wander into the living room and see the lights on in the studio. So she's home. I wonder where Emma is. And why didn't Candace come into the house before going out to her room? I stare across the yard, hoping to see some movement in one of the windows, but I can't see anything. What is she doing in there? I squint. I bet she's looking through brochures for boarding schools for me to attend, old-school stepmom style.

I slide the big glass door open and walk across the yard before I know what I'm doing, keeping my body low so she won't see me if she happens to glance out the window. She's up to something evil, I'm sure of it. Why else would she have to be so secretive? I'm going to find out what she's up to. Ana, who is the world's best eavesdropper, would be so proud.

I reach the studio and crouch down under the window facing the house. I take a deep breath. If she sees me, I'll just admit I was spying on her. It can only help my case at this point. Slowly, I push myself up so I can barely see over the edge of the windowsill. I look in and gasp.

Candace is standing in the middle of the room, wearing a long white dress. She's staring at herself in the mirror, tears in her eyes, mesmerized by her own reflection.

I can't suppress a laugh, so I duck out of sight as it escapes my lips, but when I work up the courage to peek back inside, she's still swaying in front of the mirror, holding the top in place with one hand.

She's actually wearing her wedding dress! In her room! How lame can you be?! I stifle another laugh as I watch her. She's probably imagining herself walking down the aisle, everyone staring at her and twittering about how beautiful she looks. Pathetic.

But it is kind of a pretty dress, I have to admit. It's very simple—strapless, A-line, white. It's not at all what I would have imagined her picking out. I expected something more beauty queen, with lots of pouffy layers and beads and rhinestones and feathers and stuff. This is kind of nice, actually.

I push myself up a little bit to get a better look. She runs her hand down the smooth front of the dress and grabs the skirt, swishing it forward and back.

If I'm honest, it looks good on her. She's so fit, and it accentuates her toned arms without being too revealing.

She turns a little so she can see herself from the side. She hasn't zipped the dress all the way up the back. That must be why she's holding the front. I guess she probably needs someone to help her with that part.

I bite my lip and study her face. There's something differ-ent about it. Lately she's been so stressed that's she's looked kind of pale and drawn, but now...her cheeks are a little pink, but that's not really it. It's more that she looks, well…I guess it's that she looks really happy.

She's standing there in her wedding dress, alone, two full months before the wedding, admiring her own reflection. She's clearly lost in a daydream, imagining herself on her wedding day, and she looks happier than I've ever seen her.

I duck back down and turn away, toward the house. I shake my head, but the image is seared into my eyeballs.

She's a grown woman who's been married before. She has a teenage daughter, for Pete's sake. But she's crying tears of joy over her stupid wedding dress.

I wish I hadn't seen it.

I sit there under the window, staring at the house for a long time, trying to figure out how much this changes things.

39

People always think of California as being eternally sunny and warm. In movies it's lined with palm trees and wide beaches of sparkling sand, but there aren't a lot of palm trees in Half Moon Bay, the sand is brown and rocky, and it's cool and wet almost every day, like Seattle. Even in late March, when you'd think it would finally start to get a little warmer around here, I'm still wearing a sweatshirt.

I rub my hands together and think of tropical shores as I wait out front for Riley's mom to pick me up. Riley got her license a few weeks ago, but she can't drive us without an adult in the car, and since my car decided to stall on me on the way home from school two days ago, I'm carless and powerless. I could technically hang out inside my house, but Emma's in there twirling around in her bridesmaid dress, and I can't stand to watch it anymore.

Tonight promises to be torturous. Riley's youth group is having a special event, and unfortunately for us all, this is also Ana's youth group. Three Car Garage is playing a concert, so Ana will definitely be there, and Riley has to go because her mom signed her up to help with the snack bar. Ana and Riley still aren't talking, and with Zoe pulling away more than ever, I'm not even really sure why I'm here. It's too late for us. I've started to accept it. But when Riley called to beg me to come with her, I didn't have the guts to say no. The two of us can still be friends, even if the Miracle Girls are done.

At long last, Riley's turquoise minivan turns down my street. Well, her mom's minivan, I guess. The huge color photo of Mrs. McGee's face is pasted on the door, smiling for the whole town to see. I walk down the driveway to hop in but stop short when I see someone already sitting in the backseat.

"Hey." Zoe waves as I open the door. Suddenly I'm glad she got suckered into going to church too.

"I like the RealMobile." I hop into the back and scramble onto the seat, then slide the heavy side door shut.

"Hello Christine." Riley's mom smiles, but Riley turns to face us and grimaces. I guess in the real estate world, it's perfectly normal to plaster your image and phone number on every available surface to attract potential clients, but in high school, driving a minivan with your mom's real estate ad is about the most humiliating thing you can do. Still, Riley seems to be holding up well.

We drive along in silence for a few minutes until Riley clears her throat and turns to face us. She glances at her mom, who's rocking out to some Christian contemporary music and doesn't seem to be paying attention. "So I don't know if I should spread this around or not, but I heard something about Ms. Moore, and I need to tell somebody." Zoe brightens, but I look down at my hands. I'm not sure I want to hear whatever it is Riley has to say.

"Riley, it's not nice to spread rumors." Mrs. McGee's eyes stay focused on the road, but her voice carries over the music.

"It's not a rumor, Mom." Riley pulls at her seat belt and turns to get a better angle. "I heard two teachers talking about it after practice the other day."

"What happened?" Zoe looks hopeful.

"You know how she's always butting into people's lives and stuff?" Riley meets my eye in the rearview mirror. "Apparently she lost it and yelled at the parent of one of her students, and now the parent is suing the school board." Riley nods solemnly, but my stomach drops. "That's why she's been out—because she's on suspension until they figure it all out."

My mind flashes to the scene in the grocery store. It can't be.

"Oh wow. That's crazy. Who?" Zoe asks as Mrs. McGee turns left onto Highway 1. I hold my breath.

"Don't know." Riley shrugs. "I couldn't hear."

"Is she going to get fired?" Zoe asks quietly.

"I've told you all I know." Riley shakes her head. "But I wonder what she said. Wouldn't you love to see her in action?" Riley puts up her dukes and punches the air. Mrs. McGee shakes her head. I bite my lip.

Ms. Moore must deal with other troubled students too.

She butts into everyone's life.

I can't be the only one whose parents she insulted.

He wouldn't do that to me.

"She is a little bossy," Zoe says.

"Look," I say loudly. "You don't know anything about her. She's...she's not bossy. She's just concerned."

My dad needed to hear what she said to him. Ms. Moore was the only person brave enough to do it.

Zoe's eyes widen. I've never snapped at her before, and I don't know what made me do it now, except that everything is all upside down and it's making me a little crazy. I'm hardly stable on a normal day.

"I . . . I know her."

"We know her too," Riley says.

"Yeah, but . . ." Zoe is watching me carefully. "I go to weekly counseling sessions with her so I probably know her a little better. That's all."

"Oh," Zoe says, the hurt apparent in her voice. "I . . . I always thought you went to see Mrs. Canning."

I hold my head in my hands. Why do I do this stuff to them? I never mean to keep secrets, but I have a hard time sharing, and if you don't tell your friends about something when it first happens, then as time elapses it becomes a secret, even if you didn't mean for it to be. "She's . . ." I take a deep breath. "She's been there for me."

I want to say more, to explain everything to them about how she's the only adult who seems to care about me and that's important for some reason, about how she knows my thoughts before I even think them, about how she yelled at my dad and now he's really trying . . . But I can't.

It's quite possibly the first time I've ever been excited to pull into the church parking lot. No one has breathed even a peep since my confession about Ms. Moore. Even Mrs. McGee didn't say anything. Zoe and Riley don't seem to be mad, but they're processing what I've told them, and I can't stop thinking about my dad. He wouldn't try to get

Ms. Moore fired, would he? But who else would have that kind of pull with the school board? Plus, he's been so weird lately that he might do just about anything.

The band is warming up when we walk into the youth room while Ana runs around like a chicken with her head cut off, helping the guys get set up and bringing them bottles of water. She waves at me and Zoe and gives Riley a curt nod. Zoe runs off to help her, and Riley grimaces at me. "Here goes nothing," she says and disappears into the kitchen.

I'm left alone. I walk over to examine the Three Car Garage merchandise for sale on a small table by the door. They have T-shirts in every color and a stack of CDs. Jamie, a junior who sometimes sings with the band, is manning the table. I give her an absent wave and pick up a glossy CD case. It has a black-and-white photo of Tommy Chu's house, complete with an enormous three-car garage, on the front.

I flip over the CD and examine the picture of the band on the back. They're all standing on a stretch of deserted beach, staring vacantly into the distance, trying to look like they're not posing. Dave is wearing his typical board shorts and necktie while Tyler looks like he wore an entire Abercrombie store to the shoot. There's no denying that he's the best-looking one of the bunch. I squint at the image of the drummer, Tommy Chu. I've never really paid much attention to him, but he's actually kind of cute. I scan the room and see him sitting on one of the ratty youth group couches, twirling his drumsticks and talking with some girl. Typical.

"Do you want to buy one? It's only ten dollars," Jamie says, smiling at me. "And it's really good."

"No thanks." I smile and put it back on the table. I can't

exactly tell her I already have one from my Tyler phase last year, so I just walk away. She shrugs and starts refolding the stack of T-shirts on the table.

I walk over to Ana and Zoe, who are talking to some people I don't know, and try to blend into the wall. Tyler catches my eye and nods. My stomach warms, and I smile back and then pretend to be very engrossed in the girls' conversation about highlights. It's not that I don't want to talk to him. It's just that I know from experience I get flustered and awkward and don't know what to say. He watches me for a moment, then goes back to plugging in cords for the big show.

Thankfully, it's not too long before the lights dim and the band takes the "stage," which is really a piece of plywood about six inches off the ground. The crowd—there really is a crowd—moves to the middle of the room, now cleared of chairs, and begins to clap while the guys make a show of tuning their instruments. They drink in the cheers; then Tommy smacks his drumsticks together and they launch into one of their upbeat songs. Across the room, Ana begins to dance a little and Zoe claps. All around me people are moving and dancing and laughing, but I stand at the back of the room, still.

I feel like I'm not really here. It sounds stupid, I know, because where else would I be? But it feels like my body is totally disconnected from my mind. I can see that I'm here, that I'm in the middle of this crowd of people, all of whom appear to be having the time of their lives, but I'm really a million miles away. I'm not really a part of all this.

I'm in the paper goods aisle of a grocery store, hoping my dad will give the right answer.

I'm in the deserted school, breaking into an empty art classroom.

I'm sitting on the edge of a diving board, staring into a deep pool, watching patches of sunlight move across the surface of the water.

I'm soaking in a beaten-up hot tub, wishing there was more out there in the empty night sky.

I'm watching Candace sway in a white dress, feeling all hope disappear.

I'm by the side of a wet road, staring at a wreck of twisted metal, praying that God will send someone to save my mother before it's too late. The weak gray sunlight reflects off the broken glass at my feet.

I take a step toward the door, edging my way out of the crowd. No one seems to notice as I slip past the pulsing bodies. It's already become too warm in here, with all the people moving around, and I gasp as I finally step out into the cool evening air.

Even after the door of the youth room closes behind me, the music spills out into the night. I walk into the empty courtyard in the center of the church. I don't really know where I'm headed; I just know I have to get away from there.

I don't need a grand miraculous sign, God. I don't need a flash of lightning or disembodied voice or a chorus of angels or anything. I just need something. Anything. Please. Some way to believe that we're not really in this alone.

I make my way toward a wooden bench leaning against a wall of empty classrooms. The bench is painted in a garish selection of primary colors that all look muddy in the darkening evening air.

I lower myself down and lean back, staring into the sky. The Miracle Girls are always going on about how you can see God's power in the night sky, but when I look up, I don't see evidence of a huge and powerful God. There's no cosmic collection of light. All that's up there is a gray blanket of clouds.

I take a few deep gulps of air and try to slow my breathing, but my breaths come short and fast, like I'm gasping. Why does it bother me so much? It's not that I really thought I'd find an answer in the stars. They're just tiny pinpricks of light that mean somewhere out in the cosmos something huge is on fire.

I cross my arms over my chest. The band switches songs, and a cheer goes up from the crowd as they launch into one of their slower tunes. There's a party going on inside, and once again I'm out here alone.

I shake my head and sit up, then rest my elbows on my knees and lower my head into my hands. The sting of tears burns against my eyes, and I squeeze them shut, but it doesn't stop the tears from spilling out.

I want to believe more than anything.

I listen to the music behind me and let the tears fall. Nobody's going to hear me anyway. I take a deep, gasping breath, working to get enough air into my lungs as I try to picture my mother's face. When that doesn't work, I try to think about Emma's laugh or my dad's smile.

But all I can think about is how numb I felt as I waited on that road that day. I knew, even then, that I should have died. There's no way anyone could have survived that crash, but there I was without a scratch on me, and all I could feel was a sense that there was supposed to be more.

I climbed up to the road and stood there, praying into the abyss, until a car drove by, and I flagged it down. I didn't know Zoe then, so I didn't recognize the weird hippie woman who stepped out of the car and called the ambulance for me. To this day I'm not sure if Zoe knows Dreamy was there.

I take a deep breath and try to get my breathing under control, but it doesn't keep the tears from falling. I wipe my sleeve across my face and under my nose, but more just keeps coming.

My body shakes as I remember waiting in the hospital alone. Dad came as soon as he could, but it took several hours to drive back from Sacramento. By the time he made it, I knew she was dead. They wouldn't tell me anything until he came, but I knew what their silence meant.

Something warm touches my back and I open my eyes, but all I can see is a shadow. I sit still, and an arm wraps around my back. Ana's perfume, sweet and earthy, fills the air as she takes a seat next to me on the bench. I lean in to her a little. The warmth of her body is soothing. We sit in silence for a few minutes until I feel something on my other side. A hand on my shoulder. I turn my head a little and suck in a great gulp of air. Zoe.

She slides her hand across my shoulders and rests her arm across my back and waits. I must look like a blubbering fool. I try to get under control, to stop the tears from falling, but no one says anything as I continue to bawl.

And then I feel a hand rest on my lower back. Ana quickly adjusts her position on the bench, and I catch a glimpse of blonde hair as Riley slides in next to her.

I know the music is still playing behind us, but I don't

even hear it anymore. I just hear Riley's slow breathing and Zoe's mumbled prayers under her breath and feel Ana's hand rubbing my shoulder.

No one says anything. No one has to.

I don't even know how long we sit there like that, the four of us huddled together in the cold dark night, arms around each other, but slowly I begin to notice something changing. The silence doesn't seem so empty anymore.

My eyes are so puffy they're almost sealed shut, but I open them and look to my right, then to my left, and see the girls waiting patiently with me, holding me. I guess I should be surprised they're all here, together again, but I'm not. Somehow it feels like it couldn't have happened any other way. I needed them, all of them, and they needed me too. We needed this.

"You're not in this alone," Ana says quietly. "That's why we're here."

I nod. I guess I know that. On some level, maybe I've always known that.

I don't know about all this miracle stuff. The other girls have always believed that, but I'm not sure I did until just now. Maybe that's why we're all still here. For each other. God isn't going to send a choir of angels to show me he's out there. He sent something else instead. The three of them.

No one speaks, but I have a feeling I know what we're all thinking. Something bigger than us is holding us together. We can't let our friendship break apart.

I cast my eyes up at the sky. The clouds have shifted, and the outline of the moon shines through the thin patch of clouds in front of it, reflecting light onto us all.

40

M r. Dumas coughs. I look up, but he's writing oblivi-
ously in his lesson book. I turn back to Mom's canvas and study it. It's weird to work on something she
started, but it makes me feel close to her. I pick up my brush
and get back to work. I've only got a few weeks to finish this.

I don't know why I never thought to ask Mr. Dumas about
this before. Of course he'd let me stay after school and paint.
The classroom is still and quiet, and there's no annoying
wedding chatter. With the big day a month away, there's no
peace at my house. Plus, I can't work on this there because
this painting is for Dad and Candace.

The long, thick windows by the classroom door are dark
when Mr. Dumas finally stretches, stands, and pushes his
chair under his desk.

"Far be it from me to interrupt the creative process, but I
have to head home now."

Shoot. I was just starting to get some good work done. I
lay my brush down.

"Make sure the door's locked when you leave." He pulls
his raincoat off the back of his chair and slips it around his
shoulders. "And no one in administration finds out." He
nods, then walks out the door.

Okay. I guess I get to stay. A slow smile spreads across my face. I can stay here all night if I want to. I love Mr. Dumas.

I dip the tip of my brush in rusty red paint. Just a dab is all I need.

I've only been at work for a few minutes when my phone rings. A glance at the screen tells me it's Riley.

"You home?"

"Nope. Dumas's room." I laugh. "You?"

"Oh. Great. I'm outside the gym. Practice is over. Can I come by?"

"Sure. I'll save you a seat."

"See you in a few."

As much as I love Riley, I almost wish she weren't coming. It's so peaceful, so quiet here, and I'm making good headway, but when she swings the classroom door open a few minutes later, her eyes and face are red and she has mascara running down her cheeks. I drop my brush.

"Riley, what's wrong?"

She closes the classroom door and sets her gym bag down on the desk in the front of the room.

"Are you okay?"

She nods, but tears are glistening in her eyes. "It's good news, really." She nods. "I mean, I guess."

I always feel so useless when someone else is crying. I can't tell if she's happy or sad, or a bit of both. Do I go put my arms around her? I don't know, so I sit still.

"Tom heard from his mom about a new experimental therapy program they're starting at UCSF." Riley sniffs. "It's for people with forms of high functioning autism."

"Like Michael."

She nods. "It's supposed to be really good. The guy who runs it is the world's leading therapist or whatever." Riley moves over to the desk next to me and hoists herself up so she's sitting on top of it. "And Tom's mom pulled some strings to get Michael in."

"That's great. Right?" I roll my brush around in my hand. Am I missing something? This sounds like good news to me.

Riley nods. "It's just that…" She takes a deep breath. "It's a residential program. Michael has to move there."

"What?" Michael's too young to move out. He can barely function on his own. How can they expect him to live without his family? "Like, *move there* move there?"

"For three months to start." Riley nods, and fresh tears come to her eyes. "Christine, I know it's the best thing for him, and we'll go and see him every weekend. I know that. But I don't want him to go."

Her voice becomes high and a little squeaky at the end of her sentence, and she hops down off the table and walks to Mr. Dumas's desk. She takes a tissue out of the box on the desk, and another pops right up in its place.

I try to think of some positives to the situation to cheer her up. "Well, you'll get to see Tom a lot more, right? And Michael loves to see Tom."

She blows her nose loudly and takes a deep breath. "Tom got into UC Santa Barbara. It's his dream come true. But I can't even be happy for him. I'm so upset about everything else."

I walk over and put my arm around her. Riley loops both her arms around me and pulls me into a hug.

"What's Michael going to do without us?" She holds the tissue to her nose and blows lightly. "And what am I going to do without Michael?"

41

I open my eyes and see Ana running toward my car, waving a paper over her head.

"Ana's coming."

Zoe keeps her eyes shut against the sun's warm rays and nods her head a little. It's early May and finally beginning to feel like summer. School will be out soon, and the sun broke through the clouds late this afternoon. The parking lot is full of kids hanging around, lying in the beds of trucks, enjoying the sunshine. We're sprawled on the hood of my car, hanging out until everyone's rides get here. Things aren't exactly back to normal between us all, but we're doing better. I think that night at church we all realized what we almost threw away, and we've been trying harder.

Ana sits by my feet and waves the piece of paper around frantically. "I did it! I did it!" She props her feet up on the bumper.

I yawn. "Did what?" I know what she did, but I'll let her say it herself anyway.

"Where's Cheerleader Girl?" Ana asks.

"Not here yet." Zoe puts her arm over her eyes to shield them from the sun.

"But she's coming, right? I need to know what she got on her trig test. Do you guys know what she got?"

Zoe squints at me and bites her lip.

"We don't care what she got, and I don't think you should either."

Ana flops onto her back against the windshield. "I'll be nice about it." She smiles at me. "It's not like I'm an idiot. I'll just casually ask."

Zoe pushes herself up onto her elbows. "Please don't. She doesn't like competing with you."

I raise an eyebrow at Zoe. I've never heard her be that firm with anyone, and I want to give her a high five.

Ana rolls her eyes at us. "You guys are being so dramatic. I just need to know what she got on this one last test. Trig was my only weak spot all year, and I pulled out a 100. It all comes down to this."

I sit up and make eye contact with Ana. "Seriously. Don't. Things are just getting back to normal. I don't want you to upset her. And you shouldn't be competing with her anyway." I give her a hard stare, the one I use on Emma to say, "Don't even think about it."

Ana ignores me and tries to get comfortable on the edge of the hood. Across the parking lot, I see a flash of blond hair. Andrew is walking with Kayleen. They stop in front of her silver Beemer, and Andrew smiles and gives me a goofy wave, but I pretend I don't see him.

"I was eavesdropping on my mom the other day, and I heard her coordinating car shopping with Papá. Can you believe it?" Ana leans forward and claps her hands.

"I can definitely believe it. Did you tell them you wanted a Barbie mobile?"

"I've dropped a few hints." She leans back and lays on the

shiny silver hood. The sun is making us lazy, and we sit in silence for a minute, enjoying the feel of its rays.

"Hey," Zoe says, her voice sleepy, "there's Riley."

"This is it," Ana says, sitting up quickly. "The moment of truth."

"Ana, seriously!" I'm going to throttle her myself.

She throws her hands up in the air. "I'll be nice. We'll find out soon enough anyway."

We all squint through the afternoon sun to watch Riley's approach. She's trudging to my car as if every step pains her. Finally she props a foot on the bumper and slumps over.

"What's wrong?" Zoe asks.

"Nothing." Riley sighs. She gives us a weak smile, and Ana fingers the edge of her paper.

"Cheerleader, seriously. You can't fool us." I run my hand across the smooth surface of the hood. "What's wrong?"

Riley lets out a long breath. "Whatever. I guess if I can't tell you guys, who can I tell?" She scratches at an imaginary spot on her jeans. "It's just—it's stupid I know—but I'm having a hard time with this Michael thing. It's all happening so fast."

Ana folds her paper in half.

"He's going for sure?" Zoe asks, wrinkling her nose.

Riley nods, her eyes trained on her lap. "My parents decided last night."

Out of the corner of my eye, I see Ana slip her test quietly into her bag.

"Mom's worried too. She started ironing these little labels into the seams of his clothes." Riley pulls her hair up into a ponytail. It's grown out a lot this year and is almost shoulder length now. "He's never been away from home. You can't exactly send Michael to summer camp or anything."

Behind us someone blasts a car radio.

Ana slowly slides a hand onto Riley's shoulder. "You know, I'll bet Michael will really surprise you. He's really grown up a lot this year."

Riley leans her head back, shuts her eyes, and lets the sun fall on her face. She frowns a little and sighs. "I know you're right," she says, keeping her eyes shut. "I can't stop stressing though. I even bombed that stupid trig test today."

For a moment, an awkward silence hangs in the air. I try to catch Ana's eye, but she's staring at her feet. We all know what this means, but I wonder if Riley even cares.

"Do you want us to go with you when you drop Michael off?" Ana asks quietly. Her voice falters a bit.

Riley pulls her head up and opens her eyes. "Thanks, guys." She unzips her purse and pulls out a tissue. "I'll be okay. Tom's going to be there, and that's what Michael needs."

Ana nods. "It's really great what Tom is doing for Michael."

Zoe not so subtly hits me, and I laugh a little. There it was, Ana's apology over the Tom fight—or at least as close as we'll ever get to hearing one. Even I can't help but smile.

Riley laughs and looks at a group of guys sitting on the open tailgate of a truck. They're punching each other and laughing. "Yeah, he's awesome."

We sit in silence for a moment.

"So." Riley's voice is way too bright and cheery, even for a cheerleader. She's obviously trying to change the subject. "Did you decide which of your suitors to bring to the wedding?"

I roll my eyes. "Yeah right."

Zoe bites her lip. "I still can't believe we don't get to come."

The sun glints off a twisted Diet Coke can by the tire of the car next to mine. "Emma said I could have her plus one, which was nice, but even two guests doesn't help me, obviously."

Ana shrugs. "It would be hard to get to San Francisco anyway."

"I can't believe it's only two weeks away," Riley says with something almost like excitement in her voice. "What does your dress look like?"

"I don't know. It's green. They measured me, so I guess it will fit." I shrug. "No point in putting the hideous thing on until I have solid proof that it's too late to stop this thing."

Ana laughs. "Um, the 578 wedding invitations and the huge wedding dress in your house aren't proof enough?"

"I'm..." I stare at the Diet Coke can, the way the sun warps the light on its surface. "I don't know. I'm still holding out hope."

Zoe clears her throat and puts a hand on my shoulder. "Christine, it's going to happen. It's probably time to start accepting it."

I move a little to get Zoe's hand off my shoulder. For a moment no one says anything. I hear Ana shift. "Maybe you could bring Ms. Moore." Zoe nudges me. "For support."

I press the back of my head to the windshield. "Not likely."

"I don't think she could come anyway," Ana says. "Apparently the father she upset is making big headway with the school board. She's not supposed to be in contact with any of her students."

Zoe eyes me warily. "I think you need to bring someone with you to the wedding."

I close my eyes and shake my head.

42

t seems like I've been driving forever when I finally spot the huge white dome. How long has it been since I've been here? Five years? Can it possibly have been that long? Sacramento is only two hours from Half Moon Bay, but every minute of the drive felt like a lifetime this morning, and even though I'll probably get in deep trouble for cutting school to come here, I don't care. This had to be done, and the sooner, the better.

When I get to the palatial green manicured lawn spread out around the capitol, my heart starts to race. I need to do this. People have to be held accountable for their actions.

I fork over my cash in the parking garage, pull into the first spot I see, and walk as quickly as I can to the door. My heart feels like it's going to beat out of my chest. He'd better be there.

I stumble my way up the capitol steps, then head to security. I tap my foot nervously as the uniformed police officer squints at my driver's license. He looks up at me, then back down at my license. Finally he waves me on, and I walk toward the metal detector. I hold my breath. These machines always make me nervous for some reason. My purse travels through an X-ray machine on the conveyor belt next to me.

"Bag, please?" A bored-looking cop gestures at my purse when it reaches the other side.

I lift my purse off the conveyor belt and put it on the counter. The cop digs through my bag and then nods, and finally I'm free. I think I remember where to go. I walk toward a bank of elevators and push the button, then jam my finger into it again, willing the ancient elevator to come faster.

I look behind me to make sure he's not there and let my eyes travel up, up, up to the stunning golden interior of the dome. At the very center is a circular window. It lets in light that fills the giant, ornate building. I look down to trace the light and notice I am standing on a mosaic tile reproduction of our state seal. It's a rendering of the Roman goddess Minerva sitting with a bear, and above her head is the state motto: Eureka. *I have found it.*

I set my jaw, and finally the elevator doors open. I step in with a bunch of tourists and push the button for four. After stopping on floors two and three, we make it to the fourth, and I step out into a formal stone-floored hallway lined with portraits of old dudes. It's starting to come back to me. I recognize this.

I make my way down a long hallway, then take a right and a quick left onto a smaller, carpeted hallway. The pile of the rich burgundy carpet is so deep that my footsteps are nearly silent. I pass door after identical door until finally I see it. "Assemblyman James Lee" is etched on the glass. I take a deep breath and walk inside.

"Hi, may I help— Christine Lee? Is that you?"

Darla. I had forgotten about my dad's tried-and-true secretary. "Hi," I say and freeze in the doorway. I can't talk to her now or I might back out. "Is my dad in? It's kind of an emergency." I start walking to his door. It doesn't matter what she says. I'm going in there no matter what.

"Sure, honey. I think..."

I hear her voice trail off as I turn the knob and close the door to my dad's office behind me. He's on the phone, staring at a stack of papers on his desk, but when he sees me, his eyes go wide.

"George? George? Sorry to interrupt. Can I call you back later today? Something just came up."

Something? I'm hardly something. *My daughter just appeared* would have been nice. I cross my arms over my chest. The person in Dad's ear won't shut up.

"Uh-huh." Dad holds up a finger to me. "Ha ha ha. Well that's right."

I consider walking over to his phone and hanging up for him, but I stay planted where I am. It's a better distance for what I'm about to do. I concentrate on pumping him full of poison daggers. How could he? *How could he?*

"Okay, well, we'll talk about it later. Uh-huh. Okay... good-bye." He hangs up the phone and stands, a smile spreading across his face. "Well, hey there. This is a nice surprise."

"Tell me you're not having her fired." I try to keep my voice steady and even, but I can feel my eyes filling with tears.

Dad freezes. "What?"

I walk up to his hand-carved, giant mahogany desk and grab a paperweight. As I raise it, it occurs to me that it's a wooden carving of an artichoke. Artichokes are the pride of Half Moon Bay.

"Don't you see that she was only trying to tell you the

truth?" Dad ducks like I might throw the artichoke at him. I fight the tears that spring to my eyes. I have to get this out. "Please, please, please tell me you didn't have her fired because of that. I need her. And I need to believe you wouldn't do that, but I don't really know anymore."

I back up and nearly trip over one of the high-backed upholstered visitor chairs.

"Christine. What on earth are you talking about?" Dad looks genuinely confused.

I fall back into the chair and begin to sniff, pressing the sharp edges of the artichoke into my fingers. The pain feels good.

"Christine," he says quietly, lowering himself into his chair. "I'm sorry, but I really don't know what you're talking about." He holds his palms up in the air to show his innocence.

"Everyone at school is talking about how Ms. Moore is getting fired because she made some well-connected dad angry." I steal a look at him and see what I'm saying dawning on him. "I heard her that day at the grocery store."

"Oh." His face reddens as he pulls at his tie.

"She's the only one who cared, and now she's gone." My voice cracks. I can't face next year without her. I can't face living in that town without her.

Dad gets up and comes around his desk. I try to wipe my eyes with my sleeves.

"Here, use this." Dad grabs a box of tissues and holds it out to me. "Darla makes me keep them on hand."

I take one quickly and wipe the tissue across my eyes, then look back down.

"Christine, in this line of work, I don't hear a lot of truth." He sits down in the other chair and puts his hand on my knee.

I take the artichoke from my lap and put it back on his desk, noticing that everything on it is freakishly neat and tidy. His pens are just so in a little cup, his papers stacked exactly on top of each other.

"What Ms. Moore did for me that day was really special. She, I..." His voice fails as he shakes his head. "You have to forgive me. Your mom was always so good at parenting that when she..." He takes a deep, raspy breath. "I didn't know how." He grips my knee so hard it almost hurts. "And I was messing it up horribly. Ms. Moore was right."

I try to fight it, but a tear leaks down my cheek. I stare at the floor.

"I don't want to lose you, Christine." His voice is low. "You're the most important thing in the world to me."

I've been in this office dozens of times, but I never noticed the gray flecks in the maroon carpet before.

"Do you understand that?"

They're very subtle, really, and tone it down just enough.

"Okay. You don't have to respond." He swallows and reaches out his hand to put the artichoke back into its spot. "That's fine."

I might have gone for a more bluish color, personally.

"Christine, what were you saying about Ms. Moore getting fired?"

I bite my lip. He sounds genuine. Is it possible he really doesn't know? I look up slowly.

"It really wasn't you?" My voice is high and squeaky.

"I don't know what *it* is, but no. I promise you I didn't do anything to Ms. Moore. I know how important she is to you."

I blot the sides of my eyes carefully. "You do?"

"Christine..." Dad sighs. "I see things that you don't think I see. We're the same that way." He smiles a little. "I know you feel a little protective of Zoe." He clears his throat, then continues. "I know you look up to Riley, and there's a lot more going on in her life than I hear about. I know Ana can drive you crazy, but she's who you would call in a crisis."

I laugh a little and blow my nose.

"And I know that Ms. Moore has been there for you in a way I couldn't be."

I nod.

"And she's getting fired?"

"Maybe. No one knows for sure."

Dad stands up and walks around his desk again. He sits down in front of his computer. "I wonder if I can help." He moves his mouse and clicks furiously at his screen. "There it is. I've got the home number of the head of the school board."

"Really?" I stand up and walk around the desk so I can see his screen.

"I can't make any promises. Howard is a powerful person and a bit of a grump. But I will try to help Ms. Moore any way I can."

My eyes start to well up with tears again, but I fight them back, and that's when I see it. It must have been taken when I was in fifth grade. I reach out slowly and lift it off the desk.

We were at the Monterey Bay Aquarium. I remember that

I was scared of the sharks, and Dad had to tap on the thick glass over and over to convince me they couldn't get to me.

"I love that picture." Dad smiles a little. I squint at the faded photograph. Mom is gorgeous as always, even in her outdated clothes. It's Dad and me who look different. He has his arm around her waist casually, and I'm hanging onto his hand like I never want to let go. We're both beaming at the camera like we don't have a care in the world.

I look back at him now and notice the crow's feet around his eyes and the gray streaking his hair. I shake my head. It's been a tough two years without her, but we're still here.

"But you got rid of all the other pictures."

Dad bites his lip. "I thought that was what you wanted." He lets out his breath. "I thought that would make it easier for you."

I shake my head. "No," I say simply. "That's not what I wanted."

"I'm sorry." He nods. "They're all in the attic. I'll get them down for you when I get home."

I set the frame back in its spot carefully and notice the one next to it. It's a snapshot of Dad and Candace from their cruise last summer. She's sitting on his lap, and they're laughing.

"Dad?" He glances up at me, and I force myself to ask the question, even though I don't think I want to hear the answer. "Are you really going to marry Candace?"

43

It's kind of scary how easy it is to find out where someone lives. I typed "Natalie Moore" and "Half Moon Bay" into Google, and five minutes later I'm on my way to her apartment. They even drew me a little map. I probably could have found out her blood type with a few more minutes of searching.

I check my directions again, then make a right turn into the entrance of an apartment complex on the north side of town. It's one of the older complexes, with low buildings of graying wood surrounded by evergreens. I follow a sign to number 402, then pull into an empty space in front. I walk up the covered stairs to the little porch and knock on the door before I can change my mind.

Her eyes widen when she opens the door. She's wearing jeans, a Brown University T-shirt, and red socks, and her hair is pulled back into a messy tuft of a ponytail. She looks thin, and there are dark circles under her eyes.

"Christine. You're not supposed to be here." I ignore her and step inside the apartment, then walk across the gray carpet into the living room and take a seat on the couch. I sink in a little. Most of the furniture looks secondhand, but it feels warm and comfortable in here. My eyes scan over the huge bookcases that take up most of the plain white living room walls.

"Who was it?"

"I can't tell you that." She pushes a lock of hair out of her eye and leans against the doorway to the kitchen.

"When are you coming back?" I gesture to the empty armchair next to the couch to indicate that she should sit.

"I don't know." She looks at me and lets out a sigh. "I was making dinner." She points to a package of pasta and a pot on the stove behind her. "Would you like some?"

"No thanks."

She goes to the stove to turn off the burner, then walks into the living room and takes a seat on the armchair.

"Your being here could get me in a lot of trouble." She crosses her arms over her chest, but I see the hint of a smile on her lips. "But I was sort of hoping you'd stop by."

"I don't feel like getting my head shrunk today. I just needed to get out of my house. Candace has morphed into bridezilla, and I couldn't take it anymore." I try to affect an air of calm, but I'm panicking. I didn't expect it to be so weird to be in a teacher's house.

"Listen, Christine. We need to talk."

"I can't talk today. I'm only here to hang out." I stand up, like maybe I'm about to leave.

"Sit down." She rolls her eyes. "Not about that. I need to tell you something."

I sink back into the couch cushions, but I can't bring myself to look her in the eyes.

She pulls at a thread on the hem of her jeans. She looks like a college student when she's not dressed up for work. "I wanted to tell you that there is a very real possibility that I won't be back next year."

"But—" My nose begins to prick. My dad's going to stop

this. It's not going to happen. It can't happen. A lump forms in my throat.

"Christine." I never noticed before, but Ms. Moore's hands are tiny. "Just listen."

I swallow hard, but the lump only inches forward. I can't lose her. I think that might even be what I'm here to say. I'm not sure.

"I already talked to Ms. Lovchuck." A deep crease divides her forehead in half. "I'm afraid, against my protests, you'll be reassigned to Mrs. Canning."

"Uh-uh. No way." In my first session with Mrs. Canning, she made me look at inkblots. For an hour straight I told her that every single one looked like Frank Sinatra, and she didn't crack a smile even once. She just kept writing stuff down. The second session I had her in tears when I told her my mom was haunting me. She actually left the room and never came back.

"I know." Ms. Moore gets off the chair, slides onto the couch next to me, and puts her arm around me. At first I want to shrug it off because I don't like it when adults hug me, but as tears begin to sting my eyes I decide to let her arm stay. It makes it worse and better somehow. "I wish there was something I could do."

I can't look at her. It would be too strange. But I can't move away. I can't lose her.

"It was raining," I say. I slowly lean back and stare at the carpet. She lets out a long breath. I wait, but she doesn't say anything.

"I wanted to go to San Francisco to this cool thrift store in the Mission that I'd heard about, but she didn't want to go. She thought I had enough clothes, but they were all...I don't know. Too much like what everyone else was wearing."

I see her nodding out of the corner of my eye.

"I wanted high school to be different. I was sick of being nerdy little Christine, the cello player. I was ready to be somebody. So I whined about it for weeks, and she finally took me."

Ms. Moore pulls her legs under her on the couch, and I relax a little.

"But when we got there, she wouldn't let me buy this shirt I wanted. It was too tight. And the pants I wanted had holes in the knees. So I got mad. And we were going to go out to lunch and stuff, but then I said let's just go home because I was so sick of having her tell me what to do." I smooth out my T-shirt. "She was, you know, one of those involved parents, always telling me where to go, what to wear, who to hang out with."

Ms. Moore waits while I take a deep breath.

"And she kept trying to talk about it on the way home, to explain why she was so determined to be involved in my life, how it was her job to protect me and stuff like that, but it just made me mad. I...wouldn't answer her. I refused to wear my seat belt because I knew it would make her mad. I pretended she wasn't there, and it's horrible, but I kind of wished she wasn't."

I turn my head to look out the sliding door to Ms. Moore's balcony, but the lights are on in the kitchen and all I can see is their reflection in the glass.

"So we were driving back home along Highway 1, hating life. She...she always drove old cars, boxy ones. She liked the shape better. We were on Devil's Slide. She usually took it because of the view. And a car in the other lane, going the other way, started skidding. I guess it hit a puddle or something." My breath catches, and I take a long inhale. "It started coming into our lane. She swerved to avoid it, and the brakes locked up, and we started to go over the edge."

Ms. Moore sits perfectly still, as if she's afraid moving will make me stop.

"We tumbled down the hill a little ways. I remember the car flipping over, but I don't remember anything after that. Until I was standing there, outside the car." I try to keep my voice even and steady, like I'm talking about someone else's life. "I could see that the tree we hit stopped the car from going down the cliff into the ocean. I saw the glass all over the place. I figured out I went through the windshield, but nothing really made sense. I didn't even have a scratch." I hold out my arms. No scars.

"I was really confused and disoriented. I didn't really understand how I got there, or what I was supposed to do. I tried to get her to wake up, but she wouldn't move." The image of my mother slumped over the steering wheel comes back to me. "The only thing I could think to do was go back up to the road and get help."

Ms. Moore's phone starts to ring, but she seems not to hear it.

"It took a while to climb back up to the road, and it wasn't until I flagged down a car that I remembered her cell phone. Why didn't I think to dig out her cell phone?"

Ms. Moore waits.

"The ambulance could have been there a lot sooner. I always wondered if it would have made a difference."

"Christine, no. That's not what—"

"I know. They say she died on impact. But how much can

you really believe?" I shrug. "As we were sitting there, wait-ing for the ambulance, Dreamy didn't ask any questions."

Ms. Moore's eyes go wide at the mention of Zoe's mom, but I don't stop to explain. "And she didn't try to tell me everything would be okay. I remember that. I knew every-thing wasn't going to be okay, and she didn't try to pretend it would. But she did say something I'll never forget. She said it was a miracle I survived, and God must have saved me for something special."

Ms. Moore smiles. I wait, but she doesn't say anything. Now that I've finally spilled my guts to her, she has nothing to say to me?

I scan the titles on her shelves so I won't have to look at her. Wow. How many books did Steinbeck write exactly? I glance over at her, and she's staring straight back at me.

"It doesn't matter if I don't come back next year," she finally says. Her voice is low, and I have to strain to hear her. "You don't need me anymore."

It almost sounds like she's giving up, like she doesn't even care. I open my mouth to explain that I still need her, but she holds up a hand to stop me.

"All I ever wanted to do is make a difference in my stu-dents' lives. Watching you grow this year has been one of the most inspiring experiences of my life."

Ms. Moore looks into her lap, and I hear a small sniffling sound.

"Helping you regain your life..." She wipes away a tear from under her eye, shaking her head. "If my time at Marina Vista has come to an end, it's okay."

44

"You'd better hurry."

Zoe nods, grabs her piccolo case off the backseat, and takes off toward the band room at a sprint. She has about three minutes until band practice starts.

I've been hanging out at my car after school all week, trying to kill time before going to Dumas's room. He's pretty cool for a teacher, but somehow I think it's supposed to be our secret that he lets me stay late to paint, so each day when the last bell rings, I pretend to go home like everyone else. And every day, one of the girls meets me at my car and tries to talk to me about the wedding. Today Zoe got so involved in asking me about the church that she lost track of time and almost missed practice. I didn't tell her much.

I check my watch. The wedding is this weekend, and there's still so much work left to do on the painting. It's coming along well so far, but I'm working really slowly and carefully. One false stroke and I'll ruin everything Mom started. I want to make it great for Dad and Candace—but also for Mom. It will be her last creation in the world and our first and only collaboration.

I duck a Nerf football that soars over my head and into the waiting arms of some guy with a bunch of seniors a few parking spots over. Ms. Lovchuck blows her whistle at them.

"No loitering in the parking lot, *students*," she says with her trademark distaste for the *s* word.

I watch as they climb into a nearby car and drive off. There's hardly anyone left now. I guess I can start heading over. I make sure the Volvo is locked, then weave my way through the remaining cars.

When I reach the shade of the breezeways, the sounds of the parking lot fade. I pass the B wing, my footsteps ringing in the silence. A stray piece of paper dances in the cross breeze, and I watch it scuttle down the hallway, quadratic equation over quadratic equation.

Something about the quiet of the empty school takes my thoughts back to that day with Andrew in Dumas's classroom, our only real date. I remember his hands slipping around my waist, the warm sensation of his breath on my cheek. I remember how happy I felt to be loved by someone, to be touched by Andrew.

In the distance I hear people screaming and laughing. The voices echo, distorting the sounds, snapping me out of my thoughts. I take a left and cut across the courtyard where we have lunch. I know better than to let my mind linger on Andrew. It always starts with something small, a smell, a certain déjà vu feeling that I've lived this moment before, a glimpse of him in the hallways, and I allow myself to remember the good stuff. But soon the good memories bleed into the bad ones, and I remember the way he misled me, his betrayal—and then last week, the final blow, him holding Kayleen's hand in the hall.

I make my way to Dumas's classroom. The doorknob is cold in my hand, and I turn it cautiously. If someone is still hanging out in there, I'll just pretend I left something behind and make a quick exit.

"Ah!" I cover my mouth with my hand and shut my eyes in humiliation. But really, what are the odds of seeing Andrew here, after I was just thinking about him? It feels like seeing a ghost—and I would know.

"Oh," he says, looking up from an easel, his paintbrush frozen in midair. "Dumas had to go to the front office."

I'll just leave. I can't stay here with him, and he looks like he's settled in for a while. I'll grab the sketch I've been working on and take it home. I can always bring it back tomorrow.

"Come on in. The lighting's just fine." Andrew laughs and puts down his paintbrush. He walks across the room, grabs another easel, and sets it up near his. "But now that we've established who's the better artist," he gives me a knowing look, bringing back all too clearly the last words I said to him, "no making fun of what I'm working on."

"Um, I just left..."

In the fading afternoon light, I study his lopsided grin I've been stewing over his rejection for weeks, wondering why I didn't measure up, what I don't have, what she has that's better. You know, aside from blonder hair, a perfect preppy look, and an uncomplicated life.

He waits, shifts his weight from one foot to the other, his grin fading.

I guess if I'm honest, I wasn't exactly nice to him either. That day in the gym, I unleashed on him the two most hurtful things I could find in my arsenal because I wanted to make him feel the kind of stinging pain he inflicted on me.

And yet now here he is, trying to put on a happy face, propping up an easel for me. Making an effort to be a friend.

"So. You and Kayleen?" I am careful to keep my tone even and neutral.

Andrew scuffs his foot on the floor and clears his throat. "I think you'd really like her if you got to know her."

I shut my eyes, holding back tears. He shouldn't have led me on, and maybe he should have even chosen me, but hating him isn't going to right those wrongs. I can be civil now, and I don't have to forgive him today, but maybe, someday, we'll find our way back.

"Cool," I say, careful to look him in the eye. Then, wordlessly, I walk across the room, feeling his gaze on me, and take Candace and Dad's painting from my shelf of works in progress. I set it up on the easel next to him.

Andrew leans over and studies it. Normally I hide my unfinished pieces from people. I don't want to be judged before I have a chance to make everything perfect, but for some reason I let him look for as long as he likes.

Finally he speaks, keeping his eyes glued to the canvas and his voice hushed. "I'll say I knew you when, Christine Lee."

I say the only thing that comes to mind. "Thanks."

45

The stupid photographer won't leave me alone. He keeps following me around, sticking his camera in my face, trying to capture every blessed moment. He even followed me into the bathroom downstairs. That's just sick. He kept saying, "Can I get one of you putting on lipstick?" I slammed the door in his face.

Of course, Emma is eating it up. She hasn't stopped twirling around in her fancy green dress since we got here and she was allowed to put the hideous confection on. She keeps looking at herself in the mirror and smiling because Candace let her wear some sheer lipstick. The photographer is loving her. Me, not so much.

We're all crammed into a room full of choir robes. I guess old cathedrals don't exactly have state-of-the-art bridal parlors or anything. Candace is getting ready in front of a mirror while the photographer and videographer bustle around her and her friends squeal. People keep running in and out of the room frantically, as if life depends on having the perfect hairpin. Dad, my Uncle Peter, and Candace's father are down the hall, putting on tuxedos. Once all the guests are seated and we're ready to start, we'll sneak through the outdoor courtyard to enter through the big doors at the front of the cathedral.

Last week Emma decided that if I wasn't going to bring anybody to the wedding, she wasn't going to bring anyone either, which was kind of cute before, but now I kind of wish she'd brought Sylvie along so she'd have someone else to talk to. She's driving me crazy.

"Isn't this exciting, Christine?" Emma bounces up and down on the red-velvet loveseat we're sharing, and her curls flop all over. "It's really here. It's really happening!" She stops to glance at herself in the mirror across the room again.

The photographer comes over and takes a few shots as Emma throws her thin arm around my shoulders and I attempt a smile. Finally, he moves on.

"We're finally going to be sisters. Mom looks so pretty, don't you think? Hey, are you going to call her Mom too? That would be so cool."

I shake my head, but the annoying noise doesn't go away.

Candace puts down her lipstick at long last and gestures for us to follow her. "Girls, we need you out here for pictures!" She's in her white dress, and her hair is up in a neat twist, and she's got a long filmy veil hanging down her back. Emma runs after her.

"Come on, Christine!" Emma calls over her shoulder, and I nod, but I don't move from the red couch.

I let my knees fall together and drop my white bouquet to the floor. Grabbing my head in my hands, I try to stay calm, but my throat is closing up. I can't do this. I take a long breath but feel like I'm not getting any air. One of the bridesmaids looks like she might be coming my way, so I push myself up and walk toward the door, but my breaths are short and shallow. I start to sweat. Am I having a heart attack? That would serve them right. Maybe I'll just die on them right here and now.

I stand still in the middle of the room for a moment, but when I don't drop dead, I head toward the squealing. When I get to the courtyard door, I stop short. Emma and her mom have their arms thrown around each other, smiling big beauty queen smiles for the camera in the fading afternoon light.

I can't make myself go out there and pretend to be happy. I'm here. I'm wearing the dress and I'm playing along. Isn't that enough?

I hurry back to the choir room and grab my phone, then run down the hall. My shoes slap against the hard stone floor. I'll have to sneak past Candace and Emma, but they're so wrapped up in their mommy and me portraits that they won't notice. I steal out of the door and edge quietly along a row of bushes toward the front of the church. Turning right out of the courtyard, I make it to the main front steps of the cathedral and run down them.

Around me, people are walking along the sidewalk as if this is just a normal day. The air is warm, and the city is bustling. Now that I'm out in the sunlight, away from the church, I'm just one person in a sea of people. Out here, I can breathe.

I flip my phone open and push a button. Riley answers on the third ring.

"Christine, aren't you supposed to be, like, walking down the aisle right now?"

"I can't do it, Riley. I can't do it. The wedding starts in five minutes, and I can't go back in there."

"Where are you?" I hear Michael talking in the background on her end of the line.

"Outside the church." I take a gulp of air.

"Do they know you're gone?"

"Not yet."

"Okay, listen to me, Christine. You can do this. You have to do this. You'll hate yourself if you don't." Will I? I don't think so, but I can't think clearly. "Take a deep breath. Take a few minutes. Take as long as you need. But you can do this." Her voice is coming out in short bursts, as if she's moving around.

"I'm not sure I can."

"You love them, Christine."

"No I don't." I put my hand over my eyes to shade them from the sun.

"You do. You made them that painting."

"I left it at home. I couldn't go through with it."

There's a pause. "You left it at home?"

"I told you. I can't do this," I glance back at the cathedral, silhouetted against the afternoon sun. "Any of it."

"You can do this for them." I hear creaks and footsteps, like Riley's walking across a wooden floor. "You don't have to pretend it's the best day of your life. All you have to do is be there. That's all they need."

"Uh-oh." A flash of green bursts around the corner. It's Emma. She sees me right away, gives me a sad look, and begins walking down the stairs, carefully, one at a time. Her dress floats out behind her, and I notice she's carrying my bouquet and hers. "It's Emma. I've been spotted."

"Good. Go with her."

"I have to, don't I?" My throat is starting to get that closed-up feeling again, and with every step Emma takes, it gets worse.

"Yes, Christine. You do." A car door slams. "But you don't have to do it alone."

Emma comes toward me, and I quietly hang up the phone. I stand there, waiting, hoping she will turn around and go back without me, but she comes closer with every step. When she gets to the bottom of the stairs, she stops and holds out her arm.

I watch her for a minute, then slowly reach for her outstretched hand.

"Mom says it's time to go in now."

I nod, take my bouquet, and follow her inside.

I had forgotten about the maze, but there it is, built into the cathedral's stone floor. It's a labyrinth. Whoever built this place must have known exactly how it feels to enter a church when you have so many questions.

The huge, echoing sanctuary is shaped like a cross and soars stories and stories above. It's a little dark, lit mostly by the light filtering through the high stained-glass windows, and the sounds from the huge organ seem to bounce and amplify off the rafters.

I watch as the flower girl, Emma's cousin, walks down the aisle. I could still run, turn around and head out the doors again and keep going. But would it even matter?

If I left, would they go ahead with the wedding anyway? If I ran away from this stupid church and went home, what would they do? I peek around the doors and see my dad, grinning at the end of the aisle. I know what they would do.

The wedding coordinator gives me a push, and suddenly it's my turn.

They would drop everything. They would leave their guests sitting in the pews, abandon it all, and come find me. Candace wants this more than anything, but I think, even now, she'd give it all up for me.

I take a step into the aisle. Everyone in the whole place is staring at me, and I try to breathe.

They would do this for me. I can do it for them. I take a few more steps and reach the edge of the labyrinth.

I take another couple steps, but as I reach the center of the maze, my feet fail me and I can't make them move. When I stare down at the stonework, a chill shoots through me, and I think I hear her. She's saying something, but I can't make it out. I'm vaguely aware that people are staring at me as the music continues to play, but it feels like it's happening to someone else.

Dad seems so happy down at the end of the aisle, but I can't make myself go forward. I crane my neck to hear her, hoping to feel her near me in this holy place.

I'm here.

I hear her plainly now and smile. Mom's presence begins to fill the cold air around me.

"*Christine.*"

She's here. But where has she come from? Where is she now? Then I feel a hand slip into mine.

"Christine," Emma says.

I shake my head, trying to separate Emma's voice from my mother's.

"We'll do it together," Emma says and takes a small step forward. She grips my hand tightly and waits to see if I'll follow her.

Tears sting my eyes as I nod and allow myself to be led. We march hand in hand for what seems like an eternity and finally make it to the front.

We stand in our places, on little pieces of blue painter's tape that the wedding coordinator put down during the rehearsal, but Emma keeps clutching my hand as the rest of the bridal party marches in. At first I think she's determined to make sure I don't take off again, but the way she's shaking makes me wonder. Maybe she needs this as much as I do.

Light filters through the huge stained-glass windows, casting radiant colors across the wide stone floor. They play off each other and meld together, reflecting and transforming the sun's rays. The colors are scattered and irregular, but they come together to form something beautiful. Mom would have loved it.

I stare at the dancing colors on the floor and begin to suspect that she'll always be with me. What happens today is not going to erase her. She'll always be alive in the things she loved and in my—no, *our*—memories of her. I take a deep breath, and my goose bumps start to disappear.

Maybe that's what she was trying to tell me this year. I glance up at my dad. He looks so handsome in his tuxedo, focused on the end of the aisle, his eyes dancing with anticipation. Maybe her haunting me wasn't about him or about this at all.

The cold cathedral seems to grow warm and brighter. Perhaps it was about letting go of the grief and learning to hold onto the things she loved. Maybe she needed me to understand what she always knew without a doubt, wanted to show me the goodness of the God she loved more than anything. A whisper, so low I almost don't hear it, sounds in my ear. I don't know what she's saying, but it's a sweet sound, a reassuring murmur. Maybe she's here to give me the nudge I needed to go back.

I shut my eyes and turn my face toward the light streaming in through the windows. Her presence is all around me now, and it feels... holy. Pure. Sacred. I take a deep breath. In my heart I know it's going to be all right. She's okay with this, and she's still watching out for me, holding up a lamp for my long journey home.

The music changes, and Candace moves in front of the doorway, leaning on her father's arm. Emma squeezes my hand, and I glance at Dad. I haven't seen him this happy in two years. I take a deep breath and try to smile as Candace starts the long march down the aisle.

46

The guests are long gone by the time we finish taking the formal portraits. The photographer got about a thousand shots of every possible combination of people. Bride and groom alone. Bride and groom with attendants. Me and Emma. Me, Emma, and Dad. Uncle Peter and Dad. Emma and Candace. Emma and her grandparents. The four of us together. One big happy family.

My face hurts by the time we step out of the church. Emma finally let loose her death grip after the rings were safely exchanged, and she's been chattering happily ever since the wedding party made its long retreat back down the aisle. For her sake, I'm trying, but everyone seems too wrapped up in their own bliss anyway to notice that I'm not dancing around like this is the best day of my life.

Candace holds onto Dad's arm, laughing, as they make their way to the front of the church. The reception is at the Fairmont, which is only a block away, a quick hop through a small park, so we're going to walk there. It didn't make sense to take a limo for such a short ride. I watch as Emma runs up to her mom and throws her arms around her again. Candace grabs Emma and swings her around.

I walk on ahead. The bells are still ringing behind me, and

the fading sunlight feels good on my face. I can do this. I can make it a few more hours.

I'm trudging up the circular driveway of the hotel when I see something strange. I stop. That can't be. But it really is. Mrs. McGee's face on the side of a van.

I watch as the bright blue minivan gets closer, swings into the driveway, and stops right in front of the Fairmont's big white awning. I throw my head back and laugh in disbelief as the Miracle Girls tumble out of the RealMobile.

Zoe is dressed head to toe in garnet and gold polyester. She's wearing her marching band uniform, including the little hat with the plume on top. Riley is breathless, running around the car wearing what I recognize as one of Ana's dresses, and Ana is hurriedly tucking a silky pink shirt into her black skirt. She reaches into the backseat and pulls out a box, then slides the big side door closed as Riley hands the car keys to the valet.

"We got here as soon as we could," Riley says when she sees me. "We knew we had to come."

I run over and throw my arms around them in a big group hug.

"We didn't know what to wear to crash a wedding." Ana gestures at her outfit apologetically. "When Riley showed up and kidnapped me, I grabbed a bunch of my stuff so we'd at least look sort of presentable."

"We changed in the car," Riley says. "Well, except Zoe."

"Ana's clothes don't fit me." Zoe blushes a little. "I was at a parade when they showed up. This is what I had on."

Dad, Candace, and Emma are walking up the driveway, and Dad stops short when he sees my friends. The girls fall silent as Candace walks toward us. Is she mad? She said I couldn't invite them, but I didn't invite them really. They just showed up.

I can't read her face. Surely she's not going to make a scene here, at her own wedding. Maybe they won't even stay. Just coming was enough.

"You look beautiful, Mrs. *Lee*," Ana says quickly. "Congratulations." Where did that girl learn how to kiss up so well?

"Thank you, Ana." Candace watches us, and I put my arms around my friends protectively.

"Well, come on, girls." She gestures toward the door. "How long are you going to stand around outside?" She catches my eye and smiles. "The party's just starting."

"So wait." I reach for another piece of shrimp as a waiter goes by. It melts in my mouth. Why didn't anyone ever tell me how good shrimp was? I feel like I've been missing out my whole life. "Your parents don't even know you took the van?"

"I'm sure they've figured it out by now." Riley shrugs. "They said they needed it, but they were just going to go to Costco. It's not like Costco won't be there tomorrow." I eye her and wait for her to go on. "We'll probably all get in trouble because I haven't had my license a year, but we didn't get pulled over or anything."

Zoe laughs out loud, and the sound blends into the music of the twelve-piece band playing at the front of the ballroom. This place is gorgeous, I have to admit, with its high ornate ceilings and thick carpet. Even crowded with all these tables and chock-full of people I don't know, I'm still kind of happy to be here.

"I can't believe how many rules you guys broke to get here."

"It was Zoe who was the hardest to track down." Riley takes a sip of the sparkling cider from the delicate glass in her hand.

"I couldn't answer my phone! We were lining up for the Founder's Day parade!" Thankfully, Zoe took the crazy hat off before we came into the ballroom, but she still looks out of place in her band uniform in this room of people dressed to the nines.

"Luckily, Ed told us where the parade was, and we went and got her," Ana says. "It was a good thing it hadn't actually started yet, or we would have had to physically yank you out of formation."

"I would have done it," Zoe says quietly. "For you guys."

"So are you going to be in trouble with the band leader?" I wave a waiter over. It's amazing how much power I have in this dress. Since I'm in the wedding party, the waiters are falling over themselves to bring me whatever I want. I take a whole handful of shrimp this time.

Zoe shakes her head. "Marcus was going to cover for me. He told my section to space themselves so it won't be obvious I'm not there. They'll look sloppy, but with any luck, Mr. Parker won't even notice I'm missing."

"Ah, Marcus." I shake my head. "I like that guy."

Zoe's cheeks turn pink. "I do too." She giggles a little. Riley meets my eye and bursts into laughter. Her laugh is deep and rich and so good to hear.

"Don't worry, Christine," Zoe says, her face serious. "We'll find you a guy this summer. A good one this time."

I watch as Dad and Candace walk through the crowd arm

in arm. They keep stopping to talk to people, but every once in a while, they just stop and look at each other like no one else in the room matters.

"Nah." I pop another shrimp into my mouth. "I don't think so." Maybe someday I'll find someone who will look at me like that too. But until then, I have my new family, and I have the Miracle Girls. I'll be okay.

Ms. Moore's face flashes into my head. "Besides, this summer we have other things to focus on."

We stand there for a minute, drinking it all in, but then the waiters start ushering people to their seats. Ana snaps her fingers as if she's just remembered something, then she turns and walks away.

"You don't have to go. Candace said they'd find places for you guys," I call after her. She ignores me and walks as quickly as she can manage in her heels over to the cardboard box she put down by the door. She picks it up and hurries back.

Riley takes the box from her and begins to open the flaps.

"Before everyone gets settled, we thought you should give them this." Riley and Ana pull out my painting.

"Oh my gosh." I suck in my breath. "How did you guys get this?" Ana holds the canvas out to me, and I take it gingerly. I finished it earlier this week, and it looks pretty good, if I do say so myself.

"Oh right. We owe you money for a new window." Riley smiles sheepishly. "We had to break the one by the door to get in."

I don't know whether to laugh or cry. "You guys broke into my house to get this?"

"That was before they picked me up," Zoe says, waving her hands in innocence.

"We knew you would want it after all," Ana says softly.

I look down at the canvas. Is it Mom's painting or mine? I worked harder on this than I've ever worked on anything, and it turned out better than I'd hoped.

"I'll be right back."

I thread my way through the guests, who are finding their way to their seats, and head for the big table at the front of the room. Dad and Candace are just sitting down, with Emma and assorted family members around them. I come around behind them.

"I have something for you guys." I lift the painting up onto the table and lay it down carefully in front of them.

Candace gasps. "Christine, did you paint this?"

I nod.

Dad keeps his head down, studying it silently.

"Cool!" Emma shrieks, leaning over to see.

Dad stares at the painting. It's our living room window, up close, but it's kind of stylized. You can see some of the outside of the house, but if you look in through the front window, the main stuff is going on inside.

"I remember this," Dad finally says and looks at me. He noticed. He knew what she'd been working on. That's enough for me.

"Hey, that's us!" Emma points to where four heads are peeking over the back of the couch—two black, two brown, all together. "Are we watching TV?"

I shake my head. "We're just there."

"How did you make the glass in the window look like that?" Candace turns around and looks up at me with awe.

Mom already had the glass done. It was her specialty. "I had some help."

Dad squints, focusing on the thing I knew only he would notice.

"That's her couch." He looks up at me with tears in his eyes.

I nod. Instead of the brown sectional that's actually in our living room, I painted the four figures sitting on Grandma Ba's couch instead. The flowers on that thing almost did me in. I wanted to show that she's not totally gone. There's still something of hers in it, but we're there, all of us, and we're okay.

Dad jolts up, and for a moment I'm a little worried, but he pulls me into a tight hug.

"Thank you, Christine," he whispers into my ear. "For everything you did today, but especially this."

Candace stands up and throws her arms around me, and Emma joins in too. The first official Lee family hug.

We all pull back. Candace blows her nose, then grabs my hand. I almost jump at her touch, but I notice that she has tears in her eyes. "Thank you," she whispers. In her face I see all the hopes she has for us, for healing, for the future, for our new family. Suddenly my eyes are watering too. I bite my lip and take a gasping breath.

"I'm trying." A tear rolls down my face. "I really am."

She pulls me into a huge hug and whispers, "I know you are," in my ear. Her voice is soft and sweet and sends warmth down my spine. It isn't love, but it's something. We hold each other for a long moment, and for once in my life, I'm speech-less. Finally she has to let me go to blot her face.

The wedding coordinator hands my dad a microphone and a glass of champagne, and I begin to back away. Dad flips on the microphone and stands so he can give a welcome toast. Candace gestures to my open seat next to Emma, but I shake my head and walk away, past the photographer, around to the table where the Miracle Girls are seated. Zoe is sitting next to the mayor of Half Moon Bay, but she doesn't seem to have any idea. I pull an empty chair from the next table, and the girls move over to make room for me to squeeze in with them.

Dad clinks his glass to get our attention, and we all turn as everyone in the room clinks their own glasses in response. Candace stands up and gives him a kiss, then they thank us for being part of the start of their new life together. While Dad is talking, Candace catches my eye and smiles. I know she wants me to sit with them, with her and Emma, and I will, later. They're family now, for better or for worse. They'll always be there. That won't change. But Riley, Ana, and Zoe are what I need right now.

It hasn't been an easy year for the Miracle Girls, but we made it. We scraped by through thick and thin, popular and freak, competition and boys, through the sheer torture of high school, and I think we're stronger for it.

Dad keeps blabbering away, but I'm not even listening anymore. I'm thinking about how someday we'll go off to college and move away and have weddings of our own. But I'll never forget how they were here for me today. This whole awful year, really. I wouldn't have made it through without them.

What God has joined together, Dad says from the stage, no one can separate.

As I look around at the smiling faces of my best friends, I know it's true.

about the authors

Anne Dayton graduated from Princeton and has an MA in Literature from New York University. She lives in New York City. May Vanderbilt graduated from Baylor University and has an MA in Fiction from Johns Hopkins. She lives in San Francisco. Together, they are the authors of *Emily Ever After, Consider Lily,* and *The Book of Jane.* You can find out more at www.anneandmay.com.

IF YOU LIKED

breaking up is hard to do

LOOK FOR THE BOOK THAT STARTED IT ALL:

the miracle girls

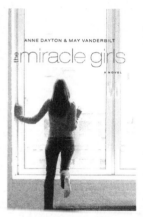

Ana Dominguez was happy in San Jose, but everything changed when her dad moved the family to Half Moon Bay, California, to open a law practice. Her parents think she's settling into her new school nicely, but she has them fooled. Riley, the most popular girl in school, has picked Ana as enemy #1, and Tyler, Ana's crush, doesn't even know Ana exists.

When Ana ends up in detention with Riley and two other classmates—Christine and Zoe—the girls discover they have more in common than they ever would have imagined. Now as Ana lives out her faith, she and Zoe are determined to befriend Riley and Christine. But the drama of high school life has only just begun...

Available now wherever books are sold.